The Trouble with Harriet

DOROTHY CANNELL

The Trouble with Harriet

WHEELER
PUBLISHING, INC.
ROCKLAND, MA

★ AN AMERICAN COMPANY ★

Published in Large Print by arrangement with Viking Penguin, a division of Penguin Putnam, Inc. in the United States and Canada

Wheeler Large Print Book Series.

Set in 16 pt Plantin.

Library of Congress Cataloging-in-Publication Data

Cannell, Dorothy.
    The trouble with Harriet / Dorothy Cannell.
        p. (large print) cm.(Wheeler large print book series)
    ISBN 1-56895-833-1 (softcover)
    1. Haskell, Ellie (Fictitious character)—Fiction. 2. Interior decorators—
England—Fiction. 3. Women detectives—England—Fiction.
4. England—Fiction. 5. Large type books. I. Title. II. Series

[PS3553.A499 T76   2000]
813'.54—dc21   99-088116
                                                                        CIP

To my daughter RACHAEL, who was the best
CHRISTMAS present her father and I ever
received and has been a blessing ever since.

ACKNOWLEDGMENT

Many thanks to my friend Rita Wilsdorf for her very special contribution.

CHAPTER I

"HOW'D YOU LIKE TO HAVE YOUR FORTUNE TOLD BY a true gypsy?"

It was a crisp autumn day, and I was traversing the market square in Chitterton Fells after purchasing traveler's checks at the bank. I had just avoided bumping into gossipy Mrs. Potter from the Hearthside Guild, knowing she was dying to have a word about our new vicar, when the thickset woman in the tobacco-brown coat beckoned to me. She was sitting on one of the stone benches under the clock tower. Having been brought up not to be rude to strangers, I walked over to her.

"You've got luck in your face, young lady."

"Do I?"

"And a pretty face it is, too." She pushed back a lock of unkempt hair before tossing down the cigarette she had been smoking and grinding it underfoot.

"Thank you."

1

She certainly had the patter down pat. It was true I was looking my best in my new heather tweed suit. But at thirty-three I had come to terms with the fact that my eyes were rainwater gray and were unlikely to turn blue as I matured. I no longer minded too much that I was sturdily built or that my hair was so straight it wouldn't maintain a hint of style unless worn long and secured with enough pins to make the metal detectors at airports go berserk. What I did mind, particularly when I looked up at the clock tower and saw that it was almost 5:00 P.M., was being sweet-talked into crossing the woman's palm with silver. Perhaps if she had demonstrated a true professionalism by producing a crystal ball, I would have felt differently.

"I see a dark, handsome man and lots of good fortune."

"That's nice." The hustle and bustle of daily life went on all around me. The doors of Tudor buildings opened and closed. Pedestrians thronged the square. There were mothers pushing prams or holding on to toddlers, elderly couples with shopping bags, and gaggles of teenagers elbowing each other amid sputters of laughter. A longhaired trio stood strumming guitars and singing "Where Have All the Flowers Gone?" Pigeons pecked their way around my feet, while I stood like someone who had nowhere to go in a hurry, watching the woman on the bench pull a battered packet of cigarettes out of her coat pocket and light up again. I had been raced off my feet the last couple of days, and it felt good to idle. But the truth was, I had always been nervously interested in having my fortune told.

The woman dropped her match and squinted at me through a wispy spiral of smoke. "No need to be scared, lady. I won't tell you nothing bad. I just said there's luck in your face. You're going to live to be ninety-three, you are, and hardly a day's sickness from now till then."

I wasn't quite that gullible. Shaking my head, I turned away. But she stopped me, although not by a hand grabbing at my sleeve or a voice that descended into a whine.

"You've had your share of sorrows," said the woman in the grubby tweed coat, most of its buttons hanging by threads. Her hair could have done with a wash. "Lost your mother, didn't you, lady? When you was only sixteen."

I had been seventeen. Suddenly I felt chilled.

"Came as a shock, it did, because it wasn't like she'd been ill, poor soul. What I see is her taking a bad fall down a steep flight of steps. They didn't think she'd die, not at first, but it was a terrible bang she'd given her head."

"She developed a blood clot." It was difficult getting the words out. The pain of memory mingled with a fearful, heady excitement. "Spellbound" best described my state of mind. Not only did time stand still; even the pigeons, along with the passersby, froze in place. Detractors claim psychics are crafty. They know how to size up their subjects.

But how could this woman, true Gypsy or not, have known about my mother? From the way I walked? Or held my handbag?

She began talking in an ordinary, chatty sort of way about the wonderful weather we had been having for October and how there were some decent shops in Chitterton Fells.

"And it's nice to be in a place where you get a blow of sea air." She tossed away another cigarette stub. "Want me to take a look at your hand?"

"How much will it cost me?" I asked.

"Ten pounds, lady."

So much for "cross my palm with silver." Perhaps I had provided her with necessary information, after all. The heather tweed suit had been a splurge, and my handbag was patently expensive, having belonged to my cousin Vanessa and given to me in a mad moment of generosity.

"Gypsies got to keep up with inflation like everyone else." The woman's eyes narrowed in amusement. "And you'll see I give value for money. Want me to tell you about your dad? Doesn't get in touch much, does he?" She leaned forward, seeming to inhale my faint gasp. "You've been worried about him, haven't you, lady?"

My hands moved, turning the brass catch of my bag, then feeling around inside for my wallet. Tucked into one of the little credit-card slots was a dog-eared snapshot of my father. It had been taken shortly before he left a note on the mantelpiece, highjacked my three-speed bicycle, and took off for parts unknown, leaving me to fend for myself at seventeen and three-quarters.

The woman took the ten-pound note I handed her and stuffed it into her coat pocket before taking my hand.

"I should've charged you twenty," she said, tracing a tobacco-stained finger across my palm.

"Because the writing's so small?"

"Aren't we the funny one?" Her lips twitched, but whether with amusement or annoyance I couldn't tell. "What I meant is there's a lot that's happened to you. I'm giving you a reading on the cheap, lady, because this old Gypsy has a heart and I liked your face from halfway across the square. I see you've got a husband."

"You see I'm wearing a wedding ring."

"He's that dark, handsome man I mentioned earlier. And you've got a big, beautiful house overlooking the sea and enough money laid by so you don't have to lay awake nights wondering where the next pot of caviar's coming from. Then there's the children." She turned my hand for a better look. "Two lovely kiddies. A boy and a girl, and I wouldn't be surprised if they was twins. Twins is lucky."

I felt quite dizzy.

"And I seem to see another child. Younger than the others. Though I'm not quite sure how she fits into the picture."

"That would be Rose." I was unable to stop the words from spilling out. "She's my cousin's daughter. But we've had her since she was a couple of months old. Her mother's a fashion model and travels abroad a lot."

5

"Some aren't cut out to be mums. Well, it takes all sorts, doesn't it? And she knows you'll take good care of her little one."

Now halfway convinced that the Gypsy woman was the true article, I almost asked if Ben and I would get to keep Rose and bring her up as our own. But I was afraid that she'd say it wouldn't happen.

"You were going to tell me about my father," I reminded her.

"Doesn't do to rush these things." She dropped my hand to light up another cigarette. "I'm getting to him, lady. He's been out of your life for years, hasn't he? Except for the letters."

"Written mostly by me." I couldn't keep the bitterness from my voice. "He does well to send the occasional postcard, and there hasn't been one for weeks."

"That's a man for you." She tapped ash onto the passing head of a pigeon. "My advice, lady, is don't hold on to hard feelings. He loves you in his own way, and times haven't been easy for him of late. True as I'm sitting here, one day soon he's going to show up on your doorstep. Sobbing his heart out. Begging you to forgive him."

"Oh, really?"

"And if I know diddle, you won't be able to send him away. Not your very own father."

She sat puffing on her cigarette, looking past me as if searching out another likely customer. When she next spoke, I sensed that her interest had dwindled and she was rounding out my ten pound's worth by resorting to a

6

tried, if not necessarily true, spiel. There was money coming to me from an unexpected quarter and a trip across the water.

"That's right!" I was jolted back to my senses. "I need to get home and finish my packing. My husband and I are leaving for France tomorrow morning."

The look of alarm that leaped into her eyes could have been faked, but it stopped me in my tracks as I turned away from her. Disposing of the cigarette, she reached again for my hand but instantly dropped it as if it were red hot.

"Listen to the Gypsy," she rasped. "Don't you take that trip! The fates are against it. And it don't never do to turn your back on them. Not if you want good fortune to be your friend. Here!" She pulled a button off her coat and handed it to me. "This'll do for a good-luck charm. Magic from a true Gypsy. But it won't work if you don't stay home."

I thanked her and put the button in my shoulder bag. What nonsense! Ben would have a lot to say if I told him we shouldn't go to France because a Gypsy had advised it.

Driving home, I rolled down the car windows to help clear my head. The woman had made a few lucky guesses about my family life, but I would not allow myself to believe she truly had the sight. Or tell myself there had been something sinister about her even as she smiled.

The golden October afternoon was fading into purple twilight, but it was still a perfect day. The air was as crisp as the first bite of a

Granny Smith apple. The leaves that scattered the winding cliff road did not resemble the soggy cornflakes so common in autumn. They were crisp and crackling, as if just poured from a cardboard box. Even better, there was hardly a cloud in the sky—until a dark mass dove across the sky. And it broke into streams of birds heading for their winter resorts. As usual, there was a laggard trailing way behind.

Hurry, befuddled, feathered soul mate! I was just the same. Always flapping to keep up. And today had been no exception. Even with the able assistance of Mrs. Malloy, who came three times a week to do the rough, as she called it, there was always plenty to do in the house. Especially when I was in the midst of packing, as was presently the case. And since the death of our beloved Jonas earlier in the year, we had been without a gardener. Ben now did all the mowing and hedge trimming. But he wasn't much good with flowers. And he didn't have the time, either. True, he had recently converted Abigail's, his cordon bleu restaurant in Chitterton Fells, into a café that served only morning coffee, light lunches, and afternoon tea. But not only was he a devoted father; he had also started work on a new cookery book. Added to which, I (after attempting for over a year to get back to working steadily as an interior designer) had landed a plum job, revamping the ancestral home of Lord and Lady Grizwolde.

It was because our lives had become increasingly busy that Ben had urged me to take his parents up on their offer to mind the children while he and I went to France. We hadn't had a holiday in years. And I wasn't going to allow an unknown woman's premonition to ruin the opportunity to bask in my husband's arms between trips to the Louvre instead of to the loo with the children, who always knew just when to interrupt us. Their grandparents had collected them that morning. It had been heart-wrenching to wave them off. But I knew they would be cosseted to the point of spoiling in the small flat above the greengrocer's shop in Tottenham.

Rounding the next bend in the road, I came within a stone's throw of home. But I had a stop to make first, at St. Anselm's Church hall. I'd promised Kathleen Ambleforth, our new vicar's wife, that I would lend her a silver serving dish with a domed lid for the dining-room scene in Murder Most Fowl, a melodrama she had written herself, with no help from William Shakespeare, and was directing (from what I'd heard) with all the determination of a sheepdog herding its woolly-witted charges into the shearing pen. She was a pleasant woman, and my heart went out to her.

It can't be easy dealing with the egos of people such as my cousin Freddy and Mrs. Roxy Malloy, who had long dreamed of making their first triumphal appearances in an amateur production to be played to thirty people sitting on hard wooden chairs. And then there was Lady Grizwolde, who had graciously agreed to take on the starring role of Malicia Stillwaters. Her ladyship had been a professional actress before her marriage to Sir Casper. Not a particularly famous one. Only two people in Chitterton Fells thought they might know someone who might have seen her in something or other. Even so, it must surely be a little intimidating giving stage directions to a pro.

Kathleen Ambleforth got even more of my sympathy when I parked on the gravel space between the church and the vicarage and spotted my friend Frizzy Taffer's teenage daughter Dawn wending her blond and leggy way between the churchyard's sagging tombstones.

"Hello, there!" I called out as I tucked the serving dish under my elbow and backed into the car door to close it.

"Oh, it's you, Mrs. Haskell." Dawn eyed me without enthusiasm. "I'm sorry I can't stop to chat, but I'm late for rehearsal."

"Freddy tells me you're very good." I fell into step beside her as she reached the path, which wound around the back of St. Anselm's to the church hall. "Your parents must be so proud."

"I should have got the lead," she said with a toss of the Godiva locks. "It was silly of Mrs. Ambleforth to say I was too young to play Malicia. I tried to tell her that I'm an old soul, but there's no talking to her. And as it is, I'm terrified of being typecast."

"Really?"

"Well, you know I played a maid in the

10

school play, and now I'm doing it again. Only this time I have fewer lines, although I do get to cry when I find Major Wagewar's body. Would you like me to show you?" Dawn suddenly scooted smack bang in front of me, almost causing me to drop the serving dish. From what her mother had told me, she was remarkably good, even for a sixteen-year-old, at producing fake tears, but I have to say that I was extremely impressed when, without any change of facial expression, the water spouted from her eyes and cascaded down her porcelain cheeks.

"That's certainly a gift," I said.

"I should run in and tell everyone you've been horrid to me." She shook her head, spraying me in the process. "But I won't because I'm really not as diabolical as Mum makes out." She darted away, and seconds later I followed her into the church hall, where we found Kathleen Ambleforth pacing below stage with a script in one hand and a whistle in the other. She was a forceful-looking woman even when glimpsed from the back. A person prone to old-fashioned tweed skirts, serviceable cardigans, and shabbily genteel hats.

"No, no, Brigadier Lester-Smith," she admonished the middle-aged man standing woodenly behind the footlights. "You cannot be shot, die, and remain standing up. You have to fall to the ground with a resounding thump. Now, let's try it again, if you please. And no more talk, there's a dear, about getting your suit rumpled when you're put in the trunk. I've been telling you for weeks to wear old clothes to rehearsal."

"This is an old suit, Mrs. Ambleforth." The brigadier sounded just a little petulant. He was a man who believed profoundly that duty to one's apparel came next only to that required toward God and country. He was known for the razor-sharp creases in his trousers. A speck of lint on a coat sleeve was a violation of everything he held dear. But clearly the acting bug had bitten him. Perhaps he had hopes of impressing a certain Miss Clarice Whitcombe, who had recently claimed his bachelor's heart. Sacrifices had to be made. He squared his shoulders and moved center stage, saying he was ready to do the scene again.

"Good man! And now"—Mrs. Ambleforth rolled the script into a paper truncheon— "where is that naughty girl?"

"I'm here!" Dawn's voice was surprisingly meek as she slid around me and scampered up the steps to stand alongside Brigadier Lester-Smith. "Sorry I'm late, but I ran into Mrs. Haskell and she kept me chatting."

I could have thrown the silver serving dish at her.

The vicar's wife turned, noticed me for the first time, and hurried my way, tossing words back over her shoulder as she came. "You've always got an excuse, Dawn. If opening night weren't just a few days away, I might have to think about replacing you. And please remember not to resonate quite so much this afternoon. I know I told you your voice has to carry to the back of the hall, but we don't want tins of Heinz tomato soup flying off shelves in Tesco's five miles away. Why don't you and the brigadier go backstage and read through your lines with the rest of the cast who are back there. I'll be ready for you in five minutes. These young girls!" She shook her head and smiled conspiratorially at me. "It's quite exhausting trying to show them who's boss. I'm glad my niece Ruth is past that trying stage. You'll enjoy her in the play. She's marvelous in the love scenes with your cousin Freddy. Strangely enough, those are the only times he doesn't seem able to get fully into his part. A bit wooden, if you know what I mean. Which, as you might guess, is how the brigadier is from curtain up to curtain down. He never comes alive until he's supposed to be dead. I just have to keep telling myself this isn't a West End production. But having Lady Grizwolde onboard is bound to build the public's expectations. Would you like to stay and watch her in action? She just took a break after shooting the brigadier for the fifth time."

"Oh, I can't," I said quickly. "I just stopped to give you the chafing dish and wish you heaps of luck on opening night."

"Such a pity you and your lovely husband will be away for it."

"Yes, isn't it?" I lied. Unfortunately, I didn't have a lot of acting ability.

"You couldn't have put off your holiday for a week or two?"

"I'm afraid not."

"Freddy must be so disappointed, but it is kind of you to let us borrow this lovely piece." The vicar's wife-cum-beleaguered-director set my silver offering down on a table marooned in the middle of the room. "Now that you're here, can't you at least stay for five minutes? Even an audience of one is such a boost for the cast." Luckily, I didn't get to answer, because a voice called out from the stage: "I'm ready if you are, Mrs. Ambleforth," and Lady Grizwolde emerged from the wings; in reality, the space where the Hoovers and floor polishers were kept.

It was hard to believe that such a woman as her ladyship coexisted in a world with domestic appliances. She was a dark-haired, classic beauty of about thirty-five, with that elusive something called presence and the sort of figure that would have caused most men to drop dead at her feet without putting her to the trouble of having to shoot them. I found myself wondering if Freddy got to kiss her during any of their scenes together and if, in the process, he was able to remember that she was married in real life to a peer of the realm.

Kathleen Ambleforth had bustled away from me in a murmuring of thanks for the chafing dish and hopes that I and my lovely husband would enjoy our holiday. And I was suddenly sorry not to have the time to stay and watch Lady Grizwolde step into her starring role in Murder Most Fowl. I had only met her a few times without any sense of getting to know her. It had been a surprise when

14

she had phoned to express an interest in hiring me to do some redecorating for her at the Old Abbey. A week later, I had come away from the consultation without high hopes. But she had got back in touch to say she liked my ideas and had chosen me over a London decorator. And after the first euphoria wore off, I wished I had a better feeling for what made her tick. That sort of understanding is crucial to doing the best possible job for a client. Now, as I was about to walk out of the church hall, I heard her ladyship speak from the stage in a throaty whisper that seemed to darken the room.

"It's one of those funny facts of life that when someone doesn't do things precisely to my satisfaction, they tend to end up very dead." Turning around slowly, I saw that she was talking to Dawn, who, in the role of the maid, ducked a trembling curtsy before backing out of sight. Then, as I walked out into the gathering dusk, I told myself that my sense of foreboding was all tied in with the Gypsy's nonsense and should be put right out of my head.

A few minutes later I reached the gates of home, standing open to the cliff road. The house had been built at the turn of the century at the whim of some distant cousin on my mother's side. What a lovely man he must have been, I thought for the umpteenth time as I drove past what had originally been the caretaker's cottage and was now my cousin Freddy's digs. In creating Merlin's Court, Eustace Grantham had brought a fairy-tale castle to life, complete with turrets, a moat, and even a miniature portcullis. It had fallen into a sad state of disrepair by the time I visited as a child. But when my Prince Charming finally showed up (they don't make white horses the way they used to), we moved in and eagerly set about removing the curses of time and neglect. We were so lucky, Ben and I, with our adorable, healthy children and this marvelous house in which to bring them up. If I had to walk around with my fingers crossed for the rest of my life, I would gladly do so. Not that I was superstitious. Far from it. I was already thinking about what I would have for my first dinner in France. The asparagus mousse or lobster bisque for a starter? Or possibly both?

It was only after I had stowed the car in the old stable that we used for a garage that I noticed another vehicle, a battered old crock, if ever there was one, parked in the courtyard. Could it belong to the Reverend Dunstan Ambleforth? He had been promising to pay us a call, and his wife had laughingly warned us not to be unduly surprised if he turned up in the middle of the night; apparently he was very much the absentminded clergyman. Especially after long hours spent in his study working on volume eleven of his Life of St. Ethelwort. But here he was, I presumed, at a perfectly seemly hour.

Crossing the moat bridge, I felt considerably cheered. Surely a spiritual visit from a man of the cloth would offset the Gypsy's warning. Being exceedingly High Church, he might even offer to come out to the stable and sprinkle the car with holy water, just to be on the safe side. I was halfway up the stone steps when Ben opened the front door. He is a man who looks good in any light, but the violet shadows cast by the onset of twilight planed his face to perfection and did marvelous things to his jawline. Even in his old corduroys and navy blue sweater he could still make my heart miss a beat.

"Ellie," he said, running lean brown fingers through his curly black hair, "there's someone here."

"I know." The wind ruffled my hair as I glanced back at the parked car.

"It's a man."

"I thought it might be." As so often was the case, I marveled that my husband's blue-green eyes were flecked with gold.

"Not just any man, Ellie."

"You're right." I understood what he was getting at. As our new vicar and a foremost authority on St. Ethelwort, Reverend Ambleforth deserved to be welcomed by Mrs. as well as Mr. Haskell on his first visit to Merlin's Court. "I'm sorry I was so long, darling. The beastly cashier acted as though I had the getaway car at the door when I asked for traveler's checks. He summoned the manager, who kept insisting, with all the authority conferred by his pinstriped suit, that our account was thousands of pounds overdrawn. Finally, he admitted that he had misplaced his bifocals and had read the plus as a minus sign, by which time I was ready to cosh him with my handbag."

"Our visitor is in the drawing room." Ben took my hand and led me through the front door into the flagstone hall.

"Well, I hope you made him a nice cup of tea," I said.

"Of course I did, and gave him a good-sized piece of chocolate cake." My husband drew me to him and kissed my cheek. "After all, sweetheart, it's not every day that your long-lost father shows up out of the blue."

CHAPTER 2

WHEN BEN AND I CAME TO LIVE AT MERLIN'S COURT, the hall was feebly illuminated by gas lamps that threw into ghastly relief the moth-eaten fox heads grinning down at us from the walls. Cobwebs had veiled the stained-glass window at the turn of the stairs. There was a strong, musty smell and mouse holes in the skirting boards. Not surprisingly, the twin suits of armor standing against the banister wall had looked as though they lived in perpetual dread of whatever melodrama would next befall the premises.

Now Felix and Fergy the foxes were gone, banished years ago to the St. Anselm's Church jumble sale, where they had failed to sell even when reduced to 10 pence each. There was a faint but encouraging smell of furniture polish. A copper vase filled with chrysanthemums and autumn leaves stood on the trestle table across from the stairs, and a Turkish rug took the chill off the flagstones.

"Could he be a figment of your imagination?" I whispered, eyeing the drawing room. "Your father?"

I nodded tremulously while clasping a hand to my heather-tweed bosom.

"If so, he's rather a large one." Ben managed to look cheerful, which couldn't have been easy given the fact that much as he loved our children, he had swept me into his arms the moment they left and proclaimed: "Alone at last!"

"How do you mean 'large'?" I asked him.

"Corpulent. Which is a good thing, Ellie. One wouldn't wish one's father-in-law to have a lean-and-hungry look."

"But Daddy was always rather slight."

"Did you only ever see him standing sideways?"

"This is no time to jest," I snapped, something I had vowed not to do during the blissful interlude of togetherness. "I'm just wondering if he really is my father. It seems such an enormous coincidence given the Gypsy's prediction."

"What Gypsy?" Ben raised a dark eyebrow.

"The one who warned me against our going to France. Which is now a moot point, because we can hardly go bunking off on holiday, leaving Daddy to fend for himself," I said, striving to sound patient.

"Perhaps he's only come on a flying visit."

"That doesn't look like an overnight bag to me." My voice faded as I looked toward the cord-bound suitcase, the size of a seaman's trunk, positioned between the two suits of armor.

For years, during my single days, I had dreamed of receiving a letter from my father asking me to join him in Cairo or Katmandu. But his brief scrawls had made it clear he preferred to roam the globe unshackled—an aging vagabond riding off on his camel into the sunset. Only my mother would have been amused. She had been such a whimsical fey creature. And Daddy had adored her. Had I failed to understand his raging grief at her loss? Tears misted my eyes as I crossed the hall at a run. So much lost time! So much to say!

Flinging open the door, I cried: "Darling Daddy!" then gulped down a breath. Ben's warning had not fully prepared me for the vast girth of the man who was endeavoring to pry himself out of the Queen Anne chair. The thought flitted through my mind that he must indeed be an impostor come here in hopes of some evil gain. A con man wearing a tropical-weight beige suit and a navy-blue-and-white-spotted bow tie. Daddy had never worn bow ties, or suits for that matter. I remembered he'd had a fondness for Nehru jackets. But at second glance I saw that his reincarnation did bear a slight family resemblance to the father I had known. His hair had thinned, revealing more of his domed head, his blue eyes had faded, and his lips were fuller (that's always one of the first places we gain weight in our family), but his voice was as of old. Rich and plummy. Mummy used to say that he could read a grocery list and leave you desperate for the sequel.

"Giselle!" He was finally up and peering at

me over the rim of his Roman nose. "The prodigal returns at last, my darling child. Alas, you see before you the pitiful ruin of a broken man; but we won't talk about me." He crossed the Persian carpet with the lightness of step often seen in people of his bulk, but there was nothing buoyant about his expression. "Homecomings are meant to be gladsome affairs, Giselle. So let it be with ours! And, ah, what a comfort it is to see that you haven't changed at all!"

It would have been tactless to point out that I had lost weight. "What's wrong?" I asked, returning his hug. "Did your father's legacy run out? Have you been forced to take a job?"

"Worse, far worse!" He sank down on the sofa, which gave an accompanying groan.

"You're not ill?" I collided with the drinks trolley in my haste to sit down across from him.

"The flesh is strong, but the spirit is weak," he proclaimed, waving his hands with a weary flourish before resting his head against a cushion and closing his eyes. "But you must not repine for me, my beloved daughter. All I ask is that I be allowed to return for a brief spell to the bosom of my family. I shall enjoy meeting your children. How many do you have now? Five? Or is it six?"

"Daddy, I haven't had a litter since I wrote to you last month."

"The mail has been slow in catching up with me."

"Well, there are only the twins, who are almost four, and little Rose, who is eight months and really Vanessa's child. Although Ben and I love her as if she were our own."

"Vanessa?"

"Fitz-Simons."

"The name does not clang a bell."

"Well, it should." I'm sure I sounded both alarmed and exasperated. "It was Mummy's maiden name."

"Was it?" My father exuded apathy.

"Vanessa is Uncle Wyndom's daughter."

"Winston?"

"Wyndom. He was Mummy's older brother. Surely you remember? He made a great deal of money on the stock exchange, possibly a euphemism for something illegal. And when he lost most of it, he and Aunt Astrid and Vanessa had to move in with us for an intolerable month."

"Was that when I left home, Giselle?"

"No, Daddy." I stood up and looked at him for a panicked moment before lifting a lap robe off one of the sofas and tucking it around his knees. When his eyes closed, I told him to rest, said I would be right back, and slipped from the room to find Ben in the hall, just putting down the telephone.

"I rang my parents," he said, "and spoke to Pop. Mother was putting dinner on the table. Probably sausages and mash. She knows that's a favorite with Abbey and Tam. And I expect it will be jelly and custard for pudding."

"Red jelly. In the shape of a cat. Your father told me, before they left, that it was waiting in the fridge." My sigh blew all the way up the staircase.

"You are pining."

"It does feel odd being without them," I heard myself say. "But your parents dote on them."

"Ellie, what's wrong?" Ben's eyes always showed more green than blue when he got that intense look on his face.

I pulled a chrysanthemum out of the bronze vase on the trestle table and snapped its stalk in two. "My only living parent shows up after being gone almost half my life and behaves in a most peculiar way—something you might have noticed if you'd been in the room with us."

"But, sweetheart"—Ben spoke in the sort of reasonable voice that would have driven any emotionally needy wife to further dismember a hapless flower—"I kept out of the way to give you and your father the opportunity for a heart-to-heart chat. And it's only been a few minutes."

"Well, it seems like hours." I perched disconsolately on the edge of the trestle table. "There's something seriously wrong with poor Daddy. He's in abysmally low spirits, describes himself as a wreck of a man, and can't seem to remember anything."

"Perhaps you were right, Ellie, about him being an impostor."

"No. If he were a sham, he would have boned up on the family history until he could recite names and dates back to the Norman Conquest. Not only couldn't he remember Uncle Wyndom, whom he used to call the abominable windbag"—my voice broke as I

depleted the chrysanthemum of its last leaf—
"he even seemed a bit fuzzy where Mummy
was concerned."

"Probably jet lag." Ben drew me off my
perch. "I couldn't remember if I had one
foot or two when we got back from America
that time."

"Is that where he came from?"

"He didn't say. Come on," he said, tucking
my hand in his. "We'll go back in together and
find out what, if anything, is wrong and how
long he plans to stay."

"Your mother moved in once," I reminded
him.

"And it was only difficult while she was here."
Ben opened the drawing-room door, and we
both peered inside like a couple of children
uncomfortably aware that we were breaking
a household rule. It was a long, rather narrow
room, made graciously inviting by the Queen
Anne furniture that I had rescued from the
attic upon our coming to live at Merlin's
Court. A portrait of Abigail Grantham, who
had been mistress here during the early
1900s, hung above the mantelpiece. Lamp-
light shed an amber glow. It mingled with the
violet shadows cast by the mullioned windows
on the ivory-silk wallpaper. That this was
now a house for children was obvious. Their
storybooks were scattered the full length of
the window seat at the far end of the room.
One of Tam's lorries peeked out from under
the skirt of the chaise longue. Abbey's doll-
house stood on a table, and the walnut cradle
we used when Rose was tiny remained in a

25

corner. But my father wasn't basking in the room's pleasant ambience. His eyes were open but completely blank.

"Did you manage to catch forty winks, Daddy," I asked as I bent to rearrange the lap robe around what parts of him it would fit.

"Alas, beloved fruit of my loins, sleep has failed me these many long days."

"We'll have to change that. Hot milk before bed and maybe some soft music playing in your room." I stroked his shoulder and felt him wince.

"What's wrong?"

"Nothing that will see me in my grave." He sounded as though he were sorry about that. "A pulled muscle is all."

"How did it happen?"

"I was about to go down the escalator at the underground station and had set my case down for a moment to get the kink out of my arm when a couple of chaps came up right behind me and one of them shoved me."

"How awful."

"Accidents will occur in this hurry-scurry world." Daddy sounded nobly resigned. "And his companion, the shorter, stockier one of the two, did try to help by grabbing my suit- case. It was as I swung back around to grab at the rail that I wrenched my shoulder. But he got the worst of it."

"Who?"

"The chap who pushed me. I missed the rail and got hold of his hand. He must have been off balance, because he went plunging forward, face smacking all the way down the escalator."

"Was he hurt?"

"No, he was hopping about on one foot when I got to the bottom."

"Would you like a couple of aspirin for your shoulder?" I asked.

"My Florence Nightingale! There is no pill on earth that can ease what ails me."

"Why don't we all have a brandy?" Ben propelled me over to the drinks trolley and, under an unnecessary clattering of decanter and glasses, whispered: "He does tend to emote. Not that I'm criticizing. It's an admirable trait in a father-in-law."

"And nothing new," I mouthed back. "He always did. He was in a lift once with Laurence Olivier, and it sort of brushed off."

Putting a brandy glass into my father's flagging hand and quickly noticing the alarming tilt, Ben propped a cushion under his elbow. "There you are! And cheers!" he said, giving a tentative tap with his own glass. "To your welcome visit and our getting to know each other, Dad. Or would you rather I called you Morley?"

"Morley, thank you, Den."

"Ben."

"Are you sure? I always thought you were a Dennis."

"I've got the most awful handwriting," I hastened to say, and Ben was as quick to agree.

"Dreadful!"

"A sound biblical name." My father took a lugubrious swig of his brandy.

"What is?" Ben was beginning to sound as worried as I felt.

"Benjamin."

"Actually his full name is Bentley," I said. "He was named after a rich relative's car. His mother is quite open in saying she hoped the gesture might result in a little something showing up in the will. But that didn't happen. And it didn't matter because we were extraordinarily blessed in inheriting this house from Uncle Merlin."

"Who?"

"Another relative on Mummy's side."

"Ah!"

"Daddy"—I rescued his brandy glass before it toppled in his lap— "you do remember Mummy, don't you?"

He roused himself to blink at me. "Of course. A wonderful woman, the salt of the earth, with the most extraordinary flaxen hair."

"It was auburn."

"So it was. Ah, memories, what anguished delight they render! But it does no good to lament. Time marches blindly on, and I must make use of the present moment." He wearily roused himself to a more upright position. "The time has come for me to introduce you to Harriet."

"Who?" Now I was the one saying it as Ben poured himself a second brandy.

"She who is the exquisite torment of my every waking moment."

"Daddy, for goodness' sake, stop talking as if you have a part in the upcoming vicarage play." I was only prevented from shaking him by the fact that my hands were already fully occupied with their own tremors. "Who is Harriet? And where is she?" I hurried to peer out the window, uselessly, as it happened, because it was now quite dark. "Did you leave her sitting in the car?"

"She is my suitcase out in the hall, Giselle." My father's face illuminated like a sun glimpsed after a long, hard winter as he rose an inch at a time to his feet. "And perhaps dear Vauxhall would be so kind as to pour me another drink while I go and fetch her."

"A funny bloke, your father," said Ben.

CHAPTER 3

"DADDY AN AX MURDERER! WHATEVER WILL THE neighbors say?" I whimpered in Ben's general direction. My knees buckled, and I had to grab hold of the knob to prevent myself from sliding down the door, which my father had closed on exiting the room as if eager to hail the first passing tumbrel. "I've seen those movies, you know, where a mild-mannered fiend of a man chops up the body of some unfortunate woman in the cellar of a seedy boardinghouse and packs her up in a trunk."

"Which he then sensibly abandons at a London railway station."

"No wonder it was such a large suitcase."

"Your father lives on the move, Ellie. Here, sweetheart." Ben's voice came at me from all sides. "Have another brandy to steady your nerves."

"I never had a first."

"Making this one all the more vital."

"What we have to remember is that Daddy is new to this sort of thing." I sipped at the glass he was holding to my lips, my mood almost as prayerful as if I had been taking communion at St. Anselm's on a lovely, untroubled Sunday morning. "At least," I said, crossing the room to fling myself down on a chair and kick out at a hassock with my feet, "we have to hope that poor Harriet is the first."

"Ellie, you're letting your imagination run riot."

"You'd rather I sat here knitting?"

"Not really." Ben's shudder could be felt from across the room. "That sweater you made me was wonderful. I could take my own blood pressure by putting on one of the sleeves. But I'd rather you stuck to doing things you really enjoy."

"Such as daydreaming about how I will redecorate Sir Casper and Lady Grizwolde's ancestral home? Forget it. That plum job is over before it began. When word gets out about Harriet, I'll never again be allowed to set foot on the hallowed grounds where an Ethelwortian monastery once stood."

"Ellie, surely you don't believe any of this nonsense you're talking."

"Well," I hedged, "perhaps it is going a bit far to think Daddy chopped her up and put her in that suitcase. He could never take the top off his egg without help."

"That's my girl."

"Harriet is probably still in one piece under presents for the children."

"Sweetheart!"

31

"Chloroformed before he put the lid down and turned the key in the lock. Oh, don't look at me like that," I protested without looking around at him. "I know there can't possibly be a body in there. But who or what is Harriet?"

"Perhaps she's a photograph."

"Of a woman other than my mother?"

"Or of your father's pet budgerigar."

"Daddy was never a great animal lover, but then again, look how he's changed in other ways!" My heart leaped along with the rest of me, and I found myself standing up and heading for the door. "Of course! Harriet must be a pet. Wrenched away from her beloved master by the quarantine laws. Perhaps she's a cat or a sweet little dog. The important thing is that darling Daddy is out in that lonely hall, probably breaking his heart right now. We should have followed him."

"He asked us not to, but—never mind. Here he is now." Ben gave my shoulder a squeeze as once more my father's corpulence reduced the room in length and breadth. He bore himself heroically erect, but his fleshy cheeks drooped, and he clutched a canvas carrier bag to his chest with trembling hands.

"Thank you, my dears"—his full lips flattened into a melancholy smile—"for allowing me to perform the reverent task of opening my suitcase in benevolent solitude. Although it need hardly be said, I am never completely alone. She who is no longer at my side in earthly form does nonetheless hover ever near. A sanguine presence, more real than the stars or moon now lighting up the sky, more soothing to my troubled breast than—"

"Yes, Daddy." I guided him over to the sofa and then watched Ben help him sit down. Both he and the springs murmured an acknowledgment. "You must tell us what's happened and let us help you."

"Bless you, Giselle." He freed a hand from the carrier bag and wiped a dollop of tear from the corner of one eye. "You were ever a rare daughter. I spoke of you often, certainly more than once, to my Harriet."

"Do you have a photo for us to see, Morley?" Ben spoke with painstaking eagerness, very much as if he had been appealing to Abbey or Tam for a glimpse of their latest artwork from nursery school. But my father did not delve instantly into the bag. Indeed, his eyes filled with more tears, which proceeded to roll unchecked down his voluminous cheeks.

"Alas," he managed, choking on a sob, "the only likeness I have of my exquisite angel is the one I carry in my broken heart."

"Then what is it you want to show us?" I was growing just a little impatient.

"Who else but my Harriet?"

"In the flesh?" I plummeted onto the chaise longue. "All of her? Or just the odd finger or thumb?" I looked wildly around at Ben. There was no misreading his expression. It was equally clear to him that my father was urgently in need of professional help. Unfortunately, a highly accredited psychiatrist did not magically appear on the spot to spell out an unpronounceable diagnosis, although for a moment, when I saw one of the mullioned windows inch open, I thought we might be lucky.

Unfortunately I immediately recognized the long leg and disreputable boot as belonging to my cousin Freddy. A moment later, the rest of him, scraggy beard, ponytail, and skull-and-crossbones earring emerged over the sill. Tucked under one arm, looking mightily miffed, was our cat Tobias.

"This house is a burglar's paradise; that window wasn't even latched," Freddy announced with his usual misplaced cheer. "I just returned from rehearsal and was sniffing around outside in hopes of inhaling a reviving breath of roast lamb and mint sauce, or at least a Welsh rabbit that had just been popped under the grill, when I spotted poor Tobias sitting forlornly under the lilac bush. Then a horrid thought occurred to me. Had you two starry-eyed lovebirds bunked off tonight instead of waiting for the morning? Didn't I merit a kiss good-bye? But that's me and my soppy insecurities! Since you're still here, I'll take you up on that unspoken offer of dinner, unless you were really serious about wanting to be alone once the children left. Afterwards, while Ben is doing the washing up, I could run through my lines for the play, Ellie."

It was Tobias leaping out of his arms that caused Freddy's head to jerk sideways so that he finally noticed my father sitting on the sofa.

"So this is what you get up to behind my back," he lamented. "Luckily playing Reginald in the play has improved my ego no end or I would be sobbing into my hanky at finding out you've got company for the evening and I wasn't included in the invite."

"Oh, stuff a sock in it!" My irritation was compounded by having to catch Tobias in mid-flight before he could land claws first in my lap. "Surely you remember my father."

"Which one?" No one could act daft better than Freddy.

"My one and only father."

"Well, if this isn't a right turn up for the book." He peered uncertainly at Daddy, who fortunately sat as if frozen in place by the click of a remote-control button. "I thought you were off riding camels in the Sahara or punting down the Nile. You were always something of a hero to me, ever since my father told me he hoped I wouldn't grow up to be a ne'er-do-well like Morley. Really quite the mythic figure." Tiptoeing over to me like a giant daddy longlegs, he lowered his voice to a conscientious whisper: "Wasn't he thinner when we knew him of yore?"

"Here's your drink." Ben pressed a glass into his hand.

"Thanks, mate."

"Freddy isn't staying," I said frigidly. "He's just remembered he has to rush home and starch his underwear."

"That's a daughter in a million you've got." My thick-skinned cousin approached the sofa and beamed a smile at Daddy's blank stare.

"Good to see you again, Morley. Here's to many chummy times together," he said, raising his glass.

"And you are?"

"Mummy's sister Lulu's son," I said. "He was an experiment, and she didn't have any more."

"It's because Ellie and I are both only children that we are so devoted to each other." My cousin did his best to look and sound soulful.

And it was true. We were very close despite the fact that he daily drove me up the wall. There was very little Freddy wouldn't have done for me or I for him, but even so, did I really want him to stay while my father continued to unburden himself? Or—and I wasn't sure which was worse—clammed up on the subject of Harriet? But it became clear I wasn't in charge of this family reunion.

"Stay put, my boy; don't dream of running off." Daddy was emerging from his trance. "Alas, given my melancholy state of mind, I cannot say the more the merrier. But I do find that congenial company enables me to face the impenetrable void with a semblance of courage. Before your arrival I was bracing myself to enlighten Giselle and...her charming husband on the tragic circumstances that necessitated my return to England."

"Did he always talk like that?" Freddy stage-whispered to me.

"Daddy," I said, "weren't you going to make a special introduction?"

"One that fills my heart to overflowing

with prideful sorrow." My father bowed his head before reaching reverently into the canvas bag and placing an object on the coffee table. "My beloved Harriet, meet your new family!"

There was a moment of profound silence.

"It's a clay pot," Freddy helpfully informed the room at large.

"A very handsome one." Ben stood nodding over by the fireplace.

It was a rather ugly-shaped pot with a lid.

"It is not a pot." My father fingered it tenderly. "It is an urn."

"Oh, one of those!" Freddy cocked an artistically knowledgeable eyebrow.

"And it contains?" I asked, already knowing the answer.

"The mortal remains of the love of my life."

"Is that what she was?" I stood up but sat back down again. It wouldn't do to give into a childish urge to hurl the urn at my father's head. Even if it didn't break, the contents would spill everywhere, and Mrs. Malloy would complain about the dust when she came tomorrow. Far better to behave like a grown-up and count my blessings. The situation might be morbid, but there was nothing sinister about it. No murder. Probably not even a customs violation. For I was sure Daddy had made the appropriate declaration. If for no other reason than he would have found it impossible not to break down when asked if he had packed the trunk himself and could attest to its whereabouts since that time.

Regaining my voice, I continued: "I do hope poor Harriet didn't die a lingering, agonizing death of some rare tropical disease that they will find a cure for next week." I avoided Ben's eyes as I spoke but could feel his look.

"Harriet and I didn't meet in the tropics." Daddy folded up the canvas bag as if it were the Union Jack and laid it beside him on the sofa. "She entered my life on a glorious evening in September. But, alas, I little guessed how soon she would be taken from me."

CHAPTER 4

SETTLING HIS BULK INTO THE SOFA, MY FATHER began his story. "On the very day I arrived in Schönbrunn, a small town in southern Germany, I was seated at a table for two in a biergarten recommended by my landlady, Frau Grundman. It was a Student Prince type of establishment, with flourishing window boxes and an old dog soaking up the sunset in the doorway. A man who looked as though he might be a goatherd by day was playing the accordion with all the usual zest of the breed. The rosy-cheeked waitress with the plait down her back had just set a foaming stein of the wheat-based Edingerbier at my elbow when in she walked.

"Oh, most heavenly creature! All heads turned. All eyes, including mine, watched her cross the cobblestones and wend her way between the rustic tables. She wore a soft, flowing dress of violet blue. It exquisitely defined her womanly figure and was the perfect foil for her platinum-blond hair. Just as she was about to glide past me, I found myself upon my feet. For the first time in my life I wished I spoke two words of German.

" 'Sprechen sie English?' My voice drowned out the accordion. Or it may be that the chap had taken a well-earned beer break. All I knew was that I was lost in the glow of her brown eyes.

" 'Thank God!' Her laugh was deliciously warm and throaty. 'A voice from bloody home. It's my birthday, and just like a stupid kid, I've been pining all day for everything that had me fed up to the gills when I left the U.K. On holiday, are you? Or did you come over for the international yodeling convention?' As she spoke, she sidled onto the chair across from me and laid her white handbag on the table. 'Is there a wife about?' She smiled impishly. 'Calm down; I promise to beat a quick retreat into traffic if she comes surging out of the loo with fire in her eyes and a toilet brush in her hands.'

" 'Regrettably, I am a widower,' I heard myself telling her.

" 'Oh, one of those poor souls.' Her expression changed from merriment to tender melancholy. 'How brave of you to come abroad in your bereaved state.'

" 'She...my wife has been gone a good many years.'

" 'Then you're over the worst, I suppose. A man as handsome as yourself will have

40

women throwing themselves at you from all angles even in Schönbrunn.'

" 'Indeed, no. I lead a solitary existence.'

" 'Not tonight you don't.' She tapped the table with a playful hand. 'Tonight you get to buy me a birthday beer. So sit yourself down, Mr....?'

" 'Simons.' I lowered myself gingerly onto my chair, which seemed to want to go one way as I went the other.

" 'I'm Mrs. Brown. But let's forget about being stiff and starchy and plunge right in. I'm Harriet. Sounds like a Victorian nurse-maid, doesn't it?' Laughing and shrugging her violet-blue shoulders, she reached for my beer.

" 'Harriet!' The very sound of it flooded my soul with music. 'No other name would do you equal justice.'

" 'Aren't you nice!' Her eyes did not leave my face as she lifted a hand and flicked one finger, bringing the rosy-cheeked waitress over in a hurry to receive the order for another Edingerbier. 'But you don't seem eager to spill the beans. Surely it can't be that bad. Let me guess?' She tilted her platinum-blond head to one side and fixed me with a mischievous smile. 'Horatio? Alginon? Rupert?'

" 'Morley.'

" 'Ideal.'

" 'You don't think it's just a little stuffy?'

" 'Not in the least. Distinguished, of course, but with playful overtones.' Harriet laid her hand on mine.

" 'How kind.' I cleared my throat and

shifted in my chair. A soft breeze rustled the plum trees against the garden wall. The air was heady with the scent of oleander, and the moon hove into view as if bowled along by an unseen hand.

" 'I sense that you're a romantic, Morley.'

" 'Do you?' I stammered.

" 'Oh, yes!' Her laugh was as light and frothy as the foam spilling down the sides of the stein that the waitress set on the table. 'I'm very good at reading people, Morley. It's one of my remarkable talents. But for now let's talk about you and what I sense has been an extraordinarily fascinating life.'

" 'I have traveled a good bit,' I told her.

" 'Tell me!' She leaned forward to wrap my hands around the frosty stein. Her perfume was sultry and exotic, like hot sun on wild red flowers blooming triumphantly in a desert oasis. I found myself telling her about my travels in the Sahara. My meeting with Sheik Abu el-Pukabbi and how only the most privileged of his wives were allowed to use the oil from those red flowers to concoct...certain lotions for nighttime use. Then I spoke of my days in the Australian bush, my sojourn in the Amazon, my trek through Napal, and how I had idled away a summer in Hawaii.

" 'My sort of man! Indomitable and care-free.' Harriet was starting a second beer and dabbed at the foam mustache she had grown that in no way diminished her charms.

" 'After my wife's death there was nothing to tie me to the flat in St. John's Wood.'

" 'No children?'

" 'A daughter, Giselle. She was then of school-leaving age, eager to make her own way in the world. It would have been a crime to burden her with a widowed father. I packed a small bag one night, emptied the money box on the mantelpiece, and blew a kiss through her bedroom keyhole. Agony for a devoted father, but all for the best, as it turned out. She is married now, with one or two children, and living in a village called Chit...something.'

" 'How charmingly domesticated.'

" 'Fells.'

" 'What?'

" 'Chitterton Fells,' I explained.

" 'Really?' Harriet took a deep sip of beer. 'I think an aunt of mine lived in a place that sounded like that. We didn't see much of her because of one of those silly family squabbles, but her name was Matilda Oaklands—yes, I'm sure that was her married name. I remember going to visit her once when I was a child. In a village near Dawlish in Devon.'

" 'That wouldn't be where Giselle lives.' I experienced a wave of sorrow at this loss of a connection, however tenuous, with Harriet's past. 'Her home is on the coast, but not in Devon. The house is turn-of-the-century and stands on a cliff, with a church for its next-door neighbor.'

"Harriet sat looking reflective while I drained my stein. Then she laughed. 'It was the house that was named Oaklands. Aunt Matilda's married name was Dawlish, and she lived on the outskirts of Cambridge. That's

43

what age does to you; first the memory goes, and then it's all to pot. Anytime now I'll have to start dyeing my hair.' She smoothed a hand over her shining platinum waves and, lips twitching mischievously, raised an enchanting eyebrow.

" 'I can't believe you're a day over thirty-five,' I assured her with fierce sincerity.

" 'Then you've been stuck in the desert talking to the coconuts way too long.' Her expression had changed to one of weary resignation. She had to raise her voice because the accordion player was heading our way as strains of 'The Happy Wanderer' engulfed us. Luckily the old dog bestirred itself from the doorway to come foraging at the fellow's heels and send him skipping, with an accompanying yodel or two, in the opposite direction. 'I enjoy a little flattery, Morley,' Harriet continued sadly, 'but I'm not a dumb blonde. So if you're hoping to sweet-talk me into going to bed with you, I'll be saying au wiedersehn.' She was on her feet, reaching for the white handbag.

" 'But I wasn't...I wouldn't...insult you for the world.' My chair went down with a bang, taking off half my foot, but my eyes never left her face. 'I beg you to believe that I am not that sort.'

" 'Perhaps not.' She sat back down and watched me pick up my chair. 'But it's not easy being a woman traveling alone. You get lonely and grasp at opportunities for a friendly chat, especially when meeting someone from home. But you can't be too careful when

44

you're fifty-seven years old.' Her smile was suddenly back in place. 'Oh, go on, you can tell me I don't look a day over forty-nine.'

"I wanted to tell her that she was beautiful at any age but settled for saying: 'I hope we can get to know each other better, Harriet.'

" 'No need to sound so humble, Morley.' She gave me a playful tap with the handbag. 'Why don't we get out of here. It's a perfect night for a stroll.'

"Such was the beginning of my all-too-short time with the woman who was to become the light of my life. The first of many rambles through the winding streets of Schönbrunn. We wandered through the parklike area, laid out with walkways, flower beds, and butterfly bushes, along the banks of the small river that meandered under buff-colored stone bridges, where Harriet said trolls hid out, plotting mischief. There was a whimsical side to her nature, a lightness of being that was the more remarkable given the fact that she had come to Germany to recover from health problems. Bravely, she wouldn't elaborate except to say that she had made an excellent convalescence, thanks to the kindness of a pair of old friends who had invited her to stay for as long as she wished. On Glatzerstrasse in Loetzinn, a town some fifty kilometers from Schönbrunn.

"I did not visit their house with Harriet. She explained that both husband and wife were of a retiring nature. She was loath to impose upon their generosity more than need be. They had an elderly housekeeper who, in addition to doing the cleaning and laundry, cooked delicious meals. Harriet insisted that she had never been so cosseted in her life.

" 'The place runs on oiled wheels,' she told me one afternoon when we were seated in a café with checked tablecloths and pots of flowers on the wall. 'It's a far cry from my flat in Wimbledon. There I would have to make my own bed and do the washing up if I didn't want to leave it until Mrs. Green came in on a Tuesday morning. You know how impossible it is to get good help in England. Well, maybe you don't, being a man and having been gone AWOL so long. But trust me, Morley, it would be silly as well as wretchedly ungrateful for me to complain about life with Anna and Ingo.'

" 'Darling, complaint isn't in you.' I felt no hesitation in using the endearment. We had progressed a long way from that first evening in the biergarten when she had feared that I was looking for a mere dalliance. We had spent so many happy days and blissful nights together. 'You won't talk about your illness.'

" 'Hush!' She leaned forward with that tantalizing revelation of womanly curves that never failed to make my soul sing. 'You promised not to bring that up again. No, I'm not upset, my gentle giant of love.' Pressing a finger tenderly to my lips. 'But I want to leave all that in the past. It you had met me a few months ago, you wouldn't have looked at me twice, or if you had, you would have hopped onto the nearest camel and headed back to the desert.'

" 'Rubbish!' My voice was gruff with emotion.

" 'Darling, I know we haven't seen any camels in Schönbrunn, but that doesn't mean there aren't any. We haven't had our eyes about us when taking our walks.'

" 'That's not what I meant, and you know it.' I had to grip the sides of the table to control my trembling. Her perfume mingled with the aroma of freshly ground coffee and hot plum cake to an intoxicating effect. The like of which I had not experienced even seated in Abu el-Pukabbi's tent, being wafted from a steaming kettle of rare oils and spices at the hands of one of his junior wives. 'What I meant, my Harriet...' I had to piece the words together from the lump in my throat. 'I would have loved you even had you been wasted to the bone, hollow-eyed and completely bald.'

" 'That's some declaration.' Her hands went to her platinum-blond hair but fell before touching it, and her eyes—in some lights brown, in others hazel, but always beautiful—misted with tears.

" 'Damn me. I should be taken out and flogged for making you cry!' I got one elbow in my strudel and another in her coffee cup in my attempt to clasp her shoulders and had to make do with her wrist. The man at the next table, a skinny fellow with a mustache too big for his face, picked up his newspaper, but I could feel him eavesdropping and experienced an uncharacteristic urge to get up and punch him. Some moments in life are sacrosanct and not to be impinged upon by the vulgarly curious. In England, of course, it wouldn't have mattered, because as a nation we have the good breeding not to aspire to fluency in other people's languages.

" 'Oh, Morley!' If Harriet heard the man's ears vibrating the newsprint, she gave no indication. 'I'm crying because I'm happy.' She righted the coffee cup and detached the strudel from my jacket elbow. 'Also, I'm feeling a little guilty because of not having anywhere of my own to take you in return for all your'—her voice dipped to a whisper—'lovely hospitality at Frau Grundman's boardinghouse. Such a nice woman. So very respectable with her print frocks and her sister, who is housekeeper to the priest at the Christ Kirche in Loetzinn. And yet so agreeably ready to believe I am your sister. Not always tapping on the door with offers of an English cup of tea or hovering about in the hall to see what time I leave of an evening. Speaking of departures, my darling one, how long before you bid Schönbrunn adieu?'

" 'How long will you remain, my Harriet?'

" 'Until October or November. There's no reason for me to rush back. Ingo and Anna are insistent that I stay until...' Harriet stared straight ahead for a moment. 'Until I have eaten them out of house and home.'

" 'But you are well again?' The man behind the newspaper couldn't have heard me. I could hardly hear myself.

" 'Completely. There's not the least need for a moment's concern. A Gypsy told me so.

A true Gypsy, she called herself, as opposed, I suppose, to the kind that has never set foot in a caravan except for a week's holiday at Skegness. She came up to me when I was sitting on a park bench a few weeks ago, just before I met you.'

" 'Did she foresee me in your future?'

" 'She told me I would meet a marvelous man who would fulfill my destiny.'

" 'Any mention of wedding bells?' Hope dangled just out of reach.

" 'She told me I had married at thirty, that there had been no children, and that he had left me eventually for a younger woman. She also pointed out that I didn't do badly financially. Which was true. The bugger didn't insist I take all of everything. But he did sign over a few investments that have kept me going in reasonable comfort. But enough about him. May he rot in peace.'

" 'He's dead?'

" 'Didn't I tell you?' Harriet shrugged her shoulders. 'It was really very sad. He collapsed on his honeymoon with the baby-doll bride. It was at one of those spa places, the doctor said he must have overexerted himself playing squash.'

" 'Did the Gypsy say anything else about the future?'

" 'Oh, just the usual silly stuff about being careful of water and watching out for black cats crossing my path; nothing to worry about.'

"And, unforgivable fool that I was, I agreed with her."

CHAPTER 5

"SOMEHOW I DON'T THINK THIS BEDTIME STORY IS going to have a happy ending." Freddy broke the silence that had settled over the drawing room like a damp set of dust covers after my father's voice faded away.

"Possibly you were helped by a very small clue." I looked pointedly at the clay pot containing the mortal remains of the woman who had stolen my mother's memory.

"Sorry, I forgot." Freddy hung his head like a child who has been scolded by his kindergarten teacher for bringing a frog to school. Making himself look utterly ridiculous, given his six-foot height and the beard, to say nothing of the earring and ponytail. I wasn't feeling particularly loving to anyone at that moment, including my husband, who was hovering over Daddy like Florence Nightingale with a brandy decanter instead of a lamp. Probably something metabolic. For surely a person's kindness level can drop, in just the same way that one's sugar level can plummet to dangerous lows in the absence of a bar of chocolate. Come to think of it, I had hardly eaten a thing all day. I had been too rattled at seeing the children off to do more than swallow a token slice of toast at breakfast. Lunch had somehow got lost in the shuffle of packing and changing the beds so that they would be fresh upon our return from the holiday, which, in Ben's and my case, was now clearly not to be.

"I think Daddy should have something to eat before he attempts to finish telling us about Harriet." I got up and stood looking around as if trying to remember where I had last put the kitchen.

"No, no! I couldn't possibly swallow a morsel."

"But you must," cajoled Miss Nightingale, administering a few drops of life-giving brandy. "I don't suppose you had much to eat on the plane."

"Just one or two peanuts and a half inch of orange juice."

"My God!" Freddy sounded close to tears. "I would think you must have lost a stone before reaching Heathrow."

"Maybe I could force down a couple of poached eggs." My father stirred valiantly into a semiupright position. "With perhaps a daub, the merest smidgen, of hollandaise sauce. On lightly toasted granary bread, if you would be so kind."

"Could you manage a few rashers of bacon?" I asked.

"If it will make you happy, Giselle." His eyes closed, and Freddy whispered that he would stay with him while I helped Ben with the cooking.

He was really telling me that I needed to work through my emotions by clattering about the kitchen putting dents in Ben's prized saucepans and dropping a bottle or two of milk. Freddy could always read me like a book. As he often said, he had the advantage of having read my girlhood diaries. Ben, on the other hand, was handicapped by the fact that he always liked to think, until faced with irrefutable evidence to the contrary, that I was a nice person.

"It breaks your heart, doesn't it?" he said, opening the fridge and taking out a carton of eggs, two lemons, and a bunch of asparagus.

"What does?" I reached around him and hauled out a plastic container of bacon and a bottle of milk.

"To think of a man your father's age falling head over heels in love, only to be pipped at the post by unkindly fate."

"Awful!" I agreed.

The kitchen was my favorite room in the house. We had modernized it when we moved in, with granite working surfaces and twentieth-century appliances, but by leaving the old brick fireplace and adding a greenhouse window above the sink, we had ensured that charm wasn't lost to convenience. Tonight, though, it failed to work its soothing magic on my troubled soul.

"You don't sound overwhelmingly sympathetic," Ben chided.

"Perhaps that's because I'm thinking about my mother."

"Sweetheart, I understand that, but you can't expect your father to spend the rest of his life in mourning." Ben was over at the sink snapping asparagus with frightening efficiency, which intimidated Tobias into thinking that shots had been fired signaling the start of World War III. He leaped from his chair at the table onto the sink edge and from there, as if yanked aloft by an invisible crane, onto the top of the Welsh dresser, where he sat looking austere. Sometimes I wished that I was a cat and could wilt the wheat sheaves on the wallpaper with a single glance.

"That's all very well for you, Ben, when your parents are both alive and well." I returned to the fridge for the makings of cheese-and-tomato sandwiches and began slicing away with slaphappy imprecision. Freddy wouldn't mind. So long as what he was given to eat didn't try to bite him first, he was happy. Chewing on a crust, I glowered at my husband's back as he finished rinsing off the asparagus and plopped it into the steamer basket of a saucepan, which he then shifted to the Aga cooker. I knew he enjoyed concentrating when he was making a routine mayonnaise, let alone a hollandaise, but the devil was in me. "Not that I begrudge you your intact family," I chirruped.

"Mother and Pop may not be quite so spry after a week with the children."

"My mother would have adored Rose and the twins."

"I'm sure she would." Ben abandoned his wire whisk with a not-too-obvious, longing glance, withdrew the double boiler from the heat, and came and put his arms around me. "Her death was a tragedy, but I'm sure she wouldn't have wanted your father to spend the rest of his life wallowing in misery."

"She was a gentle, loving spirit, which leaves me to play the heavy. A burden," I acknowledged, chomping down on another crust, "that I am only too happy to assume."

"But Harriet's dead, too."

"That is no excuse for her making a play for my father."

"He was the one talking about wedding bells."

"She thought he was a wealthy playboy." I removed myself from my husband's embrace.

"A schemer worth her salt would have realized pretty quick that he lives in tents and cheap boardinghouses because that's all he can afford."

"Why did you have to say that?" Tears stung my eyes. "I've been struggling for the last hour to forget Daddy's awful remark."

"About what?" Ben took a couple of steps toward the Aga, thought better of it, and refocused his full attention on me.

"He said Mummy was the salt of the earth."

"I'd call that a rather fine tribute."

"Would you?" The tears now spattered down my nose. "Then I dread to think what you'd say behind my back if I were dead!"

"Ellie!" Bewilderment and exasperation were written all over Ben's face.

"It's the sort of thing a man says about his painfully plain secretary of forty years who's never typed a word wrong, powders her nose with corn flour, and lives with her mother of a hundred and four."

I resented having to explain something so obvious. My mother was anything but a salt-of-the-earth woman. She was completely useless in any practical sense. She couldn't open a tin of soup without looking up the instructions in a cookbook. She thought making a bed required assemblage for which she hadn't the tools. And she was hopeless with money. She thought it grew on trees. But she was marvelous in all the important ways. She never nagged Daddy to get a job. She was great at making paper dolls and doing animal silhouettes on the walls. She thought books were the best place to live. She adored Mozart and the Beatles. And she never let other people's peculiarities bother her. Even when Freddy's mother's kleptomania was out of control between treatments, my mother didn't make a fuss when the Staffordshire dogs disappeared from our mantelpiece. She explained that Aunt Lulu wasn't well, probably because she hadn't received enough love as a child. And if she had to steal from anyone, it was better that she did it from us rather than from people who would have had her arrested, because there was Freddy to think of and Uncle Maurice, even if he was a pompous pain in the neck.

Something soft and furry landed at my feet. Tobias, despite his peculiarities, always knew when I needed him most. You can't use your children for weeping posts. And husbands may have their minds on things like hollandaise sauce. But cats are meant to be picked up and nuzzled during life's most delicate moments.

Ben wiped away a tear from my cheek and popped a piece of cheese into my mouth. I found myself feeling less like a soggy handkerchief. "Thanks," I mumbled.

"Ellie, you always told me that your father adored your mother."

"I thought he did, but I'm beginning to wonder if the reason he seems such a stranger is that I never really knew him." I stood stroking Tobias between the ears as Ben edged back toward the Aga and reached for his double boiler. "Doesn't it strike you that there's a lot more to Daddy's late-summer love affair than meets the eye?"

"In what way?"

"I didn't become a daughter to see my father caught up in something sinister."

"How, exactly, did you come up with this bizarre twist on the facts?" Ben now sounded seriously worried.

"Has the hollandaise curdled?" I asked stiffly.

"No, sweetheart, it's my blood you're curdling."

"That's right! Pooh-pooh my instincts!" Throwing my arms wide, I dropped poor Tobias, who understandably looked wounded to the quick and retreated under the table. Consumed with remorse, I filled a saucer with milk and put it under his nose. I also made an effort to get a grip on myself. How could I expect Ben to understand why I was so upset when I wasn't sure that I did myself?

"I didn't like what Daddy said about the Gypsy."

"The one who told Harriet's fortune? Sounded like the usual spiel to me." Ben was squirting lemon juice into the sauce with one hand and stirring vigorously with the other. "Water and black cats! You'd think she could have done better than that."

"She also said some things that Harriet indicated to Daddy were right on the mark."

"Anyone can make a few lucky guesses."

That was just what I had told myself that afternoon in the market square. The image of the woman on the stone bench came back to me so powerfully that I felt I was looking into her brown eyes and inhaling the smoke from her cigarette. I went back to making the cheese-and-tomato sandwiches, hacking off so much crust that there wasn't much left.

"She also told Harriet that she was a true Gypsy."

"So?"

Ben had finished with the hollandaise and was now adjusting the lid of the steamer, squinting an eye at the wall clock to time the asparagus. It took him several long-drawn-out moments to reply; when he did, it was clear he wasn't picking up on my increasingly uneasy state of mind. "She probably belonged to a Gypsy trade union, Ellie, that required its members to make it clear to customers that they weren't dealing with scabs offering palm readings on the cheap."

"She wasn't cheap."

"How do you know?"

"I'm talking about the one who spoke to me this afternoon." I pushed away the plate of sandwiches and sat down, elbows on the table, face cupped in my hands. "That's what I've been working my way up to telling you. About what has me so spooked, I mean. She used those same words: 'I'm a true Gypsy'. And she told me a number of things, about my mother's death and how many children I had, even mentioning a third one that she couldn't quite fit into the family structure. So that as much as I tried to tell myself it was all guesswork, I was unable to believe it."

"Then she got the information from someone who knew you." A chair scraped back on the other side of the table, and Ben sat down.

"That's what I thought, especially after I remembered narrowly avoiding colliding with Mrs. Potter, from the Hearthside Guild. You know what a talker she is. And even though I don't think I've ever said much to her about Daddy, she could have picked up bits and pieces from other members of the guild. Or more likely from Freddy. I've seen him carrying her shopping bag for her a couple of times in the High Street. Anyway, the most pertinent thing my Gypsy had to say about Daddy was that he was going to show up on my doorstep in the immediate future. Now what do you think of them apples?"

"Now hold on a minute." From the gleam in Ben's blue-green eyes, I sensed that he had forgotten all about the eggs Benedict. "You say 'your Gypsy,' but aren't you really suggesting that she and the one who spoke to Harriet are one and the same person?"

"I hadn't gone quite that far. I was thinking more along the lines that the two of them might be in cahoots."

"That's some stretch, Ellie, given the fact that they popped up in different countries. And what would be the motive?"

"If I knew that, I'd be a fortune-teller, wouldn't I? But can't you see it's a peculiar coincidence, to say the least? And there's more." I got up and poured myself a stiff glass of milk. "My Gypsy stopped telling me that my life was going to be smooth sailing and I'd live to be ninety-three when I mentioned that you and I were leaving for France tomorrow morning. She told me, in no uncertain terms, that if we proceeded with the trip, something dreadful would happen. Ben, I couldn't shake off a feeling of doom as I drove home. It wasn't so much when I was talking to her...perhaps because she smiled some of the time, but afterward I had the feeling that I'd had a brush with evil. I was sure you would laugh the whole thing off. I was afraid I'd end up agreeing to go. Then what if something happened to you or the children while they are with your parents?" Having drained my glass, I set it down in the sink with a rattle and waited for Ben to speak.

He rose slowly to his feet and rumpled his fingers through his black hair. "Do you now think this Gypsy woman may have had some reason, other than second sight, for trying to put the wind up you?"

"Don't you?"

"It all seems so incredibly far-fetched."

"Exactly. My father meets a women in a biergarten in Germany. A woman he knows nothing about apart from what she tells him. She won't even let him meet the people she is staying with. And within a very short time he returns to England and lands on our doorstep with her ashes."

"Ellie, surely you don't think she was murdered?"

"I haven't a clue what I think, but I'm curious to know how Harriet died."

"Then we'd better get back to the drawing room with your father's eggs Benedict. Why don't you go into him now while I finish up?" Ben didn't sound as though he were humoring me, and I gave him a grateful kiss, which was cut short when the telephone rang.

Hurrying out into the hall, I picked up the receiver, expecting to hear my mother-in-law's voice announcing that the twins wanted to say good night.

"Hello?" The voice sounded as though it had been sucking on a helium balloon. "Is this the right number?"

"What number did you want?"

"The one for Mr. Morley Simons." The voice became the merest whisper. Something else was said, but I couldn't catch the words. My aunt Astrid, Vanessa's mother, asserts that people who speak in baby-soft voices are extremely controlling because they force the listener to ask them to speak up."

"Could you speak up?" I said.

"Has he arrived yet?" The volume rose a fraction of a decibel point.

"Yes." I resisted the urge to shout.

"Then would you tell him that me and my sisters will see him tomorrow."

"And who shall I say rang?"

"Just"—I could hear voices murmuring in the background—"just tell Mr. Simons we're Harriet's relations and we're coming for her like he requested in his letter." There followed a squeak, as if someone had pinched the speaker on the bottom. "And could he please wear a red rose in his buttonhole so's we'll be sure and recognize him?"

Among all the generously built gentlemen swarming through the house as though it were Waterloo Station? I didn't pose the question because she or he had hung up, leaving me to wonder anew what madness had invaded my life.

CHAPTER 6

THERE'S ONE THING I CAN SAY ABOUT MY FATHER. HE wasn't one of those tiresome people who request something to eat and then, when it is placed before them, complete with a linen tray cloth and a chrysanthemum in a bud vase, announce that they are too tired to take even a bite. Daddy hopped all over those eggs Benedict, the steaming stack of al dente asparagus, and the accompanying rasher of crisply, curling bacon. Freddy, having been stuck with the cheese-and-tomato sandwiches, leaned over him to inhale every last whiff. But he was on sufficiently good behavior to refrain from mentioning more than once that he felt like Little Orphan Annie.

I waited to tell Daddy about the telephone message until he had mopped up the last smears of egg yolk and Ben had removed the tray to a safe distance. I was afraid he would go into a swoon that would flatten the sofa into a stretcher. But he was surprisingly heroic in contemplating his final parting from Harriet. He did sigh gustily and buried his face for a moment in his linen napkin, but he forbore staging a scene out of one of Mrs. Ambleforth's melodramas.

"My beloved would wish me to be brave." He intoned the words with mellifluous dignity.

"Want a bite of my cheese-and-tomato sandwich?" proffered Freddy.

Daddy's Roman nose twitched, either from revulsion or because the flesh (and there was a lot of it) was weak. Whatever the case, he mastered himself and declined the offer.

"And now," he said, "I shall adjourn to my bedroom. It matters not, Giselle, if it is a cramped cubbyhole at the back of the attic where rain seeps in through the broken windowpanes and death roosts upon a lampshade."

"I don't think we have anything quite that atmospheric." I got to my feet.

"Perhaps you and Ben should give Uncle Morley your room." Freddy was always the perfect host in someone else's house.

"No, no! I wouldn't hear of it," Daddy was quick to respond. "I can't imagine that Benson would wish to sleep with me. I tend to hog most of the bedclothes. At least that's what your mother used to say, Giselle." This mention of my mother was touching, but he had to ruin it. "Harriet, of course, was never one to complain."

A saint before she even passed over to the

sound of trumpets, I thought nastily as I watched Ben assist Daddy to his feet. A job that really required a couple of cranes. Freddy could have done his bit by saying he would take himself off to the cottage. Instead, he opened the drawing-room door and stood there as if he, too, aspired to canonization.

"All I require is a bed," Daddy was saying to Ben in the mournful tones of one who heard the Raven whisper, "Nevermore."

"I have no need of wallpaper or perfume bottles on the dressing table."

"Would you like a nightcap?" I asked, looking at the brandy.

He shook himself as if adjusting the mortal coil. "Perhaps Freddy would be so kind as to carry the decanter and a glass upstairs."

"Happy to oblige, Uncle." The tender-hearted fellow unpinned himself from the doorknob.

"I can do it," I said.

"But I was hoping you would bring Harriet." Daddy looked at me with anguished appeal. "Much as I would wish to do the honors myself, I am afraid these hands would shake. And it would be adding appalling insult to tragedy to spill her on the stairs."

"Sound thinking, old cock—I mean Uncle," piped in St. Freddy. "You have yet to meet the redoubtable Mrs. Malloy, but I can tell you she wouldn't appreciate the extra vacuuming."

"I'll bring Harriet." Ben headed for the coffee table.

"Why don't we leave her where she is?" I whispered when he came within inches of

64

me. "Call me a prude, but I don't like the idea of Daddy cohabiting with an urn under my roof."

"Sweetheart," he mouthed back, "the children aren't here to be shocked out of their little socks. If it makes your father happy, who are we to judge? Besides, it won't be the first time they've slept together."

Men! I turned away before he could make matters worse by imparting the information that my father had undoubtedly also had sex with my mother. What Ben hadn't grasped, although it should have stood out a mile, was that I had an ulterior motive for wanting Harriet to stay put. Call it superstitious, call it nonsensical, but I had bad vibes about that urn. And although I was somewhat put out with Daddy, I didn't want it casting some nasty spell on him while he slept. I was still fixated on Gypsy women popping up in Germany and Chitterton Fells, spouting off inside information along with the well-chosen, dire threat. Had Harriet been deathly afraid of either black cats or water when it didn't come in a glass?

Daddy's suitcase was no longer in the hall, but this small matter was cleared up when Freddy took us through a step-by-step account of how he had carried it aloft. Not that, he insisted, he was complaining about the weight. Trooping upstairs at an appropriate funeral pace, I mulled over the problem of how to ask my father if anything untoward, other than the obvious, had occurred in Schönbrunn during his stay.

It had been a long day, and my thoughts kept slithering off in different directions. One minute I was picturing scenes out of spy novels. The next it was hit men who had been paid by a spurned lover or an ex-husband to get rid of Harriet for what he considered good and sufficient financial reasons. Had she latched on to Daddy because she felt safer with a man in tow? And what if—I stumbled on taking the last stair—those creeps were now after him because he knew something he didn't realize he knew that would land them in the soup? I was suddenly thinking about that man who had given Daddy a push getting on the escalator at the airport. And how his companion had picked up Daddy's suitcase. Talk about losing my fragile grip on common sense! Did I need to remind myself that such accidents happened? Hadn't my mother died from a fall down a flight of stairs at a London railway station?

I was brought back to the moment by a thud. It was incurred by Ben's walking into the suitcase that Freddy had left standing in the middle of the landing, which we rather grandly referred to as the gallery. That's what Mrs. Malloy had insisted it should be called. In hopes, I think, that her portrait would one day hang on its main wall and people with guidebooks in their hands would strain against the velvet ropes in attempts to glean what lay behind her enigmatic smile. There was, however, nothing ambiguous about Daddy's bellow of alarm as the urn—to give the clay pot its due—tilted sideways with a bounce of its lid before Ben righted himself in what could easily have passed for slow motion.

"Whoops!" Freddy shook his head, smacking me in the eye with his ponytail. Fortunately, he didn't lose contact with the decanter.

"That was a silly place to leave the case," I told him, being in one of those moods when I had to nitpick.

"Where else could I have put it?" He looked at me with reproach.

"Up against the wall wouldn't have been a bad idea."

"I didn't know which room you had picked for Uncle."

"Do you two want to stand around quarreling while Morley and I take a taxi the rest of the way?" Ben sounded thoroughly fed up, and it belatedly occurred to me that this hadn't been the best of all days for him, either. He'd been looking forward to the trip to France even more than I had. Yet in the blink of an eye he'd had to come to terms with the fact that not only wasn't he going to Gay Paree; his home had been turned into a morgue.

Opening the door closest to me, I said: "I thought Daddy could sleep in here. The bed's made up, and it has the best view of the sea."

A silly thing to have mentioned. Given his present disconsolate state, my father probably shouldn't be encouraged to hang out of second-floor windows. He had talked about ending it all when Mummy had died but had decided to wait until he had lost a few pounds so that I wouldn't be put to the expense of a

67

large coffin. Not that he'd been a fifth of his present size at that time. Fortunately, the mood had passed, possibly because Freddy's mother had pointed out that my mother might be enjoying the opportunity to make her own way in the next world. Aunt Lulu was a twit in many ways, but she had her moments. It cheered me a little to remember that Daddy hadn't made light of Mummy's passing.

The bedroom we entered had neutral wallpaper with matching curtains and a beige carpet. Innocuous would best describe it. But my father immediately prowled around the space between the foot of the bed and the dressing table like a disgruntled bear in a cage while never taking his eyes off Ben, who was still holding the urn.

"What's the prob, Uncle?" Freddy put the coffeepot and decanter down on a trunk that served for a table and elbowed me aside to flop down in an easy chair.

"Harriet wouldn't have liked this room." Daddy's lips flapped in distaste.

"Wouldn't she?" I was tempted to say that it was fortunate her powers of observation had been curtailed, but with the urn right there in our midst, that would have made me a poor hostess.

"She wouldn't have liked that fox-hunting picture."

"She didn't have the killer instinct?"

"Harriet was one of life's fragile blossoms! She disliked violence." Daddy's eyes took on a glow, as if reflecting a distant sunset. "I remember sitting with her one evening in the biergarten where we first met and her saying to me in that wonderful voice of hers that she had always shunned situations where someone was liable to be physically injured. She asked me to remember that; one of those woman things, I suppose, because Harriet wouldn't have upset a teacup, let alone a person." He rescued the urn from Ben and stood stroking it with the soft touch of a man who was swathed in clouds of contemplation.

He now deposited the treasured repository on the bedside table and surveyed it tenderly before touching two fingers to his lips and transferring a butterfly kiss to the clay lid.

"Sweet dreams, beloved." He lay down on the bed, folding his hands across his chest.

"Don't go easy on the brandy, Bentwick," he found the strength to murmur.

"Coming up." Ben got busy pouring, and I had just opened the wardrobe to make sure there were sufficient clothes hangers when the telephone rang—a muffled, almost apologetic sound coming from the extension in our bedroom and the one downstairs in the hall. This time it would surely be in-laws reporting on the children. Probably just to say that they were tucked in bed, sound asleep, but my mother's heart smote me. What if Rose wouldn't take her bottle? Or Abbey was homesick? Or Tam had put the tablecloth over his head and tried to parachute out the window?

"Freddy must have gotten it." Ben was handing Daddy his coffee when the telephone stopped ringing.

"Yes, but..." I headed for the door.

"He'll be back up in a jiff, Ellie, if it's anything that he can't take a message on."

"And in the meantime"—Daddy hoisted himself up on the pillows and took a sip, as if bravely endeavoring to follow doctor's orders—"I will continue with the heart-wrenching story of my final days with Harriet."

"Yes, you must, if not immediately...very soon." I was swaying like a pendulum between the bed and the doorway when Freddy reappeared, looking glum.

"That was the pater."

"Uncle Maurice?"

"He's the only father I've got, so far as I know."

"What did he have to say?" Ben eyed my cousin—his friend—with man-to-man concern.

"Could I please have a decanter of brandy?" Freddy held out his hand, and when nothing found its way into it, he sagged against the chest of drawers. "I suppose I've got to be a man about this, but it's not going to be easy." His voice cracked. "To break it to you gently, my mother's in a bad way."

"Dying?" Eyebrows going up in alarm, Ben handed over the decanter.

"Oh, poor Aunt Lulu!" I whispered.

"It's not that"—Freddy dragged himself over to the bed and planted himself on Daddy's feet—"although to hear the pater talk he'd much rather she was breathing her last. And I must say that the Mum has really done it this time." Taking the stopper out of the decanter, he inhaled deeply. "She's got mixed up in bad company. Big-time shoplifters, forgers, even a couple of train robbers."

"Wherever did she meet these people?" Ben and I asked as one.

"At the rehab place where she had gone for the latest cure."

"Aunt Lulu's a kleptomaniac," I informed Daddy, who was trying to reclaim his feet.

"That's the problem with this modern age," he rasped. "Every woman has to have a career."

"Uncle Maurice couldn't have expected Aunt Lulu to stay at home changing nappies at nearly sixty," I pointed out.

"It was the pater's idea to pack her off to Oaklands." Freddy sounded understandably aggrieved. "And now he's all het up because he walked in tonight on the mum hosting an aftercare group session in the sitting room. Apparently, such meetings are a strict requirement of being released into one's own custody after finishing the program."

"Then I can't see your father has anything to complain about," Ben consoled him.

"My thinking." Freddy took another sniff of brandy. "But the pater gave me an earful about how Mum and her gang were talking about holding up the local Lloyds bank—Barclays or the Midland being out of the question because several of the group had deposits with them and they seemed to have a moral objection to stealing their own money."

Daddy shuddered. I was rather surprised he didn't reach over to cover the urn's ears.

"What it comes down to," Freddy continued bravely, "is that somehow this is all my fault. If I'd been a better son instead of a complete lughead, Mum would have found fulfillment bottling fruit or playing bridge. So now it's time to pay the piper."

"Meaning?" Ben's left eyebrow went up.

"The pater is bringing Mum down here tomorrow, handcuffed to his wrist, no doubt, and she's to live with me at the cottage—confined to the spare bedroom on a diet of bread and water—until I have drummed some sense in her head. I'm even expected to take her to church." My favorite cousin looked at me with anguished eyes. "Ellie, I don't know that I can stand it. Not with the new vicar spouting off about St. Ethelwort, or whatever the bloke's name is, for hours on end. Mrs. Vicar's all right. She did give me the lead in Murder Most Fowl. But if I start showing up at church like it's opening time at the local, she'll start thinking I'm just the one to marry her pie-faced niece Ruth. And it's bad enough having to kiss the girl for art's sake in the play."

My heart went out to him, although I reserved some pity for myself. Aunt Lulu, in addition to her talent for sleight of hand, was an accomplished escape artist and would doubtless show up at Merlin's Court with increasing frequency as the days went by. And to think that tomorrow morning Ben and I should have been leaving for France! I was about to tell Freddy to look at the silver lining when my father embarked on the final chapter of Life with Harriet.

CHAPTER 7

" 'IF I HAD MY WAY,' I TOLD HER TENDERLY, 'I WOULD shower you with summer days all our lives long. But as God did not put me in charge of the weather, you must tell me, sweetest of all Harriets, what I can do to complete your happiness.'

" 'Darling, you can buy me another Edingerbier.' She gave me one of her most mischievous smiles as she leaned across the table and tippy-toed her fingers across my hand. It was a sunny afternoon with just the right amount of breeze. She was wearing a frock that looked wonderful with the golden tan she had added to her charms during our weeks together. We were seated in the biergarten where we had first met. The old dog lay bathed in golden shadows in the doorway. The air was ripened to an intoxicating brew by the scent of oleander, And there was not a woman at any of the other tables who fulfilled the ideal of womanhood as did my Harriet.

"I beckoned to the waitress—the same young girl with the plait down her back who had waited on us the first time. By now she knew us very well, was always full of smiles for the verlieben, as she called us, and within minutes she returned with a brimming stein that she set down at Harriet's elbow.

" 'You two together, so happy in your faces, it always makes my day go better.' She stood wiping her hands on her white apron, her eyes pleased, like those of a child with a present to open. 'I tell my Albert about you and say: "We must be like that when we are old. Our hearts must beat fast, and the songbirds must sing in our heads." '

"She went skipping off, and Harriet, taking note of my frown, laughed. 'Darling Morley, I know you think of me as little more than a babe in arms, but the truth of the matter is that I am at the very least a middle-aged woman. To a girl as young as that, I must appear quite ancient. And perhaps it is time I made a few home improvements. Try a new shade of mascara, for instance.'

" 'Don't change a thing!' My heart threatened to burst with emotion.

" 'How very fierce of you!' she cried, drawing back in her seat in mock terror.

" 'Only because I adore you.'

" I know you do.' Harriet's hazel eyes darkened to brown as they gazed deep into mine. 'I really believe that you would do anything in the world for me.'

" 'I'd give you the moon on a star-studded platter.'

" 'What I really want'—she spoke into the frosted stein—'is a promise.'

" 'Anything!'

" 'It has to be a solemn vow.'

" 'You have it.'

" 'Without even knowing what it is I ask?'

" 'I only wish...' I could not hold back the sigh. 'I only wish, my adored one, that it was my vow to honor you and keep you as my wife from this day forward.'

" 'Morley, we've talked about all that. I thought you understood that I can't marry you. Not now...not until I am quite sure my illness won't come back. I know I'm being irrational, but the fear doesn't go away the moment you are told you're cured. In a few months, perhaps, I'll really believe it. Here...' Harriet pressed a hand to her heart. 'Believe what my doctor has told me. That I am a walking miracle destined to live forever. And'—her mischievous smile reasserted itself—'they do tend to believe in miracles in these parts. It's a cultural requirement, just like edelweiss and strudel and old men who look like Heidi's grandfather. But just in case something befalls me, will you promise, Morley, to take me—my ashes, that is—back to England?'

" 'My angel!'

" 'Darling, don't rush me!' She stroked my hand and sat biting her lip for a moment. 'I've never thought of myself as sentimental, but then I've never had a brush with death before.' She started to cry, her face working itself into a shape that was unfamiliar to me, so that I felt that I had already lost some essential part of her, or would if I didn't bring her back from the brink of the infernal abyss.

" 'Harriet, you have my solemn word that I will do as you ask.'

" 'Thank you, Morley.'

" 'But nothing is going to happen to you.'

" 'No, of course it isn't. I'm just being a woman, that's all.' She took a few token sips of beer and got to her feet. 'Let's go for one of our walks, darling. And you can tell me some more about your wonderful little family in England. After all,' she said, gathering up her handbag, 'if I am going to meet them one day, I ought to know all about their likes and dislikes.'

" 'They couldn't possibly dislike you.' I placed the money on the table for our drinks and stood looking down at her with moist eyes.

" 'Your daughter could resent me.'

" 'Why ever would she? Giselle has her own life.'

" 'She might not relish the idea of anyone taking her mother's place, especially a total stranger.' Harriet took my arm, and we went out into the street lined with Fachwerhoesen, those charming gabled houses with their multicolored, leaded windows. To the passersby, we probably looked like an ideally happy couple. And suddenly I was walking on air. An amazing feat for a man of my size.

" 'My beloved,' I said, gazing ardently at her

exquisite profile, 'may I take these foolish concerns as an indication that you will one day, in the not too distant future, relent and marry me?'

" 'Darling Morley!' She stopped in the middle of the pavement, placed her hands on my shoulders, and looked up at me with eyes darkened with incipient tears. 'How I wish it could be that way! You and me adventuring on together, soaking up the sunshine, sharing life's umbrella when it rains. It would be all I've never allowed myself to hope for. I always thought dreams were for other people—decent, honest, hardworking sorts who deserved to be rewarded for never putting a foot wrong.'

" 'Foolish heart,' I said, kissing her for every gawker to see. 'There is no one more deserving of happiness than you, sweet Harriet.'

"She drew breath for a shaky laugh. 'Perhaps I should marry you. That might teach you not to be taken in by women with platinum-blond hair and a fondness for country walks.' Tucking her hand into my elbow, she drew me on down the street, and by exercising all the restraint at my disposal, I mastered the passionate desire to press the matter further. Savor the moment, Morley, I told myself as we walked toward our favorite spot on the riverbank, where fir trees grew in shady clusters and red and white fairy toadstools nestled among the rocks. I thought, of course, that there would be many more such halcyon afternoons, as well as daffodil-yellow mornings and evenings of star-spangled enchantment.

"'But not tomorrow,' Harriet said as we leaned against the moss-covered trunk of a weeping willow, watching a troop of ducks, led by a matriarchal figure, ease themselves into the umber waters and paddle off under the little stone bridge. 'Tomorrow I won't be able to see you during the day because I have an appointment and I don't know how much time it will take.'

"'With your doctor?' The bird that had been serenading us for the last five minutes stopped in mid-trill, and the sun drifted behind a cloud that hadn't been there a moment before.

"'No, darling. But it's a secret, and I refuse to say another word about it. Oh, all right!' She smoothed a gossamer finger across my troubled brow. 'It's a good secret; at least I hope you will really like it. Now,' she said, looking up, 'did I imagine that drop of rain that just fell on my head, or is it getting ready to pelt?' A rumble of thunder answered her before I could. The weeping willow swayed like a fan in the hands of a swooning debutante. The sky turned to lead. And, alas, before you could say umbrella, we were in the midst of a downpour. And even though we were able to secure a taxi right away, we returned to my boardinghouse in a very damp state indeed.

"Frau Grundman, that most congenial of landladies, quickly appeared with cups of cocoa. And handing Harriet a candlewick dressing gown, she urged her to take a hot bath down the hall. This kindness was followed by the offer to take her garments downstairs and put them in the clothes dryer. Meanwhile, I had difficulty controlling my agitation. I was convinced that my angel was about to catch her death of cold. When I told her so, she called me a silly. But when I returned from Frau Grundman's kitchen, where I had borrowed a bottle of aspirin, I discovered to my anguish that Harriet's eyes were already reddened. Naturally, I urged her to get into bed. I extolled the virtues of the down comforter, which Frau Grundman called a fetterbett. I filled a hot-water bottle from the electric kettle that I used for my morning tea. I even offered to read to her from the Oxford Book of English Verse while she settled down to sleep. Her favorite poem was 'To Althea from Prison,' the one about stone walls and iron bars and so on. She always adored the pathos I imparted to every noble syllable, the way my voice would rumble on the threshold of tears. But not this time. Today there would be no Richard Lovelace.

"My adored one insisted that it was best for her to return to Glatzerstrasse in Loetzinn. She had promised her friends, the Voelkels, that she would spend the evening with them. She had seen so little of them recently and would be gone all day tomorrow. Again that reference to the surprise she had in store for me. But now I felt no inclination to press for details. My every thought was of profoundest concern for her well-being. Beg as I might, she would not take the hot bath so wisely suggested by the good Frau. It was as much as I could do to persuade Harriet to finish her cocoa. She was eager, as never before, to head down the narrow stairs into the street. Once on the pavement, I quickened my steps to match hers. It was no longer raining, but there was no saying that it might not start again at any moment. And even though I was carrying an umbrella, I felt powerless to protect her either from the elements or whatever fate had in store. I both hoped and dreaded that a taxi would come gliding to a stop as we reached the corner.

" 'Darling, don't look so worried.' Harriet tucked her hand into my elbow as a couple of cars went splashing past. 'I promise you I'm not going to catch pneumonia. Truly, I'm a lot tougher than you think. Perhaps I shouldn't have been in such a rush to leave. But I really didn't like to put Frau Grundman to all the bother of drying my clothes. I'll be able to have a long laze in the bath when I get back to Loetzinn without worrying that I'm using up all the hot water.'

" 'How can I help but worry, knowing how ill you've been.' A passing lorry further muffled my voice.

" 'Morley, you're going to make yourself ill fretting about me.' Harriet stepped off the curb to hail a taxi. It stopped within inches of her feet. Before I could move, she was inside and rolling down the window. Just a couple of inches so I couldn't see her face as well as I wanted to. 'Good-bye, darling, it's been wonderful from start to finish. An absolutely perfect day, I mean.

Now hurry back to Frau Grundman's and have her make you some more cocoa.'

" 'Harriet!' I moved to press a hand to the glass, but she was already a blur moving off into traffic. As I trod disconsolately back to the boardinghouse, the rain came down again in stinging darts, and I continued on under the black canopy of the umbrella.

"My bleak mood continued throughout what was left of the afternoon into the evening. Before turning in for the night, I partook of a glass of Frau Grundman's homemade peppermint schnapps, and I woke in the morning feeling groggy and still out of sorts. My soul was further soured by the sunshine streaming through the window, for what was sunshine without Harriet?

Oh, to have phoned her! But her hosts, the Voelkels, were not on the telephone. Harriet had explained early in our relationship that this was one of their eccentricities and not to be weighed against their supreme generosity. When the noon hour approached, I forced myself to take a constitutional through the town and even stopped at the bakery for a confection or two. Replete with flaky pastry and plump, juicy raisins, they rallied my spirits. I even ventured into a nearby cinema where I watched an American film that made me proud to be all things British. On this high note I returned to the boardinghouse, to be somewhat deflated on being informed by the kindly Frau that Harriet had not telephoned. My beloved had indicated that she was liable to be occupied for the better part of the day.

Patience was called for, I told myself whilst tucking—somewhat languidly it must be said—into an early dinner of schweinerhaxe-pork with sauerkraut and dumplings. Frau Grundman's repertoire was not extensive, but she was an excellent cook and very generous with the second helpings. There were only a couple of other guests staying at the time. Both Japanese. Still, I lingered in the dining room at the conclusion of the meal to sip a glass of cherry brandy (it was not as good as the schnapps) and toss out the occasional, congenial snippet of conversation. My efforts appeared to be well received, if incompletely understood. A pity, for I recall mentioning that I had a daughter living in Chitterton Fells, a charming village by the sea in England, and I was sure that the Japanese gentlemen would be welcome to pay an extensive visit if ever they were in the neighborhood. One always wishes to take one's ambassadorial duties seriously.

"I reentered my room moderately restored. But as the evening dwindled from dusk to darkness, my heart grew heavy once more. Perhaps part of the blame may be laid upon the dumplings. But oh, how I repined for my absent Harriet. My ears strained for the sound of the phone. It did not ring that whole long night. I dreamed I heard it when I finally sank into the stupor of troubled sleep. Every couple of hours I would start up in my bed, but all was still and silent as the grave. At last dawn came and with it the renewed optimism that I was a fool. Harriet must have returned very late to Glatzerstrasse in Loetzinn. She would soon be with me, delighting my ears with all the details of her yesterday. When she had not arrived by midmorning I assured myself that she had slept late.

"When afternoon came without her, I went for an hour's walk around my room. By evening I was so distraught, I swore at the toll-painted wardrobe and could not face the thought of food, although Frau Grundman begged me to let her feed me a spoonful of Wiener schnitzel. There followed a sleepless night, and by the next day I was bedridden. Time became a drifting sea upon which I floated in utter hopelessness, save for enfeebled flounderings back to life and hope when a knock came at my door. But it was always the Frau, never she who I yearned to clasp in my arms once more.

" 'This cannot go on so, Herr Simons.' Frau Grundman stood over me with tears in her eyes on the afternoon of the third day. "You must shake yourself together, sit your feet to the floor, and get on the trousers; then you go into Loetzinn, find Glatzerstrasse, and see these people where your friend lives.'

" 'I have never been there. They are of a reclusive nature, and Harriet felt obliged to maintain their privacy,' I fretted.

" 'Then you go up and down the street till you find the right place.'

" 'I had thought of that.' I lay pleating the sheet with my hands. 'But it could take days. I understand it is a long street, and Harriet never told me the number.'

" 'So you just stay here to look up at the ceiling?'

"I was about to concede that she had a point when the telephone rang and Frau Grundman went plodding downstairs to the old-fashioned instrument in the hall. My heart had started beating again—uncertainly, as if trying to refamiliarize itself with the tempo. It would be her daughter, I told myself. Or, just possibly—the summer rush being over—someone inquiring about room rates. Despite such rationalizations, I sat forward on my pillows and was even extending a foot out of bed when back she came.

" 'Herr Simons!' Her voice came and went in gasps.

" 'Yes, Frau Grundman?' It was all I could manage.

" 'That telephone call, it's from Herr Voelkel.'

"I could neither move nor speak.

" 'He gave me the message; you are to go right of this minute to number 84 Glatzerstrasse. Or if not so soon, when you are able. It was not a friendly voice he has, but that could be because he was upset and looking all around inside his head for the words.'

" 'What did he say about Harriet?' I flung off the bedclothes, and Frau Grundman retreated with averted eyes to the door.

" 'Nothing. He did not speak her name.'

"A sob bubbled its way up my throat.

" 'Get dressed, Herr Simons. All will turn out for the better; you will see it is so.'

" 'Yes,' I whispered. When the door closed,

I endeavored to gain some mastery over my emotions. The eternity of waiting was near an end. Perchance the picture was not as black as I had painted it. I would discover that Harriet had been ill, felled by a violent infection of the lungs from being caught in the rain, but she was rallying and asking for me. Or it could be her old illness that was the culprit. I must fasten on the fact that I now would be there to nurse her back to vitality. The terrible, foolish fear that she had chosen to vanish from my life would be set aside. That she, a goddess, had chosen to love a mere mortal would always be the sweetest of bewilderments!

"I do not have a clear memory of dressing and leaving Frau Grundman's establishment. Did I have socks on my feet, let alone a matching pair, when I got into the taxi that bore me away to Loetzinn? I could not describe that ride, or the direction it took or how long it lasted. All that is certain is that I found myself standing outside a tall, narrow house in Glatzerstrasse with a yellowish white front door and an iron railing at the basement windows. A pale, solemn house that seemed ill-fitted to contain Harriet's lustrous presence. An old woman garbed in servile black answered my knock and, without inquiring who I was or waiting for me to introduce myself, beckoned me inside and closed the door with a soft click. Her heavy-lidded eyes were as dark and forbidding as the hall in which we stood. Its walls were papered in a red flock with speckles of black and gold, the staircase was almost monstrous in its elaborate carving, and a stuffed black bear loomed large in a shadowy corner. The old woman opened a door to our left, pointed a gnarled finger, gabbled something incomprehensible, and slipped away the moment I entered the room.

"This was no more cheery than the hall. Indeed, if possible, it was more oppressive to the human spirit. The walls were paneled in black oak; the narrow window was draped in heavy plush. There were cigarette butts in the ashtrays, and the fireplace looked as though it had not been cleaned in years. Above it hung a portrait of a lifeless-looking cat that appeared to have been stretched to cover the width of the canvas. Alas, my poor Harriet! Such were my thoughts as footsteps sounded behind me, and as I turned, I saw a small man, with a foxy face, wearing an Edwardian-style black suit with a wine-colored velvet waistcoat and a silk cravat at the neck of his dandified shirt.

" 'Mr. Simons, I presume?' His German accent had slight Cockney overtones. "I am Ingo Voelkel. My housekeeper, Fraulein Stoppe, told me of your arrival. And I ask that you will accept my wife's apologies for not coming down to greet you. Anna is reclusive by nature and at present unable to face seeing anyone. It is good of you to come so promptly. But of course you will have been anxious about our dear Harriet.'

" 'She is...?' I strove to keep my voice level.

" 'Dead.' Herr Voelkel spoke the word as if it were a day of the week.

" 'Oh, my God!' I fell back against a piece of furniture.

" 'I only wish there had been a way to break this to you gently. May I offer you a drink, Mr. Simons?'

" 'Nothing!' I shook my head violently.

" 'Then do please take a seat.' He was beside me, and I found myself being lowered onto the sofa. 'You will of course want to know how it happened.'

" 'She was always loath to talk about her illness,' I moaned from the depths of the horsehair cushions. 'But when she did, she was optimistic; indeed, she assured me there was every indication that she was cured.'

" 'You need a drink, Mr. Simons.' A glass of sherry was pressed into my hand.

" 'Her doctors were mistaken or untruthful?'

" 'Neither. Harriet was well on her way to full health when misfortune struck.'

" 'It is what I feared,' I said, shaking sherry all over my trousers. 'She was brought low by a cold after being caught in the rain when out walking with me the other day.'

" 'My dear man, you wrong yourself.' Herr Voelkel stood over me, his reddish brown eyes boring into mine. 'Harriet was killed when the car she was driving on her way back here from Koblenz ran off a country road along the Moselle River and plunged into the Elzabach, a creek in the area of Metternich and Zell. There was a heavy fog. It was, tragically, one of those things. A terrible, unforeseeable accident.' "

CHAPTER 8

THE SALMON PINK SATIN NIGHTDRESS LAY ACROSS THE bedspread, looking inappropriately optimistic. It was a lovely thing with a tucked bodice and a handkerchief hem. Not at all my usual sleepwear. I had bought it earlier in the week with blissful thoughts of the trip to France in mind. That afternoon, before going into Chitterton Fells, I had been about to put it in my case when I decided that there was no good reason why my second honeymoon with the husband of my dreams should not begin that night. So I had sprayed it with my very best perfume and left it out, picturing how it would look when moonlight silvered its folds. Now I rolled it into a ball, stuffed it in the top drawer of my dressing table, and got into my flannel pajamas with the Peter Pan collar. I was sitting up against the four-poster headboard when Ben came into the room with a cup of hot milk that he handed to me before shedding his dressing gown and getting in beside me.

"This beats champagne any night of the week." I took a comforting sip and smiled at him. His pajamas were of the same burgundy shade as the velvet curtains, and his hair looked very black against the white pillow-case. The selfish part of me wished that Daddy hadn't shown up with Harriet. At least not until we had returned from our holiday, complete with new T-shirts and enough renewed energy to support him as he worked through his grief.

"I wonder what she was really like?" I set down my empty cup on the bedside table.

"Your father painted a pretty clear picture."

"He gave us his impressions and told us what Harriet told him."

"That's all he could do."

"I know." I watched Ben turn off his lamp, did the same with mine, and lay back, staring up at the shadowy ceiling. "It's that Gypsy business that still has me unsettled. The one in Germany warned Harriet to be careful of water."

"They always do."

"Her car went into the river."

"Accidents happen all the time."

"If it was an accident." I sat up and poked at my pillow.

"Why wouldn't it be? Visibility was poor, and she probably didn't know the road. Also, her mind may have been filled with Morley's pleasure when she showed up with her surprise. She was probably planning the trips they would take together. Voelkel told him that Harriet had gone to considerable trouble to find a big old American convertible because your father had mentioned that he had always wanted to drive one."

Moonlight pierced the curtains. "Maybe it was so old that the sleeving was gone," I conceded. "Or just maybe Harriet was mixed up in some sort of shady business that led an interested party to follow her and drive her off the road."

"Ellie!" Ben, never at his most patient late at night, was sucking in a breath and holding his head.

"I didn't at all like the sound of the foxy-faced Herr Voelkel," I continued relentlessly. "It seems awfully fishy to me that there was no telephone. And nice people," I added as Tobias's furry form settled at the bottom of the bed, "do not have pictures of dead cats above their mantelpieces."

"What sort of shady business?" Ben chomped down on a yawn.

"How should I know?" I turned on my side and tucked a hand under my pillow. But I kept my eyes open. As sleep crept closer, so did the image of Harriet's car swerving off the foggy road and taking a nosedive into the Moselle. How long did she remain conscious? How fiercely did she struggle to free herself? Did she have a moment of false hope, thinking she could open the door? Did she think of my father as she gasped her last breath? It was time to think of something else. "What did Freddy have to say when you saw him off the premises?" I asked.

"He didn't support your outrageous theory, if that's what you mean." Ben sounded very much the long-suffering husband.

"I don't have a theory."

"Then let's say Freddy's only mention of murder plots was when he talked about his role in the St. Anselm's play. He asked me if I could spare an hour or two to hear him run through his lines. I told him that he should go home and lie awake all night anticipating his mother's visit. So he slunk off, but only after I promised not to bolt the front door in case he took fright and decided to come back here with his teddy bear."

"That was kind," I said.

"Thank you, sweetheart. And now, if you won't think me a spoilsport, I'll snuggle down and think about what a wonderful time we could be having if your poor father weren't three doors down with only a funeral urn to take into bed for a cuddle."

"Now who's displaying a penchant for melodrama?" I moved closer and stroked his hair, but the moment I guessed what he was thinking—that Merlin's Court was built in the good old-fashioned way, with walls several feet thick—I popped a kiss on his ear and turned over. Who could even consider the possibility of romance under the present circumstances? Like it or not, we had become a house of mourning. At least until Harriet's relatives arrived to claim her remains.

It took a while and the counting of many

sheep on my part, but at last Ben fell asleep. I looked at the face of the illuminated clock, closed my eyes, and looked at it again. Almost midnight. Maybe I dozed, because the house seemed to shift, and I felt myself falling and sinking deep into rolling shadows. Jerking upright, I gulped down deep breaths that got forced painfully back up into my throat by the frantic beating of my heart. Afraid to lie back down, I slid out of bed, felt around for my dressing gown, and picked up the empty milk cup before tiptoeing from the room.

As I was descending the last couple of stairs, I noticed that Ben hadn't put the bolt on the front door. A closer inspection, while standing with shivering feet on the flag-stones, showed that he hadn't even locked it. I hadn't taken his promise to Freddy seriously and now decided that he had probably just for-gotten. Ben tended to be a little cavalier in making his nightly round of securing doors and windows. (Hence, my cousin's remark ear-lier in the evening, upon climbing through the sitting-room window, that Merlin's Court was a burglar's paradise.) Shaking my head, I remedied matters before nipping down the hall into the kitchen, where I found the light left on. Well, we had all been pretty emo-tionally drained by evening's end, I thought, while pouring milk into the saucepan that Ben had left beside the sink. He had also left out a tin of cocoa and a half-opened packet of diges-tive biscuits. Or was it possible that Daddy had come downstairs for a nightcap?

Deciding that I preferred the sofa to sitting on a hard kitchen chair, I put a couple of the digestives onto a plate, which I carried along with my steaming cup back out into the hall. As I reached the drawing room, I saw a light in the crack under the door. Fully expecting to see my parent installed within, I shifted everything to one hand and turned the knob. And immediately realized I should have done a better job of balancing cup and plate, because I almost dropped the lot.

I had not previously seen the Reverend Dunstan Ambleforth attired in anything other than a cassock and surplice, but even in his present baggy trousers and elderly cardigan he was every bit the cleric. He was a man with one foot firmly entrenched in a bygone century and the other planted on the path to the heavenly kingdom above. His white hair stood away from his head as though he were perpetually being caught by surprise. A false impression. At our first meeting, I had been convinced that had the church organist parachuted off the balcony, Mr. Ambleforth would have gone right on announcing that the next hymn would be 342. Certainly he did not look one whit discombobulated when he now raised his watery blue eyes and saw me standing three feet away.

"Ah, there you are, my dear." He smiled in a kindly if somewhat abstracted manner. "I've been sitting here contemplating the effect of the tonsure upon monastic life. As you know, the good St. Ethelwort opposed the practice and had quite a spat with Rome on the subject in 1031. I am surprised that his bishop did not give him the boot"—Reverend Ambleforth chuckled softly—"or perhaps I should say the sandal, and order him to take the next boat back to the principality from which he came, in what we now call Germany."

"Excuse me," I began.

"One can appreciate, my dear, why the Barbers Guild would not have him for their saint."

"I'm just not sure why you're here," I floundered on.

"I have no doubt, however, that its members flocked to his shrine along with the multitudes of goldsmiths and stonemasons and so on when word of his miracles made it clear he was a saint for all men."

Mr. Ambleforth's eyes were now fixed on the days when hair shirts were the height of fashion. I could see I was about to lose him completely. But all I could do was stand there clearing my throat.

"Yes, what is it, Kathleen, my dear?" he murmured dreamily.

"Kathleen?" I exclaimed. The man actually blinked at me.

"My goodness! He sounded mildly perplexed. "You're not my wife."

"No, I'm Ellie Haskell."

"So you are." He rose from his chair and extended a courtly hand way off to my right. "How very good of you to drop in for a chat. Do have a seat and unburden yourself. Be assured, my dear child, that nothing you say, of however private a nature, will shock me. Think of me only as your confessor. A vicar hears it all. You are not the first remorseful soul to come to me in need of guidance. Indeed, you are not the first to have helped yourself to the contents of the Missions to Defrocked Clergy fund."

"The what?" I sat down with a bump on the arm of the sofa.

Again he blinked, this time with more emphasis. "What did you say your name was?"

"Ellie Haskell."

"Ah, I'm afraid I was thinking of an Edie Hubbell from my previous parish. Sometimes one's mind goes back in time..."

I had to halt him before he reached the Middle Ages. "I'm afraid, Vicar, that you're a little confused. You see—" My voice was cut off by the clock striking one.

"Perhaps you're here about the girl guides," he suggested hopefully while resuming his seat. "In which case it is my wife you should see. Kathleen still has her own guide's uniform and will thus be delighted to welcome you to the vicarage."

"But this isn't the vicarage."

"It isn't?" He got up again and peered around him like a man slowly defrosting after being frozen for fifty years. His eyes took in the portrait of Abigail above the mantelpiece, the turquoise-and-rose Aubusson carpet, and the ivory damask on the Queen Anne chairs. His forehead creased in deep perplexity as he contemplated the yellow Chinese vases on the mantelpiece and the decanters on the drinks table. But I could tell he wasn't entirely convinced that he had wandered in through the wrong front door.

"This is Merlin's Court," I was saying when the doorbell rang. After hurriedly excusing myself to Reverend Ambleforth, I raced out into the hall to find out who else thought our household never slept. I opened the door just as our visitor was about to punch the bell again. As I stepped back, she advanced into the hall as if leading an expedition to the Arctic Circle. The twin suits of armor quaked in their metal boots as if expecting to be ordered to brave polar bears for the glory that was Britain.

Confronting Kathleen Ambleforth, or Mrs. Vicar, as she liked to be called, for the second time in one day, I was struck anew by the fact that she was a woman who had undoubtedly taken life by the throat from the moment she emerged from the womb. Her boundless energy made the average person look in need of an immediate blood transfusion. Upon her arrival in Chitterton Fells, she had unloaded the moving van while two strong men in cloth caps sat drinking the cups of tea she provided for them. Within an hour she had the furniture in place, the pictures hung, and the ornaments arranged to her satisfaction. Whereupon she settled her husband in his study, made a batch of cheese scones, and went back outside to dig up most of the garden.

I'd heard all this from Mrs. Malloy when she was sitting in my kitchen trying to get the point across that coming to clean for me three mornings a week would be a lot more fun if I would only get everything shipshape before her arrival. She had become an even greater admirer of Mrs. Ambleforth after auditioning for a role in Murder Most Fowl and being given a walk-on part, along with the opportunity to understudy the lead. Her only criticism being that Mrs. Vicar had no fashion sense. This said while Mrs. M. was wearing purple velvet that allowed for more cleavage than the San Andreas Fault. Tonight Kathleen was wearing a tweed coat with inches of pink nightie showing below the hem, a curler above each ear, and a pair of brogues on her bare feet.

As usual, she exuded the desire to get life sorted back to her satisfaction.

"I'm sorry to knock you up at this hour." She closed the front door for me and looked around as if searching out pictures that needed straightening. "But the thing is, Ellie, Dunstan has got himself misplaced again. I left him in his study while I went into the kitchen to whip up half a dozen sponge cakes for the Women's Institute tea, and when I got back, he was gone. At first I didn't worry because he often goes off on a walk to sort out St. Ethelwort in his head. But when he didn't come back after a couple of hours, I said to Ruth, 'If I know your uncle Dunstie, he's gone wandering into the wrong house. And the one closest to us is Merlin's Court.' "

"He's in the sitting room," I said.

"Silly old dear!" Mrs. Ambleforth shook her

head fondly. "The neighbors at our former parish got quite used to his little visits. They even used to leave the cocoa tin out for him."

"I'm afraid he had to look in the pantry tonight."

"That must have been a blow! Dunstan isn't used to fending for himself. Not with me and Ruth to look after him. Such a wonderful girl. She does all her uncle's typing for him—his sermons as well as the manuscripts. Her living with us suits all of us for now. And it's not as though she never gets to meet any eligible men. There's Freddy, for instance. As I may have mentioned this afternoon, he's really quite outstanding in the play. Of course, I do think it's one of the best I've written. And we are very lucky to have Lady Grizwolde in the lead. You know she was on the stage before her marriage?"

"Yes, I heard that."

"Dunstan wasn't the only lucky one"— Mrs. Ambleforth had found a picture to straighten—"in coming to live here, I mean. I expect you realize that the reason he was so keen on the move is because it puts him right on the spot with St. Ethelwort." Turning in time to catch my perplexed expression, she continued: "The ruins of the monastery he founded in 1014 stand on the grounds of the Grizwolde ancestral home. You'll have to excuse me, my dear. The trouble with living with Dunstan is one expects everyone to know these things."

Watching her move on to reposition the vase of flowers on the trestle table, I tried not to sound defensive. "I knew about the ruins, but I tend to think of all monks as Benedictines."

"Just don't ever say that to Dunstan or he might come out of one of his trances to murder you." Mrs. Ambleforth gave another of her fond chuckles and, taking my arm, led me toward the drawing room, where her spouse sat in apparent oblivion with his cup of cocoa on his knee. "Dear old thing!" She stood in the doorway, looking at him fondly. "He really is just a little potty on the subject of his eleventh-century hero. The saint only a man could love is what I call him. But that's husbands for you! They all have their little quirks, don't they?"

Before I could answer, my father came downstairs. He wore a blue-and-white striped nightshirt and, with arms outstretched, glided right up to this seemingly imperturbable woman. Glassy-eyed and larger than life, he extolled her in a voice that should have been accompanied by the clanking of chains: "Cast off death's embrace and return to my empty arms, oh, most exquisite of passion flowers!" It was a bright spot of the evening that, unmindful of the cocoa, Mrs. Ambleforth, fearful of being ravaged by a madman, charged into the room and sat down on her husband's venerable knee.

CHAPTER 9

I WAS STANDING AT THE LATTICED WINDOW OF A house by the sea on a breezy October morning, watching a dark-haired man descending the steps into the courtyard. He was my every dream come true: handsome, witty, charming, and best of all, endearingly in love with ordinary, everyday me. There was only one problem. He should have been loading cases into the car for a trip to France. Instead, he was about to drive Daddy's Rent-A-Wreck into the stable before the man who delivered fish on Tuesdays could plow into it.

"You're a selfish, spiteful cow; that's what you are!" The female voice spoke from behind me, enunciating every syllable with brutal relish." It's not love he feels for you but pity! After all, it can't be said you're either use or ornament in this house. Only because he's a gentleman born and bred did he agree to take you away to foreign parts in the first place."

My hand gripped the curtain as the voice flowed over me, softening just a little, making it even more unpleasant. And for some reason reminding me of the Gypsy. "When he comes through that door, I expect you to tell him you have remembered where your duty lies. Wish him happiness with a woman better suited to a man of his virile good looks and speed him on his way."

For another couple of seconds I remained too stunned to move, but when I mustered the wherewithal to turn around, I saw Mrs. Roxie Malloy planted on one of the drawing-room sofas. Her dyed black head, showing two inches of white roots, was bent over the sheaf of papers she was holding.

"I trust you understand me, Clarabelle!" she proclaimed. The sweep of her arm made the table lamp quiver.

Clarabelle! I had long ago shortened my name to Ellie. But as my father had unfortunately remembered, the full version was Giselle. Something Mrs. Malloy knew. Indeed, there was very little she didn't know about me, having been my household helper from the time she arrived to serve canapés on my wedding day and agreed to stay on in the hope of adding a little tone to the establishment. It was understood between us that she ruled the roost at Merlin's Court. But even if she hadn't called me by the wrong name, I would have realized something was seriously amiss. It was only eight-thirty, and she never arrived before nine unless she had occasion to report a death. Preferably a murder.

"Mrs. Malloy!" I bent to touch her arm.

"Get away from me, you miserable upstart!" Tossing down the papers so that half of them fell on the floor, she sprang to her feet. A risky maneuver given the fact that she wore extremely high heels and had an hourglass figure with more sand in the top than the bottom. "Fetch me a cup of tea this instant! And remember, I don't take milk, sugar, or arsenic!"

I was wondering whether to ring for the doctor or look in the yellow pages to see if there were any exorcists listed when Mrs. Malloy blinked her purple-shadowed lids. As if coming out of a trance induced from drinking something stronger than tea, she brought my face into focus.

"Oh, it's you, Mrs. H. Almost gave me a heart attack, you did, creeping up on me like that. If this was America, I'd probably sue you for everything you've got." She shook her head and pursed her magenta lips. "Who'd have thought you'd be back from Gay Paree already!"

"I haven't been."

"Are you sure?" Dropping back down on the sofa, she pressed a hand to her black-taffeta bosom. She always dressed as if going out for a night on the town. If rhinestones were diamonds, she would have had to put herself in a safety-deposit box. "Well, I suppose I've got to take your word for it, although I could swear on a stack of Bibles that you told me you was leaving today at the crack of dawn. The last time I was here, you said good-bye at least three times. I can't think what could have happened, short of an earthquake, to keep you from setting off on your holiday the minute you got up." She suddenly turned her head sideways as a rumble sounded from above and the pictures on the walls shifted to cockeyed angles.

"That'll be my father," I told her, "coming downstairs."

"Your what?" Mrs. Malloy sounded as though I had made a purchase without discussing it with her first.

"He arrived last night out of the blue."

"So that's why you haven't bunked off to France." She sat thinking the matter over. "What's he look like? One of those rugged, be-damned-to-you-woman types?"

"You've been reading too many romance novels," I chided.

"No, I haven't. Leastways not for a week or two." She gathered up a few sheets of the scattered papers. "But I know what you're thinking, Mrs. H. Me and your dad probably wouldn't suit. He's bound to be years too old for me. And I'm not the sort to enjoy pushing a man around in a bath chair the way Lady Grizwolde is stuck doing with Sir Casper. Not even to live in a bloody great mansion, I wouldn't. And besides"—her expression turned frosty—"it didn't do my son George much good marrying into your family. What does he find out but that Vanessa has done the dirty on him and little Rose isn't his! And I'm sent bringing her down here in my weekend bag. It's a wonder I didn't turn to the gin bottle." This was spoken as if she had never touched a drop in her life except under doctor's orders.

"It was all terribly hard on you." I knelt to pick up the rest of the papers and hand them to her. "But you won't have to worry about Daddy making a nuisance of himself. Ben and I will be here to keep an eye on him because we aren't going to France. Also, he's involved with somebody else."

Mrs. Molloy bridled. "There's not a woman alive, Mrs. H., that I couldn't knock out of the running if I was to set me mind to it."

I didn't tell her that in this case the other woman was dead. "I'm surprised you didn't notice me when you came in here," I said, settling myself on the sofa across from the one on which she was seated.

"I was reading, Mrs. H., and had the pages up to me nose."

"You certainly startled me with the things you said! You were very good. Really a powerful performance."

Her attempt at appearing nonchalant failed because she was blushing through three layers of makeup. "Well, there's no denying I always wanted to be on the stage. My old ma used to say I was another little Shirley Temple." Reaching out a heavily ringed hand, she made a production of rearranging the papers on her fishnet knees.

"And here you are about to take Chitterton Fells by storm," I said enthusiastically, although I had been under the impression that hers was only a walk-on part. Little more than a black hat and a veil in the funeral scene. Although I was sure she could pack a lot of pathos into standing with a hanky in her hand, it was unlikely that this scene would bring down the house.

"There's a lot to keep straight when you're understudying for the role of Malicia Stillwaters. It's the role of a lifetime, Mrs. H.! Can't you just picture me on opening night? There I'll be standing in the wings, two minutes before the curtain is due to go up, when someone throws Malicia's costume over me head and shoves me onstage." Mrs. Malloy was being sucked back into her trance. "It'll turn out that Lady Grizwolde didn't show up. Poor thing! Her car will have run out of petrol miles from anywhere, just like always happens in the movies."

"Really?" I evinced appropriate surprise. Tobias had leaped out of nowhere onto my lap, embedding his claws in my thighs. Now he settled down to give Mrs. M. the evil eye. They had never been terribly keen on each other, each always being wishful of having the upper paw. "Her ladyship could then break her ankle slogging across the marshes in search of a telephone," I suggested, entering fully into the fantasy. "That way you would get to take over for all three performances. Of course, I'm sure that in reality she has a car phone, but you can't let details ruin the big picture."

"Whatever happens happens." Mrs. Malloy assumed a philosophical mien. "At least you and Mr. H. will be here to see the play, unless you change your minds about going to France, that is." This was punctuated by a deprecating snort. "Pretty rotten I thought it was your bunking off when—leaving me right out of it—Freddy should have been able to count on your claps."

"The trip was already planned by the time he told us that he'd auditioned and got a part. And we did offer to go a week later, but he wouldn't hear of it. He said that having Ben and me there could be a drawback because we'd be bound to jump up and down in our seats, obscuring the view of the talent scout lurking in the back."

Mrs. Malloy looked as though this possibility had not previously occurred to her, while I hoped that the crowd that poured into the church hall wouldn't be expecting Andrew Lloyd Weber. Unfortunately, there was no banishing the image of the three Miss Richards who routinely terrorized children's piano recitals. Or that of Mr. Briggs, who wrote a review column of local events for the weekly newspaper.

"People enjoy a lighthearted comedy," I said hopefully.

"A what?" Mrs. Malloy's painted brows shot up. "Wherever did you get the idea that Murder Most Fowl is a barrel of laughs? It's a tragedy right up there with Hamlet. Only in English and without the men hopping around in tights. Hasn't Freddy filled you in on the plot?"

"Just his part."

"Men!" She looked at Tobias, who understandably took the huff and stalked off to the other end of the room. "As if I don't have enough to do, Mrs. H., it's left all up to me to fill you in from beginning to end. And this is a three-act play we're talking about. Well, there goes the hoovering for this morning!" Her sigh sounded as though she had worked on it for weeks. "The curtain goes up on Malicia Stillwaters sitting at a little green desk, writing a blackmail letter to Major Wagewar."

"How does the audience know that's what she's doing?"

"It's that big word for talking out loud that Hamlet invented."

"A soliloquy."

"Always have to show off, don't you, Mrs. H.?" Mrs. Malloy looked more pitying than condemning. "Malicia has just moved to the small seaside village of Chatterton Dells, and she's gone and upset all the neighbors by turning the grounds of the ancestral home into a chicken farm. Not that she gives a bloody hoot. She's always got what she's wanted by fair means or foul. The Malicias of this world always do. And she really has the major by the regimentals because she knows that Reginald Rakehell, that's played by Freddy, is his son from the wrong side of the blanket. But then she falls head over heels for Reg and tries to break up his marriage to Clarabelle. When the major turns the tables on her blackmailing scheme, she has to murder him. Only he's left a letter telling what she's been up to in a jar he's brought back from India. In the final scene, Clarabelle shows up waving a gun, meaning to shoot Reg, but she aims all wild like and hits the jar. It breaks all over the mantelpiece. And Detective Inspector Allbright arrives just as Clarabelle turns the gun on herself. In the final scene, Reg is sobbing over her lifeless body, with the major's letter in his hand."

"A man who dumps his wife for a villainess deserves to suffer." Such was my unsentimental view of things.

Mrs. Malloy sat drained of all emotion. "The audience will know when the curtain comes down that Reg is going to put on the old stiff upper lip and go outside and shoot himself. All very British. Mustn't let the old school down and all that."

"What happens to Malicia?"

"She goes to jump out the window, but the vicar stops her and tells her that when she comes out of prison, she can come and work for him and do the typing for a book he's writing on the life of St. Cuthbert."

"Mrs. Ambleforth appears to have drawn rather largely from life in writing this play."

"All great art is partly autobiographical," Mrs. Malloy pronounced with the authority of a six-former who has just received an acceptance from Cambridge.

I turned the conversation back to my father. "Just now I said that Daddy was involved with someone," I began, "but what I didn't tell you is that he has brought her to Merlin's Court."

"Well"—Mrs. Malloy bristled as she got to her feet—"I hope she won't go putting on airs and expecting to be waited on."

"She's not that sort of woman."

"That's what they all say."

"This one's not saying anything."

"Lost her voice?" Mrs. Malloy tried not to sound interested. "Or is she in a snit?"

"Neither. She's dead."

"And she's here in this house? Well!" With a deep intake of breath, she pronounced, "If there's one thing you should know by now, Mrs. H., it's that I don't work with bodies cluttering up the place. For starters it's not allowed by the C.F.C.W.A. In case you've forgotten, that's the Chitterton Fells Charwomen's Association."

"Harriet isn't laid out on Daddy's bed. Her ashes are in an urn that looks like quite an ordinary clay pot, and although I don't think he'll let it out of his sight for long, I thought you ought to be forewarned."

"In case I thought it was a jar of freeze-dried coffee?" Mrs. Malloy could be quick on the uptake.

"There is that," I said, "along with the problem of Aunt Lulu."

"Freddy's mother?"

"That's right. She's arriving today to stay with him at the cottage for a while. And, of course, she will be in and out of this house. You knew about her being a recovering kleptomaniac; it just wouldn't do at all if she were to make off with Harriet. For one thing, Daddy would be beside himself. Plus, her relations are coming sometime today to collect the urn."

"So you want me to keep an eye on old feather fingers?"

"I'd be most awfully grateful, Mrs. Malloy."

"Story of my life, that is. One of these days you'll notice that I don't have a Dior frock to me name. But in the meantime tell me more about this Harriet," she urged, patting my shoulder invitingly. Where did your dad meet her?"

"In Germany."

"And what's her last name?"

"Brown." I thought this over. "About as common a name as you can get other than Smith. I'm sure he'll be more than willing to tell you the whole story. I think he needs to continue to work it out of his system. Something happened last night that was really quite disturbing. Daddy came downstairs when Reverend Ambleforth and his wife were here. He was sleepwalking and looked quite scary, especially when he started babbling at Mrs. Vicar, thinking she was Harriet. I don't suppose they will be inclined to say anything. I certainly hope not. You will keep mum on this, Mrs. Malloy?"

The woman I had long regarded as my right hand eyed me severely from under neon lids. "I trust that was a joke, Mrs. H., because as well you know, it's against the ethics of me profession to breathe a word to a living soul about what goes on here at Merlin's Court. Except," she amended, "to immediate friends and the occasional person in the bus queue."

"I just don't want it going round that my father is batty." I had been prowling around the room as I spoke and ended up in front of the window in time to see a taxi halt in the driveway and deposit three passengers.

"That'll be Harriet's relatives," I informed Mrs. Malloy over my shoulder as I hurried from the room. If she replied, I didn't hear her because on winged feet I was through the hall and down the outside steps. Perhaps I had been letting my imagination run wild last night. Perhaps there was nothing more to the Harriet situation than a sad little love affair. But I was enormously relieved that the end was in sight. I would invite these people in for a cup of coffee, Ben and I would offer condolences, Daddy would emote, and they and the urn would go away, never to be seen again. This may sound hard, but I wasn't only thinking of how glad I would be to have the funeral pall lifted from the house. I really believed my father's emotional recovery depended on making an immediate break.

Unfortunately, the best-laid plans of daughters often run amuck. When I reached the three people standing alongside the taxi, Ben had already joined them. It took a moment for me to sort them out into a man and two women, for they looked oddly like those egg-shaped Russian dolls that fit one inside the other. Short and round with shiny black hair and eyes. Also a bit wobbly. That could have been because they were bundled up in jackets better suited to a Siberian winter. Or because they were upset.

Ben gathered me forward. "Ellie, these are the Hoppers, Harriet's cousins, and I've just been telling them that your father isn't here."

"What do you mean?" My face suddenly felt as if it, too, had been produced in a doll factory. "I heard him come downstairs a few moments ago when I was talking to Mrs. Malloy."

"And I just saw him go whizzing off on the back of Freddy's motorbike."

"Did they say where they were going?"

"No, but your father shouted back that he had the urn with him."

"Oh, my goodness! What if they have a spill?" It was an unfortunate suggestion to make in front of the Hoppers. All three mouths rounded into O's of alarm.

"I'm sure Freddy will be careful to avoid any big bumps in the road. But it is too bad they went off without letting us know when they'll be back." Ben was doing a better job of keeping a grip on his temper than I was of holding down my hair, which the wind was trying to rip off my head.

"We're so sorry about this," I said. "Why don't you come into the house and wait a least a little while."

"Yes, do," Ben urged them. "If you haven't eaten yet, I can make us all a big breakfast to take the chill out of our bones. And with luck my father-in-law will be back before we're finished with the toast and marmalade."

The response was a threefold stare; then the Hoppers went into a huddle, their heads so close together that they seemed to merge into a black bowling ball. Whispers drifted our way, punctuated by miniature snuffles and snorts. It seemed to take ages, but at last

113

they separated back into their clonelike entities.

"We'll come back later," said the man.

"This afternoon," added a female voice.

"At about three," piped up another.

"It wouldn't do to keep the taxi waiting indefinitely." The man flexed the fingers of his red mittens. A signal, perhaps, to his companions. And before Ben and I could get out more than a few words in reply, they had all bundled aboard and were being driven away at a lumbering pace.

"It really is too bad of Daddy." I stood shivering in my cardigan, which wasn't made for Siberia. "He bunked off on purpose."

"I didn't think he got on Freddy's bike by accident." Ben wrapped an arm around me as we made our way back to the house.

"I meant that he wanted to put off handing over the urn for as long as possible."

"To be fair to him, Ellie, the Hoppers could have been more precise about when he was to expect them. They could have set a time last night or rung again this morning. But they are understandably upset and not thinking clearly. This has to be an unhappy experience for them. And somehow I don't think they're too bright, do you?"

"I don't want to think about them at all," I said. "I know it sounds horribly selfish, but I'd like to forget about Harriet and go off to France as we planned. But of course I can't blithely abandon Daddy."

"Not today or even tomorrow. But in a couple of days he may perk up and begin to feel at home here." We were standing on the little bridge that spanned the ornamental moat, and Ben swung me around to face him. "And we wouldn't be abandoning him, sweetheart. Freddy would be around to help keep his spirits up."

"Freddy will have enough on his plate with Aunt Lulu and the play."

"That's true, but—" Before Ben could cajole me further, we heard a mighty roar and turned to see a motorbike slithering and sliding down the drive. A couple of birds shot up in the air, squawking for dear life. Moments later, as the vibrations faded into the wind, my father staggered to the ground and blundered toward us. As he brushed up against me, in passing I saw that his eyes were squeezed shut. I was afraid to say anything to him in case he was sleepwalking again. Isn't it supposed to be dangerous to rouse someone when they are in that state? Ben may have been thinking along those lines, or he may have noticed that Daddy's face was avocado green. Anyway, he let him go into the house without a word.

"Back safe and sound," Freddy shouted from the drive with inappropriate cheer. "Although I suspect Uncle Morley's life flashed before him when we were taking the worst of the hairpin bends going up and down the cliff road. But that's not all bad, because I think he was hoping at the start to have me drive him around for hours so he could be gone when Harriet's relatives showed up."

"They came and left. Empty-handed.

Where's the urn?" Ben called down from the moat bridge.

"Still up in Uncle Morley's bedroom. He only said he had taken it so you or Ellie wouldn't go looking for it and hand it over while his back was turned."

"You're a disloyal toad, Freddy, and I hope your mother stays with you for months and robs you of every dish in the sink." I would have said more, but Mrs. Malloy came out the front door to announce that Lady Grizwolde was on the phone and wanted to talk to me.

"It'll be about the decorating," I told Ben.

"You would go thinking that. You and your career!" Mrs. Malloy followed me back into the house. "And there's me all in a state that she's rung to say she broke her leg and would you please break it to me gently that I'll have to take over as Malicia Stillwaters and risk seeing me name up in lights when Hollywood comes calling."

CHAPTER 10

MRS. MALLOY WOULD PROBABLY HAVE CONTINUED to hover beside me, listening in on my attempts at conversation with Lady Grizwolde, if my father had not come downstairs. His complexion was back to normal, and he was carrying the urn with all the pomp and circumstance of the archbishop of Canterbury preparing to anoint his monarch at the coronation. Mrs. Malloy came as close to genuflecting as I had ever seen her, in or out of church.

"If I had known you had a dad like that, Mrs. H.," she whispered in a voice that carried to the rafters, "I would have worked for you free of charge. Of course, it's too late now because you chose to be sneaky. But I won't hold the sins of the daughter against the father." Upon which parting thrust she proceeded reverently across the flagstones to the kitchen door, which she opened as if she were one of St. Peter's underlings manning the Pearly Gates. Stepping aside, black and white head bent, she allowed my father to pass through.

I spoke into the receiver. "I'm sorry, Lady Grizwolde. I didn't catch what you said."

"I've been wondering when you are setting off for France?" Her voice was that of a woman who knows she is beautiful. It was easy to picture her standing in the vast hall of the Old Abbey with the light from the stained-glass windows illuminating her perfect features to a medieval perfection beloved of kings and struggling artists alike. I immediately wished I were wearing something smarter than my old skirt, striped blouse, and camel-colored cardigan.

"We were supposed to leave today, but my father arrived unexpectedly. So the trip is off." I stood peering into the mirror above the trestle table, fiddling with my hair, and in the process almost knocked over the bronze vase filled with chrysanthemums and autumn leaves. "Ben and I will just have to go to France another time."

"I'm sure it's lovely having your father with you." Lady Grizwolde's voice had grown faint, and I hastily adjusted the receiver to my ear.

"Oh, yes! Daddy's quite a character."

"You'll have to bring him over here. Perhaps even this morning, if you can spare the time, because I'm eager for you to come out and look over some of the magazines I was telling you about; the House Beautiful ones, with those rooms I liked. Remember I couldn't find them when you came last time? Timothia—you'll remember my husband's cousin—had put them away in an old chest. She's a bit vague at the best of times, and it seems to have gone over her head that I've been looking for those magazines for days."

"It's so annoying to lose things," I agreed. "What time would you like me to come?"

"How about eleven-thirty? And then you can stay for lunch. Cook always rustles up something more exciting when we have visitors. And do bring your father, if he would like to come."

"Thank you, Lady Grizwolde. I'm sure he'll appreciate the invitation even if he decides that he's best to stay put for today."

"Try and persuade him; I'll tell Cook to prepare for one more, just in case."

"That is kind of you."

"And if he doesn't come, we can have his share." Lady Grizwolde's mellow laugh had the faint ring of one that had been perfected during hours of rehearsals. I hung up with mixed feelings. I wasn't really keen on working from pictures. I much preferred to get the feel of the house I was to work on and integrate that with the owner's taste.

Idly, I wondered if my relationship with Lady Grizwolde would open up into something approaching friendship. Would the day come when she'd ask me to call her Phyllis? Somehow I doubted it, although not because I suspected her of snobbism. It was more the feeling that she was a woman who, for all her graciousness of manner, didn't choose to get close to people. Maybe she was shy. I knew all about putting up defenses. Unfortunately, I'd discovered that the shields used to protect ourselves tend to be made out of glass. Doomed to shatter at a thrust from an unexpected quarter.

Mrs. Malloy was a woman who knew how to parry life's slings and arrows. She wore the armor of her taffeta cocktail frocks and heavy makeup with the indomitable courage of Henry V preparing to trounce on French heads at Agincourt. When I entered the kitchen, she was seated at the table across from my father. Ben stood at the Aga frying bacon and eggs as if playing a bit part in Murder Most Fowl.

"Your Harriet wasn't German is what you're telling me." Mrs. M. poured orange juice for Daddy as if to spill a drop would be a sacrilege demanding immediate excommunication.

"She was a true English rose." He studied the urn in front of his plate and caressed its oddly shaped curves with a lover's hand.

"From London, you say?" The glass of juice was set down reverently at his elbow.

"That's where Harriet lived when she was married. But she much preferred the countryside."

"So did my third husband before he passed on." Mrs. Malloy was patently committed to making this a truly bonding experience.

"How did he die?" Daddy asked in the manner of one whose burden is imperceptibly lightened on meeting a fellow voyager through the vales of misfortune.

"He didn't. He passed on to his fourth wife."

"Ah!" Daddy retreated back into the shadows.

"Harriet's such a beautiful name. If I'd had a daughter, that's what I would have called her. I've often said so to Mrs. H." My prized daily helper ignored me as I walked past her to join Ben at the Aga.

"Would you really?" Daddy peeked out again.

"And Brown is a lovely surname."

"It didn't do my exquisite Harriet justice."

"Well, if you don't mind me saying so, neither does that pot you've got her in." Mrs. Malloy could only be sweetness and light for so long. "But," she added, remembering to gush, "perhaps it's got sentimental value."

"Her friends the Voelkels selected it." Daddy viewed the urn over the rim of his Roman nose. His pale blue eyes grew troubled. It was as though he were seeing it for the first time as a vessel rather than an extension of Harriet's earthly being.

"You don't think it's suitable?" He appealed to Mrs. M's superior knowledge.

"Doesn't do a thing for her."

"What would you say is wrong with it?"

"Well, for starters, you said she was a platinum blonde, didn't you? And that sort of clay is absolutely the wrong color for blondes." Mrs. Malloy spoke with the authority of one who imagined herself to have hobnobbed with the likes of Yves Saint Laurent. "And besides"—she had decided not to mince words—"it's a horrible shape."

Daddy pursed his fleshy lips. "Harriet had a perfect figure."

"Then she should have something with nice graceful lines instead of those funny bulges. Not that I'm trying to make meself out to be an authority." Mrs. Malloy suddenly remembered to be humble. "But I do remember when my third husband once removed—"

"Your what?" My startled voice almost made Ben drop the frying pan while in the process of pouring off the bacon fat into a Pyrex bowl. It was, however, Daddy and Mrs. Malloy who looked most put out by the untimely interruption.

"They tend to do that, your daughter and son-in-law," she informed him sympathetically. "Creep about the kitchen, I mean, as if they owned it. Listening in on other people's private conversations. But that's the price you're going to have to pay for breakfast, I suppose. At least the children aren't underfoot. Not that they aren't dear little things, all of them." A smile settled like a purple butterfly on her lips, and I knew she was thinking of little Rose, who would have been her granddaughter if my cousin Vanessa hadn't put one over on her son George. "Life can be rotten at times," said Mrs. Malloy.

"What did you mean about your third husband?" I prompted as Ben slid a fried egg onto the plate I was holding out to him. "How exactly was he removed?"

"By a couple of very rude policemen. They came bang at teatime and wasn't even nice enough to let Alfie (or was it Bert?) finish his toad-in-the-hole. Well, that's what you get for splurging on pork sausages when beef ones would have done just as well is what I had to tell meself." She shook her head at the vagaries of life. "They charged him with trafficking in stolen goods. Though you tell me how much trafficking he could have done when he didn't so much as own a bike, let alone a car! Of course, looking back, it does seem a bit odd the sort of presents he bought me that year. A pram for me fiftieth birthday, an airline stewardess's uniform for our wedding anniversary, and a barber's sink for Christmas. But men never have a clue what to get, do they?"

"I know enough not to buy anything for the kitchen." Ben smiled at me in a somewhat abstracted manner as he added several rashers of bacon, a couple of slices of fried bread, and a large spoonful of sautéed mushrooms to the plate.

"Did Alfie...or Bert, go to prison?" I asked, setting Mrs. Malloy's breakfast down in front of her.

"I've remembered it was Gerry." She picked up her knife and fork. "And for your information, Mrs. H., he got off. His lawyer told the jury to take a look at the defendant seated in the dock and ask themselves if here was a man with enough smarts to steam off a postage stamp that had gone through the meter. Boiling a kettle engages the thought processes, is what he said, and some people don't have

123

it in them to think. He called Gerry the biggest patsy he had ever come across."

"It is a terrible thing to be deceived," my father murmured into his orange juice.

"Well, the reason I brought Gerry up," Mrs. Malloy explained, "is that when he died, his wife—the one that he married after him and me parted ways—she went and had him cremated. Said it was more hygienic. Silly cow! It's not like most people leave the body in the front room, sat up in the easy chair, looking at the telly, now is it? What she wanted was to do things on the cheap. Just like I would have expected, she bought the urn at a going-out-of-business sale. So what was there for me to do but put our differences aside and go out and get one that looked like something? Solid brass, it was, and I hope that every time she looks at it up there on her mantelpiece, the bugger realizes that Roxie Malloy saved her from being labeled the world's worst cheapskate."

"And I don't see anything wrong with Harriet's urn." I put Daddy's breakfast in front of him.

"I'm sure I'd be proud to be in one just like it." Ben flipped out the last two eggs; one for him and one for me.

"Why don't you tell my father about the play," I suggested to Mrs. Malloy. "It might help take his mind off things." Truth be told, I was feeling just a little bit spooked. Hour by hour Harriet was becoming more of a presence in the house. Before much longer I would be laying a place for her at the table and smelling her perfume when I went into the bathroom. Oleander, I thought; that's what it would smell like. Just like in the biergarten in Schönbrunn. I opened a window to let in some fresh air, and the sharpness of the breeze, coupled with the fact that what I smelled was damp earth and chrysanthemums—flowers typical of autumn funerals—snapped me back to my senses. Harriet's relatives would be back this afternoon. They would take the urn away. And Daddy, having fulfilled his promise, would be able to get on with his life. Perhaps one day he would even meet someone else. Someone kind and sensible. Named something like Agnes or Mary. Who would cook him wholesome meals and remind him to wear his nice woolly scarf in bad weather. Taking my place at the table, I again encouraged Mrs. Malloy, who might not have heard me the first time, to fill my father in on Murder Most Fowl.

"I hardly think that's likely to help cheer him up." Ben scraped back the chair alongside mine and sat down with his plate. "It's far more liable to put him off chicken for life. And I would be sorry about that because I woke in the middle of the night with the most marvelous recipe, with pictures included, spread out in my mind. It was all there, right down to the quarter of a teaspoonful of white pepper. It even had a name. Chicken à la Marie Antoinette."

"That sounds fabulous!" I was tucking into my bacon and eggs with renewed good cheer.

"And this morning I still feel inspired."

"I can't wait to read it when you get it down on paper."

"I must have fallen asleep thinking about our not going to France."

"Always the silver lining."

"I think I'll use Madeira cake crumbs instead of bread for the dressing." Ben fetched the coffeepot and returned to fill all four cups. "I'll season it with orange rind and freshly grated ginger. And while it's roasting the chicken will be basted with Grand Marnier and sesame-seed oil." Ben sat back down and pronged a piece of bacon. "Would you think me selfish, sweetheart, if after we're through with breakfast I go and hole up in the study? I really do want to work on this recipe while it's white hot in my mind."

"Of course you must." I was about to tell him that I would be going out shortly to the Old Abbey, but Mrs. Malloy's voice caught my ear. She had finally picked up on my suggestion and was filling Daddy in on the play.

"As things stand, Mr. Simons, I don't have a huge part. But it's all what you make of it, is what I say. And I'll get to play Malicia Stillwaters should Lady Grizwolde come a cropper between now and opening night. So we'll just have to keep our fingers crossed, won't we? That nothing nasty happens to her," she added piously. "Of course, I'm of a more mature age than her ladyship. Although there's many that wouldn't notice. Seeing I'm often taken for twenty years younger than me proper age. And as Mrs. Vicar says, me and her ladyship are both dark, stunningly good looking women, with an air of mystery about us that'll set the audience back on its ears. She picked me for the understudy, Mrs. Vicar did, because of how well I do the cat meowing offstage. I put a lot into that meow. Would you like to hear me?" Unfortunately, she demonstrated before my father could respond, and Tobias came prowling out of the pantry to register his disgust. Mrs. Malloy ignored the flinching going on all around her. "The cat knows, you see, that Malicia has poisoned Clarabelle, just like she did Major Wagewar, and is trying to put her in the trunk, where she's got him hidden. But she's having trouble—"

"I'm not surprised." Ben poured more coffee. "From what you have told me about poor Clarabelle, she isn't at all the sort of woman to cohabit with a man outside of marriage inside a trunk."

"That's not the problem, Mr. H." Mrs. Malloy eyed him austerely. "And it isn't that the trunk isn't big enough for two. It's the one Malicia used for packing her household stuff when she moved to Chatterton Dells. But something's gone wrong with the lid, and every time she lifts it up, it comes banging down. So she has to put Clarabelle in the wardrobe. But as it turns out"—Mrs. M. was back to addressing my father—"the woman isn't dead at all. She'd poured most of the poisoned milk into a saucer for the cat."

"Poor cat," I said.

"Anyway," Mrs. Malloy informed Daddy,

"Clarabelle comes back to life in the last scene." She didn't get to add that this was only a brief reprieve before Reginald Rakehell's hapless wife shot herself because my father spoke up in his most mournful voice.

"I only wish such could be the case with my Harriet. Ah, to hold her in my arms once more! Alas, I hardly know how I will find the courage to part with her when the dreadful hour arrives. Will my hands falter when I am forced to hand over her sacred remains?" He picked up his serviette to mop up the tears flowing like the Nile down his full cheeks. "How, I ask you all, am I to get through the hours until three o'clock. That is when the relatives are to return?" He eyed Ben, who nodded.

"You could come with me to the Old Abbey," I suggested. "Lady Grizwolde is a new client of mine. She rang up just now to ask if I could stop by this morning, and when I mentioned, Daddy, that you were here on a visit, she urged me to bring you along. We've been invited to stay for lunch. She and Sir Casper have a cook, so we might get served something quite delectable." I saw him moisten his lips and nibble on the idea. But then he wrapped his hands around the urn and shook his head.

"You're a good daughter, Giselle! Always so quick to try and lighten your poor father's load, but in my present state I can hardly be acceptable to these lofty-sounding people. 'Tis better by far that I remain here with Bentwick and while away the dreary hours talking to him."

"That's fine with me." Ben responded cheerfully, as if chicken à la Marie Antoinette were the furthest thing from his mind. Without glancing at me, he settled back in his chair and folded his arms for the long haul. I was thinking that Mr. Ambleforth's revered St. Ethelwort had nothing on my husband when Mrs. Malloy came to the rescue as well as to her feet.

"No need for you to take time away from your cookery book, Mr. H. Your father-in-law can sit with me while I do the dusting. Being the sympathetic soul I am, it will thrill me no end to hear more about his troubles."

"That's awfully good of you, Mrs. Malloy," I said. "But now that I think about it, I can't be sure how long I'll be gone, and I wouldn't like to rush the visit and give Lady Grizwolde the feeling that I'm not fully committed to the job."

"You mean we might not get back until well into the afternoon?" Daddy looked slightly more animated than I had yet seen him. "It would certainly be unfortunate if Harriet's relatives were to arrive early and not be able to wait for our return. But surely they would understand that I needed to get away for a brief change of scene. They can always come another day."

"But, Daddy, you wouldn't want them to show up for the second time to find you gone." Seeing that he would, I sighed. "Let's plan it this way. If we're still at the Old Abbey when they arrive, Ben can telephone. Lady Grizwolde is bound to be understanding under those circumstances, and it won't take us ten minutes to get back."

"Off you go, then, and enjoy yourselves." It was clear from the way Mrs. Malloy rattled together the breakfast dishes and banged the cutlery on top that her nose had been put seriously out of joint. Daddy, bestirring himself to notice, thanked her for her kindly overture, but I knew what he was thinking. She had a fatal flaw as a listener. She enjoyed the sound of her own voice. For every three words he might get out on the subject of Harriet, she would have six to spill about the play. But, she was far too magnanimous by nature to allow resentment free rein. "So," she asked him, "do I take the urn around with me while I'm doing me hoovering?"

Understandably, my father blanched, but he recovered most of his voice to say he would take Harriet with him, adding that he was sure that Lady Grizwolde would have no objection to one more at, or perhaps it should be said on, the luncheon table.

"Maybe not," I said as Ben busied himself at the sink. "But, Daddy, wouldn't it be best to leave the urn here?"

"Giselle, I'm surprised at you. Harriet so enjoyed an outing."

"I know, but—"

"And when I think of how happy she was at the prospect of surprising me with that car, it breaks my heart all over again." Daddy murmured something about putting on his ascot and navy blue blazer and disappeared into the hall.

"Oh, I do love to see a grown man cry," Mrs. Malloy positively simpered. "It gives you hope, doesn't it, that they're not all beasts only interested in getting their Sunday dinner on time? So's they can be off to the pub with their mates. Sensitive and sexy all in one package. You don't get to see that every day of the week."

"My father? Sexy?" I gaped at her.

"Why not?" Ben inquired without turning around from the sink. "I plan to go on being wildly desirable after I turn sixty."

"I can see why Harriet fell for him like a ton of bricks," Mrs. Malloy murmured dreamily, "and I could just sob me eyes out to think the two of them didn't get to live happily every after. Or," she said, trudging into the alcove, where we kept the buckets and mops, "I could get a grip and think about putting the moves on him meself."

Half an hour later, her languishing sigh replayed itself in my head as I drove through our wrought-iron gates with my father beside me and the urn in the canvas bag on his knee. It wasn't that I thought it impossible for a man of over sixty to still be attractive to the opposite sex. And I didn't doubt that a woman could develop a fondness for Daddy over time. But to think of him as a man who would make female hearts beat like drums and their legs turn to jelly was an adjustment!

The sky was overcast, and as the cliff road narrowed, I had to concentrate on its twists and turns. There were rocks and shrubs on one side and the drop-off to the sea on the other, with only the occasional strip of iron railing to mark the most dangerous places. Even so, the thoughts kept coming. Had I really heard anything about Harriet that justified my disliking her? Was it only the jealousy on my mother's behalf that had sparked my suspicions that there had been something fishy about her relationship with my father?

Daddy hadn't said a word as we drove along. But suddenly he gave a strangled gasp and cradled the canvas bag to his chest in the manner of a mother protecting her newborn infant from a pack of advancing hyenas. We had just passed the rather spooky old inn, now a B and B operated by Mrs. Potter's sister, and were within yards of the Old Abbey's gates when we saw a bicycle wobbling along just ahead of us, smack in the middle of the road. I saw a flash of rounded back and a flutter of white hair before I spun the steering wheel to the left, grazed the brick wall, and felt the car slide around in slow motion to face the cliff's edge, as if hoping for one final glimpse of the sea.

CHAPTER II

THE MOMENT I HAD THE CAR SAFELY BACK ON THE appropriate side of the road, Daddy changed his tune about wanting to live and began talking about how there would have been something sublimely apt about meeting his end in the very same manner as had his beloved Harriet. Luckily, my hands were laminated to the steering wheel or I might have been tempted to strangle my own father. Every part of me was shaking, including my teeth.

"Look, Daddy," I croaked as my foot hit one of the pedals, killing the engine. "I'm really not in the mood for this. Heaven may be a very nice place to visit, but I really don't want to live there right now. I wouldn't get to see Ben or the children. So if you don't mind, I would like to savor this reprieve instead of wallowing in regret that I'm not in a watery grave."

"Forgive me, Giselle." He studied my face somberly. "Your continued existence means a great deal to me. Such being the case, I must endeavor to temper my grief with more awareness of your feelings. I shall strive to be cheerful." He spoke with resolution and nobility. "Harriet would have wished it."

"I hope our near miss hasn't shaken her up too badly?" My voice verged on the hysterical as I looked at the canvas bag he was still clutching as if it were a baby yet to be weaned. "But is it too much to ask that just this once you think of the living?"

Before he could reply, a face appeared at the open car window. The face of a man holding on to a bicycle that was almost as elderly as he.

"Having car trouble?" he inquired kindly. "Not that I can be of much help, I'm afraid. No mechanical knowledge whatsoever. But I couldn't pass by on the other side of the road without at least offering you a blessing."

"That's awfully nice of you, Mr. Ambleforth." I produced a smile and refrained from mentioning I had narrowly missed running him over and killing my father and myself in the process. To have disturbed the tranquillity of his expression would have seemed truly wicked. "I do hope," I continued, "that you and your wife have recovered from your late night."

"Which night was that, my dear?"

"Last night," I said, wishing I hadn't brought up the subject. I was about to introduce Daddy to him when the vicar nodded his venerable white head.

"Ah, yes. So kind of you to have invited us to your home for an evening of chamber music. We appreciate these overtures to welcome us into the lives of our parishioners. My wife," he said, recalling himself with commendable effort to modern times, "is very partial to the cello. Or am I thinking of compost? Kathleen has always been an extraordinarily keen gardener. She's won a great number of prizes at flower shows for her daffodils. No, I do believe—am indeed quite sure—it was for her marigolds. It is a great blessing to have a green thumb. One remembers, of course, what Jesus had to say about the lilies of the field. Or was it the...?"

I seized the pause to say that my husband and I would love to have him and his wife over for dinner one evening soon while my father was staying with us. And Daddy, assuming his most lugubrious expression, leaned around me to extend his hand out the window.

"Morley Simons, not of this parish."

"A sheep from another fold," Mr. Ambleforth murmured.

"I have, in fact, never been much of churchgoer, Vicar." Daddy addressed the clerical collar. "But one reaches a time in life when the attractions of the hereafter are undeniable. It occurs to me that perhaps I have been remiss in not warming a pew on the occasional Sunday morning."

"He who is last shall be first, my son."

I had always thought that concept just a little bit unfair, and now, being already peevish, I wished the two men would go off to the nearest pub for a beer and a word of prayer. That way I could go on alone through the gates of the Old Abbey.

"Perhaps I could call in and see you during office hours, Vicar," Daddy suggested. "My spirit is much in need of the soothing balm that you men of the cloth are paid to administer. My dear daughter Giselle may have told you of my recent agonizing loss..."

Hearing the sound of approaching traffic, I suggested, somewhat belatedly, that Mr. Ambleforth step onto the verge. He did so without appearing to be in fear and trembling for himself or the bicycle. After a couple of cars had gone whizzing past us, he wisely announced that he would proceed to the Old Abbey, where he intended to repose among the monastery ruins and commune with the spirit of St. Ethelwort.

"We're going there ourselves," I told him. "Up to the house, I mean. I have an appointment with Lady Grizwolde."

"Ah," said Mr. Ambleforth, "a most charming young woman. Such a very great pity that she and Sir Casper have not been blessed with offspring. One cannot but suppose that the legend holds true." And on this tantalizing tidbit he pedaled off and soon passed through the gates in the brick wall.

"What a decidedly odd sort of chap," my father remarked, clasping the urn in its canvas bag more tightly as I turned the key in the ignition and we followed at a cautious pace in the vicar's wake.

Within moments we were on a tree-lined

drive, the house rising up before us. Built in the reign of George II, it appeared at first glance to be the sort of house that a child would draw. Its beauty was all about purity of line and exquisite proportion. The brick had weathered to a buttery yellow, and the roof was the color of a pair of moleskin gloves, changing to lavender in places where brushed with shadow. I was breathing a sigh of relief that the Victorians had not done terrible things to it with factory-sized additions when I almost ran over Mr. Ambleforth's bike, which had been abandoned smack in my path. Hitting the brake and killing the engine for the second time that morning, I glanced to my right and saw the ruins of St. Ethelwort's monastery.

Such places tend to come into their own at night, with moonbeams silvering the maze of broken-down walls and the jutting remnant of a stone staircase. But I experienced a thrill at seeing this one in daylight. The vicar sat entranced under what was left of a Gothic archway. Meanwhile, Daddy looked far from happy. I could see his point. All this jostling had to be most upsetting to Harriet. It was amazing she had succeeded so far in keeping her lid on! I was just about to get out of the car and lean the bike up against a tree when a man appeared from behind some shrubs.

He had a pair of pruning shears in his hands, and when he came up to the window, I decided that he had to be at least ninety. His face was wizened and yellowed, his back so bent that he probably hadn't seen the sky in a decade. But his birdlike eyes were as inquisitive as those of a child, and every other step he took was a little hop.

"Good day to you, missus." His nose almost touched mine as he leaned into the car. "Are you the one come to see Lady Grizwolde about fancying up the old place?"

"That's right. I'm Ellie Haskell."

"Aye, that'll be you." It hardly seemed possible, but more lines crinkled his face as his bright eyes searched mine. "I've been on the lookout for you. And if you won't take it as impertinence, I'd like to put a word in your ear about not changing too much up at the house. It might not go down well, you see. I've worked here since I was a boy, no bigger than that there tree stump," he said, pointing it out with the shears. "I knows what I'm talking about."

"Sir Casper will be upset that Lady Grizwolde wants to redecorate?"

"Not him; he's all for it. Anything to make her ladyship smile pretty at him; that's the master's way. It's him that mustn't on no account be vexed." The little old man cowered against the car as he glanced toward the ruins where Mr. Ambleforth still sat.

"The vicar?" I gave a surprised start and accidentally elbowed Daddy, who had hitherto sat oblivious to the conversation. "What does redecorating the Old Abbey have to do with him?"

"Nowt."

"Then I don't understand."

"It be old Worty I'm talking about. Him that built the old monastery where all you now see is rubble."

"Oh, you mean St. Ethelwort!"

"To be giving him his proper title." The old man gave another of his funny little hops, almost catching himself in the chin with the point of the shears. "Growing up around this place, I got to thinking of him the way I did my uncle Ned that I was named for, half-fond, half-fearful, if you get my meaning. Do things to suit the old boy's fancy is what I says about old Worty, and no harm done."

"What sort of harm could he do?" I discovered I was shivering, just as I had in the market square when talking to the Gypsy.

"It all goes back to when the old house was here," Ned informed me. "The one as was built after Henry VIII went and got rid of all the monks. The lady of the house in Elizabethan times—I've forgot her name—saw a vision of the saint in the chapel one night. And it's said she made him a solemn vow, and in return he promised there'd always be Grizwoldes at the Old Abbey. But Sir Casper's father—him that was Sir Walter—went and broke faith. And Old Worty showed he wasn't the sort of saint you can thumb your nose at. Not without getting your comeuppance you can't."

"Mr. Ambleforth was saying, when we met him on the road just now, that it was a pity Sir Casper and Lady Grizwolde haven't been blessed with children. And you think that's because Sir Walter upset St. Ethelwort?" I looked expectantly into Ned's face. My father sat with remarkable placidity at my side. It occurred to me later that he was content for me to extend my visit to the Old Abbey indefinitely in the hope that Harriet's relations would have come and gone before we got back home.

"Sir Casper's first wife didn't bring no children, neither, though it be said she broke her heart and her health trying." Ned lifted his eyes heavenward.

"What was it the Elizabethan lady promised St. Ethelwort?" I asked.

Either he didn't hear me correctly, because there was a clap of thunder close by, or he chose to give a garbled reply. "Sir Casper's mother. She was German, and like they say, blood will tell."

"But what does any of this"—I approached from a different angle—"have to do with Lady Grizwolde's plans to redecorate the house?"

"Old Worty, being already vexed, mustn't be put out more. He don't like change." Stepping back from the car, Ned cupped a hand over his eyes and peered in the direction of the house. "Every time her ladyship moves something to a new spot, like a picture or a vase, it gets put back where it was before. Always in the middle of the night. And it wouldn't be Sir Casper doing it because Lady Grizwolde's wish is his command. Neither would it likely be his cousin Miss Finch-peck. Afraid of her own shadow, poor lady. I thinks that's her standing out on the steps looking this way. So I'd best not keep you no longer."

"It's been interesting talking to you," I said.

"Looks like its starting up to rain." Ned

wiped at his forehead. "You leave the keys in your car when you get up to the house, lady, and I'll park it in the garage for you. I'll do the same with Vicar's bike. Not that a mite more rust will make it a whole lot of difference." Shifting the offending vehicle to the side of the drive, he stood watching as I got the car moving, with a jostle or two that caused the canvas bag to bounce up and down on my father's knee.

I drove the tree-lined distance to the forecourt. Two stone lions guarded the base of the steps leading up to the front door, where a thin, gray woman hovered with a watering can in her hands.

"The welcoming committee?" my father intoned as we disembarked under lowering skies. The wind had sharpened to a wintry chill, and dry leaves eddied about our heads like feathers being plucked by a nimble-fingered farm wife. I was almost sure that I felt a spatter of rain on my neck and wished my camel cardigan was thicker. It would be good to get inside and be offered a cup of tea or coffee. But not if the urn came, too. I wasn't up to its morbid company. Perhaps I was still shaken by the close call out on the cliff road. Perhaps I was just being small-minded. All I can say for sure is that I wasn't about to sit across from my father and watch him dandle that piece of pottery on his knee.

"Daddy, you're going to have to leave Harriet in the car."

"My dear Giselle, I can't do that." He looked at me as if I had sprung more snakes than Medusa. "My darling had a horror of enclosed places. She told me so once."

"Such fears are behind her now." I refused to wilt under his parental disapproval. "I'm here on a professional visit, and I don't think it right to distract Lady Grizwolde from the business of discussing fabrics and wallpaper. Yes, I know," I added, seeing his mouth open in protest. "I did say that you could bring the urn. And perhaps it is unfair of me to change my mind. But won't you please try and put yourself in my place?"

"Very well." My father sucked in a breath and billowed to even more mammoth proportions. "Then I shall remain in the car with Harriet."

"Oh, that's splendid!" I said, losing what was left of my temper. "That way I'll have to rush through the consultation, creating the impression that I'm not really interested in the job of a lifetime, and Lady Grizwolde will have second thoughts about hiring me. Some father you've turned out to be!" My nerves were still in shreds from our close call on the road, and Ned's talk about visions and broken vows had left me feeling spooked. But that was no excuse. I was instantly horribly ashamed of myself and wouldn't have blamed Daddy if he had climbed back into the car. Instead, he opened the door and deposited the canvas bag gently on the driver's seat.

"You are entirely right, Giselle." He forced a smile that only made his face appear more mournful. "You must look to your career as modern women do. Her ladyship should get her money's worth even if it means our spending all afternoon here. I do see that if I were to present the urn to her notice, she might not encourage us to prolong our visit."

"Thank you, Daddy." I turned to head for the stone steps and saw the gray lady coming down them. When I told her who we were, she set her watering can down where we were liable to collide with it and tugged the two fronts of her cardigan around her wispy middle.

"There you are, the decorator people. I'm Timothia Finchpeck, Sir Casper's cousin. I'll take you to her ladyship. It's no bother." Her voice was as small and pinched as her face and equally without expression. "I was only going out to the rain barrel to fetch water. My mother was always most particular that I never wash my hair from the tap. All those harsh chemicals. But I hadn't realized how cold it had become and was debating whether to go back inside for my coat."

Would she have dithered on the steps for an hour if Daddy and I had not shown up? Following her into the house, we passed through a square hall with ancestral portraits on the walls, sumptuous rugs on the parquet floor, and graceful balustrades rising to a semicircular gallery above. We then entered a delightfully comfortable sitting room. It was paneled from floor to ceiling in honey-colored pine. The fireplace, where flames licked cheerfully around a large log, was a simple stone affair with pewter mugs and candlesticks on the polished mantel. Positioned around it was a dusky green sofa and an assortment of chintz-covered chairs interspersed with small tables just waiting to have cups and saucers and perhaps a bundle of knitting placed upon them. The windows were long and narrow and draped in amber velvet. Two corner cabinets displayed Toby jugs and silver riding cups. I stood breathing it all in, wondering what changes I could suggest without bringing the ancestors down from the walls to chase me off the premises.

Switching on a couple of table lamps, Timothia Finchpeck indicated that Daddy and I be seated close to the fire. "This room was always a favorite with Sir Casper's first wife, and the present Lady Grizwolde uses it as her personal sitting room, although I think she would prefer one to the back of the house, away from people coming and going. But I expect you have been here before, Mrs. Haskell, although I don't remember the occasion."

"I was here a couple of weeks ago," I said, settling into one of the chintz chairs, "but not in this room. Lady Grizwolde and I had our discussion in the library."

"That must have been when I was in bed with a cold," Miss Finchpeck informed us in a nasal whisper. "I am prone to being chesty. My mother said it was because I was born during a terrible fog and the damp got into my lungs before I took my first breath."

"It is a great burden to have a frail constitution," my father opined while sucking in his stomach in a futile attempt not to look quite so shamelessly robust. "Alas, one must play the card life deals us. And you should take heart

144

in the knowledge that it is sometimes the wilting rose that outlasts us all."

"One has the hope." Miss Finchpeck couldn't have looked less cheerful. "I certainly do my best with gentle exercise and daily tonics to improve upon what nature has bestowed. What did you think of the library, Mrs. Haskell?" The pale eyes wavered in my direction.

"Wonderful," I replied. "Such a beautiful room, and all those leather-bound volumes!"

"Some of them came from the old house."

"The one built when Henry VIII made a grant of the land to the family? What did they do to win royal favor." I was eager for a history lesson, even though I doubted I would get the scurrilous version, but Miss Finchpeck flinched like a Victorian governess being cornered in a dark corridor by the master of the house.

"It is not a matter that has ever concerned me, Mrs. Haskell. My father strongly disapproved of women talking politics. Even though he has been dead many years, I abide by his convictions. Please don't ask me about St. Ethelwort, as so many visitors do, because I also adhere to the rule of never discussing religion. And now, if you will excuse me, I will go and fetch her ladyship." She vanished like a wisp of dust being swept out of sight by an efficient housemaid, and my father and I were left looking at each other from our chintz chairs.

"Thank goodness you and Mummy allowed me to think and speak for myself," I said.

Waving a magnanimous hand, Daddy heaved

his legs onto an ottoman that had previously been sitting around looking ornamental. "My dearest girl, I understand that your nerves must be frayed to shreds at witnessing my suffering, and perhaps I have languished more than is becoming in a parent. But I trust that I have not been a bore. That poor Miss Finchpenny—"

"Finchpeck."

"A sad little name for a sad little woman." Daddy rolled the words around on his tongue. "Imagine having her about all day and every day like a fog that never lifts."

"Yes, she did seem a little depressing," I said quickly before he could add that Harriet had been a perpetual ray of sunshine. But he surprised me.

"Your mother washed her hair in rainwater." Daddy smiled directly at me, and I felt as though a door were about to open up between us. At the same moment, the sitting-room door was pushed open, and Lady Grizwolde came into the room. It was an entrance worthy of both an actress and a stunningly beautiful woman. The thought crossed my mind that it would be understandable if Timothia Finchpeck resented her with all the silent malice of the poor relation destined to wait out her life in the shadows with the other ghosts of the Old Abbey.

CHAPTER 12

EVEN DADDY, WEDDED AS HE WAS TO THE MEMORY
of Harriet, could not hide a glimmer of admiration as he rose to his feet and watched
Lady Grizwolde shake my hand before turning
to take his. Her movements were elegant,
her smile gracious, and I sat back down again
feeling that her satin-smooth black hair and
dark eyes were all wrong. She should have been
a cool blonde wearing blue or sea-green silk
rather than the deep-rust skirt and high-
necked black sweater belted at the waist with
a narrow gold chain that, other than her
wedding and engagement rings, was her only
ornament.

"How very nice that your daughter could
bring you with her today," she was telling
Daddy. Her voice was melodious but expres-
sionless.

"Morley Simons. It is most good of you to

allow my intrusion, your ladyship." He bowed as far as his stomach permitted, over her hand.

"Please call me Phyllis. As your daughter may have gleaned from the local gossips, I wasn't born to the aristocracy." She settled down on the sofa, legs neatly crossed at the ankles, and watched Daddy and me return to our chairs. "My father was a postman, and my mother worked in a launderette. And though I have always aspired to a life of ease, I haven't forgotten my roots, as might be expected." She didn't add, You may take that back to tattle mongers if you choose, but I sensed that was her message.

"We're very lucky to have you living here." I sat smoothing out the wrinkles in my skirt, wishing that I hadn't worn my hair in a style similar to hers and wondering if she had any idea that she inevitably made the people around her feel hopelessly rumpled. "Kathleen Ambleforth told me when I stopped in at rehearsal yesterday that she is thrilled to have you in her play."

"She's very enthusiastic about the entire production." Lady Grizwolde readjusted a sofa cushion. "Murder Most Fowl is really not a bad little farce—as these amateur things go. Of course, it wasn't intended to be funny; they never are. But your cousin Freddy has a real talent for campiness. The perfect choice for the hero who can't see the bodies for the trees. Luckily, Mrs. Ambleforth took the discovery that she wouldn't have the audience sobbing in their seats very much in stride. I imagine she's an adaptable woman in all areas of her life. How else could she survive being married to that extraordinarily odd man with his obsession for St. Ethelwort? I wouldn't be a bit surprised if he's out there now, sitting like a man turned to stone among the ruins."

"My dear lady, you do not deceive yourself." My father's voice erupted from the depths of his armchair with all the delight of a man delivering bad news that in no way related to him. "Giselle and I encountered the vicar as we were about to enter your gates. He was on a most disreputable bicycle and almost ran our car off the road."

"That's a bad curve. I'm surprised there aren't more accidents there." Lady Grizwolde's face remained smooth, unmarred by any expression other than sociability. "But I don't suppose," she continued, "that Mr. Ambleforth was unnerved enough to take himself off home. He's usually here for hours. Before too long he'll come knocking on the door asking for the hundredth time to view the chapel. Casper has been avoiding him like the plague."

"The reverend chap makes a habit of mooning about the grounds, does he?" Daddy shook his head and flexed his lips as if excess of any sort were foreign to his nature.

"I've seen him from my window in the middle of the night. And poor Timmy once phoned the police thinking he was a burglar. You've met my husband's cousin?"

"She let us in," I said.

"So she did. I thought you might have mistaken her for the housekeeper; people often do. Her mother was Casper's aunt. And Timmy's lived here most of her adult life. Where else was she to go? And as Casper's first wife didn't object to her wafting about the place, I've tried to be as accommodating." This was said without any discernible trace of malice. "I sent her to fetch those magazines with the decorating concepts I've been wanting you to look at, Ellie. You don't mind my calling you that, do you?"

"Of course not. I'm eager to see what you have in mind."

"To have such a daughter with such a career! One bubbles with pride as a parent!" Daddy might only have been prattling on to spin out the visit, but my heart was touched, and Lady Grizwolde turned to him with a trace of animation in her dark eyes.

"How charming, and what a pleasure it must be for the entire family to have you come and visit. Did you have to travel far to get here?"

"From southern Germany, the village of Schönbrunn." My father sank low in his chair and managed to look as if he had aged ten years in as many seconds. But he didn't produce a hanky and mop his eyes.

"I don't think I've heard of it." Lady Grizwolde actually leaned forward a little in her seat and cupped her chin in a slim, long-fingered hand. "What is it near?"

"The closest town is Loetzinn."

"And is this Schönbrunn a picturesque place?"

"The most beautiful place in the world!" Daddy now produced the handkerchief with a snowy flourish, and I found myself wondering if Frau Grundman had done his laundry for him while he stayed in her guest house.

"Loetzinn, you said." Her ladyship now appeared reflective. "Maybe I have heard or read about it. Doesn't it have a rather beautiful church? A Roman Catholic one, that was built after the Second World War and is celebrated for its nave or stained-glass windows or some such thing?"

"Alas, I have heretofore not been much of a churchgoer." Daddy was now wielding the hanky with such vigor that the curtains stirred all the way across the room. "But now that my eyes are turned heavenward, I shall be more devout in my observances." I held my breath waiting for him to sound off about his recent bereavement, but her ladyship spoke before he could say Harriet.

"Was there some scandal—a fairly recent one—that made the newspapers? The priest absconding with the missionary money and running off to Monte Carlo to play the casinos? Or am I getting it mixed up with somewhere else?"

"Does any of this ring a bell, Daddy?" I asked.

"A what?" He might have been floating on the ceiling from the faraway sound of his voice, but he drifted back down to us after a couple of seconds and drew his pale eyes together over his Roman nose. "Some reprehensible happening occurring at a church in Loetzinn, is that what we are discussing? Nothing to do with choirboys, I hope. Or rude scribbles on the frescoes. My beloved Harriet would have been deeply distressed. She revered antiquities."

"Daddy, Lady Grizwolde—Phyllis—was talking about a robbery."

"Maybe it wasn't money that disappeared." She regarded him steadily. "Perhaps it was a chalice or a statue that wept when the clock struck a certain hour. I'm not very religious myself, but living here, on the grounds of an ancient monastery, it's impossible not to become a little interested in ecclesiastical matters. But if you didn't hear anything being right on the spot, I must have the place wrong. And yet"—she placed a finger between her perfectly arched black brows—"the name Loetzinn does seem to have stuck in my head." Before Daddy could respond she continued!

"And who, Morley, is this Harriet of whom you speak so fondly?"

"The goddess of all earthly delights, a diamond of the utmost radiance, a flower such as the world's greatest horticulturist could not hope to produce. Pardon me, Phyllis, but I tend to break down when speaking of her!"

But never to be at a loss for words, I thought. Unkind of me. But to be fair, I was here to do a job, and unless choked with the hanky, Daddy would be in full flood for an hour. As he swallowed a noisy parade of sobs, I hastily provided a synopsis.

"My father and Harriet met in Schönbrunn and fell deeply in love. Tragically, she was killed in a car accident. He arrived home last night with her ashes, which he has the sad duty of handing over to her relatives this afternoon."

"It goes without saying that my life ended with my adored one's death!" Daddy was off and running, and there was no way I could step on his tongue without looking like the most unfeeling daughter alive. Her ladyship was the one who broke in on him.

"Her ashes are in your house?" Was she making polite conversation? Or did her fastidiousness find the idea repellent?

"Not presently," he told her before I could open my mouth. "They're on the front seat of Giselle's car."

"In a nice little urn with a good tight lid," I heard myself say.

"Harriet often spoke of how she loved a run in the car." Daddy's eyes turned dreamily reminiscent. But I knew it would be only a matter of seconds before he remembered that she had met her death in one. And we would have the whole story of the trip to Koblenz. Luckily, the door opened, and Timothia Finchpeck came into the room with a bundle of magazines in her arms.

"I'm sorry it took me so long to find these, Phyllis." Her whispery voice made me long for a hearing aid, but Lady Grizwolde barely turned her head in her direction.

"That's all right, Timmy. There's no need to stand there looking like a fly to be swatted."

"They weren't in your bedroom where you said they'd be." The faintest flicker of defi-

153

ance showed in Miss Finchpeck's eyes. But what emanated most was a dreariness that seemed to sap so much of the color out of the green sofa and chintz chairs that they appeared almost as gray as she was. It was raining quite hard now, and a rumble or two of thunder indicated that it was likely we were in for a real storm. "I had to search all over the house for them, Phyllis, until I found them under the towels in your bathroom," she said, handing over the magazines.

"You should have come back before wearing yourself out" was the cool reply. However, looking at Lady Grizwolde, I was sure she knew that such wasn't Miss Finchpeck's way. Either from doggedness or a fear of looking stupid, the poor woman would never return empty-handed after being dispatched on an errand. My heart went out to her. What a horrible way to live! I didn't like how Lady Grizwolde talked to her. But perhaps her ladyship had her own point of view. Maybe she thought Miss Finchpeck could have made a life for herself either through a career or marriage instead of installing herself at the Old Abbey like the ghost of a martyr from the days of the Reformation. Even so, there was such a thing as common kindness. I looked over at my father and felt a major pang of guilt. When we got home, I would let him talk about Harriet for as long as he liked and regardless of whether I reached the screaming point. It was, I thought a shade virtuously, what my mother would have wished.

"But Timmy, you didn't bring them all."

Lady Grizwolde looked up from the magazines she had been sorting through on the knees of her rust suit. "There was one that I particularly wanted to show Mrs. Haskell—with pictures of a library from a town house in New York. It had some wonderful iron chairs with the seats upholstered in modern tapestry. Are you sure you didn't drop it?"

"Those are all the magazines I found, Phyllis." Miss Finchpeck gathered herself together as if from stray strands of ectoplasm. "I really don't know why you wish to change the library, or if you must, why you can't just add a few new books to the shelves. So long as the leather bindings match, the effect wouldn't be too jarring. Anything else would be unkind to the memory of all the Grizwoldes who came before us and put their hearts and souls into this house."

"Exactly." Her ladyship got to her elegant feet. "They changed things, and so shall I. Never mind. With a little luck the place will be yours one day, and you will get to redo things back to the way you like them." Giving Daddy and me one of her manicured smiles, she said she would go and have a quick look for the magazine herself. "And while I'm gone, Timmy"—she turned back on reaching the door—"perhaps you would ring for Sarah and have her bring in the quiche Mrs. Johnson made for lunch. Mrs. Haskell and her father are expecting guests at their home this afternoon, so I think it would work best, given the time constraints, if we eat casually in here rather than the dining room."

"Ah, most gracious," Daddy said, raising up in his chair, "but one would not wish to disrupt any arrangements you have made. Giselle's husband is at home with nothing to occupy him and thus more than eager to be at the disposal of our visitors until our return. Indeed," he added, exuding magnanimity, "being a chef by profession, Bentwick will no doubt relish the opportunity to twitter about with the cucumber sandwiches and pour cups of Earl Grey into Royal Doulton cups."

"Lunch in here will be lovely," I interrupted firmly.

"I'll be back in a couple of moments." Lady Grizwolde went out the door, closing it behind her. Whereupon Miss Finchpeck gave a little twitch, but whether from relief or irritation wasn't clear. Reaching for a needlepoint bellpull, installed between two landscapes that looked like genuine Constables to me, she gave it a tug. A distant ringing sounded, after which the only sounds to be heard were the crackling of the fire and the lashing of rain against the long, velvet-clad windows. My father overflowed his chair, his feet extending beyond the ottoman. An enormous man flopped out as if waiting to be removed for immediate embalming. A man who, if I were prepared to be truthful, I hardly knew. Even so, I suddenly found him the most comforting thing in this room, which I had found so inviting just a short time before.

"My mother, who was Sir Casper's father's— Sir Walter's—sister"—Miss Finchpeck raised her voice slightly to be heard above the rain—

"instilled in me a sense of duty toward this house. It was her belief that to betray that duty was a sin against God and country." The small, dull eyes found mine, and it was their lack of expression that made me feel it would be warmer outside in the rain. What must life be like for Sir Casper, I wondered, living with a wife who had all the vivacity of a store mannequin and a cousin with fog in her lungs? "In saying this, I make no criticism of Lady Grizwolde." The voice had dropped back to a whisper. "She was not reared on warnings of the dangers in store for those who tamper with what our traditions hold dear. And she has not yet realized the house has no liking for beautiful women."

"Oh, dear!" was all I could come up with.

My father managed an eloquent stare.

"Sir Casper's mother was beautiful, and she used the power such looks bestow to persuade poor Uncle Wallie to betray a holy trust." Miss Finchpeck drifted over to a seat under the windows. "I should not be saying any of this, but I have to appeal to you, Mrs. Haskell. Discourage her ladyship from making changes at the Old Abbey, especially now that Sir Casper has such high hopes for the righting of that old wrong."

In the silence that resettled over the room I thought about old Ned and his talk of broken vows. He'd also said he didn't believe Miss Finchpeck responsible for the middle-of-the-night replacement of furnishings Lady Grizwolde had moved to different locations. But I thought him wrong. I suspected that beneath her timidity Miss Finchpeck had a will of iron. It was tempting, but I knew it would be useless, to ask what Sir Casper's father had done to break faith or how Sir Casper planned to set matters right. She would recognize my vulgar curiosity for what it was, and she might already regret having spoken at all.

"It's not my decorating style to tear down what works just for the sake of change unless that's what the client wants." I sounded as if I were reciting lines from a manual, but I did understand this peculiar woman's thinking. I believed that houses are like people. If you dress them up in clothes that don't fit properly or are in styles that don't suit them or colors they hate, they will be very unhappy, and no one could enjoy living in them. But unlike Timmy, where I stopped short was in thinking a structure capable of exacting revenge upon its inhabitants. At least, jumping as thunder shook the room like a bag of bones, I thought I did.

The door opened, and a curly-haired young woman in a black frock and white apron came with springing steps into the room. Hers was the first merry face I'd seen since leaving home. And that was beginning to seem ages ago.

"Hallo." She stood with hands on her hips looking Daddy and me over as if we were contestants on a game show and she had to decide which one was sitting on the chair with "Prize" written on the seat.

"Hallo," we said back, and she gave us a cheeky thumbs-up before looking over at

Miss Finchpeck, who had picked up some knitting and was silently moving the needles. "You rang, miss? Just passing the time? Or was there something I can do for you?"

"Lady Grizwolde would like lunch brought in here, Sarah."

"What's that you say?"

"Lunch in here, Sarah."

"Well, you've got to learn to speak up the first time, haven't you, my funny old duck?" The girl bounced forward, picked up the ball of wool that had fallen to the floor, dropped it in Miss Finchpeck's lap, and actually patted her on the head before skipping out of the room.

My father and I exchanged wide-eyed stares.

"She needs training," the thin voice informed us, "but it's so difficult to get staff, and she wants to be here because of her grandfather and because she loves this house. Ned practically brought her up. So she was always about the place."

"It exhausts me to even think about being young." Daddy shifted his feet more firmly onto the ottoman as the door again opened and Lady Grizwolde reappeared. Her dark hair had an added shine; her complexion, a more dewy radiance. Or so I thought, but perhaps it was only because her youth and beauty were in such utter contrast to the figure looming over her shoulder.

I had known that Sir Casper was many years his wife's senior. But not ever having met him or even seen him in passing, I had pictured him as distinguished, very possibly handsome. There is always something romantic about the wealthy, titled man—a widower no less—marrying a beautiful woman for love. So I had wanted to believe. The reality entering the room was more than disappointing. The old man hobbling my way, leaning heavily on two canes, looked as though he wore an ill-fitting facial mask of yellowish rubber with a few wisps of gray hair sprouting from the wrinkled scalp. His eyes were watery slits; his lips, practically invisible. It was the sort of face that a makeup artist might have produced to scare young children and grown-ups alike into waking nightmares. Standing up to shake the fleshless hand he had laboriously removed from one cane, I pondered the inevitable question. Why had Phyllis Grizwolde—who must have had eligible men falling over each other to marry her—married this one? Was he so incredibly wealthy? Or—I tried to be kind— an incredibly wonderful human being? Loving and sympathetic, a witty conversationalist, a sporting backgammon opponent. The touch of his skin on mine was icy, and his voice was a wheezing rasp that, because of his bent posture, hit me in the chest.

"I'm pleased to welcome you to the Old Abbey, Mrs. Haskell." He was now speaking to my shoes and was yet to appear aware of my father's presence or that of Miss Finchpeck. "My dear wife tells me that you have an excellent reputation as a decorator, or whatever they call you people who help pick out new curtains and other flummeries that women so delight in. I have told her to spare no expense, especially when it comes to the master-bedroom suite. To date"—he lifted his head and wheezed in my face—"her ladyship and I have occupied separate quarters, but that is shortly to be changed!" He uttered a fusty chuckle and kept a clawlike grasp of my hand as I took an automatic step backward. His lipless mouth worked, and his red-rimmed eyes grew more watery.

"We can talk about this over lunch, Casper." Her ladyship spoke from behind him.

"No, no, my dear! I must seize the moment." He wagged a stick and sent a couple of magazines flying. "I must make it clear to this young woman that I wish her to create a pink-and-white fantasy of a room with fairy lights over the bed and mirrors everywhere. There must be canopies and frills and velvety carpeting."

"It is what I would have wished for my honeymoon with Harriet." My father's voice flooded the room, but no one paid him any attention.

"Casper, you must not tire yourself." Her ladyship moved within five or six feet of her husband and extended a hand without touching him. "Now that you have seen Mrs. Haskell, why don't you retire for a good long rest?"

"Rest!" He threw back his rubbery bald head and cackled a laugh. "Rest is something for the old and decrepit, and I feel youth creeping back upon me. Am I not out of my wheelchair for the first time in months? Have I not lost the tremors that have so long afflicted me? Timothia"—he addressed Miss Finchpeck without looking her way—"tell Phyllis that you see in me the vital man I was before the years chewed me up and spat me out."

"You look remarkably fit, dear Casper," responded the voice from the shadows.

"Aye, and I shall be ready to cast off at least one of these sticks," he said, tapping it on the floor, "after a hearty luncheon."

"But you never eat anything but clear broth midday, and always in your room." Lady Grizwolde's voice was so cold, I wished I had a coat to put on. "If you are making this change in your routine because you think Mrs. Haskell is staying for lunch, it is unnecessary." She turned to me. "I couldn't find that magazine I wanted you to see, but I will get it to you another day. I do understand that as you and your father are expecting visitors this afternoon, you must get home as quickly as possible."

"Yes, isn't it a shame," I managed to say just as Sarah wheeled in a trolley with a delectable-looking quiche—all golden and puffy, taking pride of place among dishes of fruit and marinated vegetables. I took some comfort in Daddy's anguished expression. He was thinking about his stomach, not Harriet.

CHAPTER 13

SOME THINGS SHOULDN'T HAPPEN TO A PERSON ON an empty stomach, and discovering that the vicar had driven off in my car was one of them. Daddy, of course, was beside himself that Harriet had gone along for the ride. Being a responsible daughter, I had felt duty bound to suggest that my elderly parent take Mr. Ambleforth's bicycle while I walked home, and I would have appreciated a little gratitude. Needless to say, none was forthcoming. Poor old Ned stood looking as if he expected to be hauled off and stuck in the stocks. He was now telling me for the third time that he had driven the car into the garage, as he had promised.

"Right there is where it was." He pointed a gnarled finger at a sizable space between two cars, an elderly Rolls-Royce and a Honda Prelude. "Drove it in most careful, I did. And then I went and brought in Vicar's bike and leaned it, just as you sees, up against the wall just inside the door, where he wouldn't have to fall all over his self looking for it. It don't take going to Oxford University to tell he's an absentminded gent. Goes with the job, don't it? And he's been around here quite a bit of late, sitting like a nesting bird in them ruins and trying to talk to Sir Casper about Old Worty every blamed chance he gets. You could have knocked me down with a feather when I looks out from the greenhouse not ten minutes ago and sees the blighter—if you'll pardon my language when talking about a gentleman that hangs over the pulpit of a Sunday—speeding off down the drive as if Lucifer his self was after him."

"I don't see a greenhouse," I said.

"It be over round t'other side of the house." Ned flagged a gnarled hand to our left. "Lady Grizwolde, that was Sir Casper's mother, had it built. A very keen gardener, she was. Designed a lot of the beds, she did, and most of the arbors and rock pools was her doing. And, not surprising, some of it rubbed off on the son. Most mornings, before his health got so bad, he'd be out in that there greenhouse."

"My esteemed fellow"—Daddy ballooned up to ferocious proportions—"I would not wish you to labor under the misapprehension that I do not delight in your discourse. I am, however, impelled to inform you that I wish to know how you plan to retrieve my daughter's vehicle and its precious cargo."

"I'm sure Ned was coming to that," I said

164

with a shake of my head that sent raindrops spraying right and left. Standing in the open garage doorway with the wind blowing our way, I had got quite wet. "He'll take us to a telephone, and I'll phone the vicarage. It's a straight road there and no great distance, so with any luck Mr. Ambleforth will already have walked in the door."

"And he can come right back for you." Ned's wizened face widened into the smile of a man who had just heard that the executioner was in bed with the flu.

"I think I'd rather it was Mrs. Ambleforth."

"Likely you're right." He nodded at me before ducking out into the downpour.

"There isn't an entrance to the house through the garage?" My father did not sound like a man who had cheerfully lived in grass huts and trotted across the burning desert on flea-ridden camels. But perhaps life in Frau Grundman's well-run guest house has ruined him for life in the raw.

"If you come down here and around this corner, avoiding the drainpipe that's come loose, we'll be in the dry in two ticks." Ned plowed forward like the Hunchback of Notre Dame, with Daddy and me sloshing along behind. I collided with a rain barrel, possibly the one from which Miss Finchpeck drew water to wash her hair. But before I could bend to rub my bruised shin, Ned had opened a door, and the three of us were stepping into a narrow whitewashed corridor with a green linoleum floor and an archway ahead. This led into a red-carpeted area with a flight of steps at one end, a dark trestle table against one wall, and several varnished doors bearing enameled signs. The one closest to me as I stood drip-drying read: Housekeeper. Ned passed this by and nipped nimbly over to another that stood ajar. But he stepped back just as he was about to go in and pressed a finger to his lips.

"Mr. Jarrow's in there on the phone," he whispered, guiding us all over to the wall, where we huddled like policemen about to pull our guns and burst in on a couple of bank robbers "Sometimes he can be nice as you please. And of another he can be as carpy as the dickens."

"Who is he?" I turned my head to mouth back.

"Sir Casper's secretary. And to be fair, he's had his plate full this year. Just got back, he did, after being gone a month at least down in Colchester looking after his old sick Mum that's got a nasty, grudging tongue in her head from what Cook tells me. So best to toss sonny boy a piece of raw meat before sticking a finger in his cage as of now is my thoughts. All for the quiet life, I am." Ned's low voice faded away. And being at the front of our little group, I couldn't resist the impulse to contort my neck until it felt as though it were being stretched to the snapping point in the hands of one of those people who twist balloons into animal shapes. Unfortunately, destiny hadn't meant me for a swan. So I took the other approach, inching forward until I could stick my nose, which had never given me any difficulty, around the door frame.

What I saw was an office that was like most offices where people do a lot of dull, necessary work instead of sitting, with feet propped up, absorbing the smell of leather and the gloss of mahogany. There was a desk and a number of file cabinets, several wastepaper baskets, an electric typewriter sitting like a replaced wife across from a word processor, and of course a telephone. A slender man of medium height in a gray suit with a pale blue tie was standing with the receiver to his ear. What jumped out at you was his mustache, which was much too big for his narrow face; so much so that it looked as though it might have landed there by mistake after being dropped from a great height and he might be asked to return it at any given moment.

If he saw me peeking in on him, Mr. Jarrow took no notice. He continued talking into the receiver in the firm but mollifying voice so highly prized in a secretary.

"I shall certainly convey to Sir Casper that the business entailed unforeseen complications which lead you to believe you should be more handsomely compensated for your job performance. That way he will have time to consider his response before your meeting with him. Which is scheduled for...Yes, that is correct, this evening at..." Mr. Jarrow looked down at the calendar on his desk. Because my father chose that moment to tread heavily down on my heel, requiring me to bite my lips off to refrain from screaming, the next thing I heard was the telephone being replaced. And before I could lead the march into the office, a door that was partially blocked from view by two filing cabinets opened, and Lady Grizwolde moved to confront the secretary at his desk.

"I was on the other line," she informed him.

"If you choose to eavesdrop in your own house, your ladyship," he responded with slightly more expression in his voice, "that is entirely your prerogative."

"Indeed. I am, after all, closely concerned in the matter."

"Pivotal, one might say."

The lady of the manor and the hireling. She, a woman of elegance and beauty with dark eyes and smooth black-satin hair. He, a man who wouldn't have merited a second glance but for that ridiculous mustache. But it was she who moved restlessly around the desk, her rust skirt the only spot of color in an otherwise drab room.

"Perhaps you and I can come to some arrangement, John?" She paused to pick up a pencil and twirl it between her long fingers. "I've already tried to put a spoke in the wheel this morning and even for a few moments thought I might be able to take direct action. Blame my horoscope; it said my luck was out. But surely you must have some under-standing of how I feel...."

"You didn't have to marry him." Jarrow was rearranging papers on his desk.

"At the time, he seemed the ideal candidate.

You of all people should know how I am and what I require in a husband."

"You got the wealth and a title to boot."

"All that and a bedroom of my own when the exceedingly long honeymoon was over."

"And you expect me to have pity?"

The rain beat upon the window high on the rear wall, making for a dreary accompaniment to the scene being played out before my spying eyes and those of my father, who was leaning over my shoulder with increasing heaviness. Another moment and we would have gone sprawling down in the doorway. But before we could show family solidarity by disgracing ourselves equally, Ned popped around from behind us, hacking out a disgusting cough into an even more disgusting handkerchief. Having announced to her ladyship and Mr. Jarrow that they were not destined to continue enjoying their tête-à-tête, he stuffed the rag back into his trouser pocket and scooted into the office, plucking at a tuft of his hair as he went.

"Morning, your ladyship." He turned one of his little hops into a bow.

"Actually, it's afternoon," interjected the secretary, glancing up at a round wall clock.

"So it be, Mr. Jarrow, so it be! And I'll not be taking up more'n a few minutes of your valued time; nor her ladyship's, neither. We just come along—me and this pair of folks," he explained, beckoning Daddy and me into the room, "to ask if you'd be so good as to let them use the phone. There was a mishap,

169

you see. The vicar that's so dotty about Old Worty drove off in their car."

"Oh, so that explains it," said Lady Grizwolde.

"Explains what, your ladyship?" Ned stood scratching his head.

"Why they're still here."

"Aye, that do be the point."

"It's really like something out of a bad play," I murmured.

"Oh, please don't say that to Mrs. Ambleforth or she'll write in a new scene. And I'm really not up to learning any more lines." Lady Grizwolde gave a laugh that contained absolutely no merriment and held out the phone to me. "You do know the vicarage number?"

I nodded and dialed, but without luck. After listening to a prolonged series of rings, I hung up and announced the obvious: "No answer."

"Most annoying." Mr. Jarrow sounded efficiently regretful.

"It's a great deal more than that, sir." Daddy commanded center stage with an operatic fire in his eyes and a stride suggestive of a billowing cloak and a rapier about to be drawn in a sizzle of steel. "It is an occurrence fraught with the most anguishing of possibilities, the most excruciating of regrets...." He broke off just as his voice swelled to such a volume that I expected him to burst into an aria—completely in Italian, with no stinting of notes held till his face turned blue. "Don't I know you from somewhere?" he inquired of Mr. Jarrow.

"Not that I am aware of, Mr....?"

"Simons. Morley Simons."

"I regret neither the name nor your appearance are familiar to me."

"You weren't perchance in Germany recently?"

"Not unless I was sleepwalking." The mustache weighed down Mr. Jarrow's attempt at a perfunctory smile. "I do have a cousin who resembles me closely. And he does travel quite a bit. It would make for rather a coincidence if you had run into him. However, these things do happen, I suppose."

While Daddy stood with furrowed brow and I was about to suggest that we ring for a taxi, Sir Casper came through the door. He had the two walking sticks with him. Instead of leaning on them, as we had seen him do earlier, he had them tucked under his armpits. Although it couldn't be said that he was entirely steady on his pins—indeed he progressed more sideways than forwards—his steps had an elongated prance to them that made him look rather like an aged ballet dancer attempting to relive a performance in Swan Lake. Had a couple of glasses of red wine got the blood flowing through his veins? Or had his doctor paid him a visit and broken the happy news that, all evidence to the contrary, he wasn't dead yet?

"Phyllis, my darling." His eyes watered with delight in his yellow face as he made for her with increasing, if haphazard, speed. "I have been looking all over the house for you." A lilt had been added to his quavering voice.

"On such a glorious day we should be outside smelling the roses."

"It is raining, Casper." Lady Grizwolde pointed out without looking at him or anyone else.

"All the better for the sort of romp I have in mind!" He wagged a stick and cackled a roguish laugh. "First we can play hide-and-seek among the trees, and when I catch you, we can dry each other off in the green-house."

"You mustn't miss your nap, Casper."

"No forty winks for me today, Phyllis!"

"I believe what her ladyship is suggesting," Mr. Jarrow interposed in a softly persuasive voice, "is that you should reserve your strength, for it would be a pity to do yourself an injury just when you have the promise of a full return to vitality."

"But where is the harm in feeling frisky?" Spoken like an elderly spoiled brat who's nanny had always given him everything he wanted.

"You are understandably buoyed up, sir, by the realization that the medicine you require is shortly to be made available to you." The secretary looked down, but not before I glimpsed the malicious glance he gave her lady-ship. "But you may damage your chances of a recovery if you mistake a psychological lift for the real miracle."

I can't say anything about Daddy's reaction to standing in on this conversation or describe Ned's demeanor, for I had kept them out of my line of vision, but I was certainly feeling

172

off-kilter, even before Sir Casper wobbled up against me.

"Perhaps you are right, Jarrow," he bleated from my arms. "I must endeavor to be patient. It will make the rewards all the sweeter, my Phyllis."

He went suddenly, horribly limp. My knees sagged as I backed up against the desk. Help was slow in coming. My father, Ned, Lady Grizwolde, and Mr. Jarrow all stood fixed in place, as if wondering what was the proper etiquette in a situation such as this. Who was the appropriated person to step forward? Did it depend on whether Sir Casper was living or dead? I was getting ready to drop him when he let out a snore that shook him awake, and finally Mr. Jarrow took custody of him.

In the ensuing reshuffling of our positions I found myself on the other side of the desk staring blankly at a daily calendar. It was the notebook kind with the date and the day of the week on the top of the two pages spread open. There were a number of entries recorded in neat black handwriting, but nothing as my eyes skimmed the lines on any of the black lines about an appointment for this evening between Sir Casper and the caller. And yet when speaking on the phone, Mr. Jarrow had looked down at the calendar and spoken as if he saw one noted there. I looked more closely and spotted a tiny jotting on the topmost outer corner of the page. I had to squint to make it out: R. to be D. 9. Or it could have been a 7.

I was jostled several paces to the right by

Ned, who was struggling to help Mr. Jarrow. Sir Casper had come to like a drowning man hell-bent on dragging his rescuer and possibly a couple of passing liners underwater. My father had very sensibly stepped out of the way. Now he caught my eye, and I would have had to be a dolt not to have realized that he was desperate to get out of there and recover the urn. Luckily, Lady Grizwolde was every bit as eager to be rid of us. She reached into a drawer and withdrew several key rings. Selecting the one she wanted, she dropped it into my hand.

"Take my car—not the Rolls, the other one. And don't worry about getting it back to us today. I know you are expecting visitors. Tomorrow will do just fine. No, I wouldn't dream of letting you wait for a taxi," she insisted, cutting off my protest. "Just go off and enjoy the rest of the day. And now if you will excuse me," she added, having guided Daddy and me firmly out the door, "I really must help Ned and Mr. Jarrow with Casper."

"Of course." I had trouble putting the breaks on my feet after being given such an emotional, if not physical, shove out the door.

"And I hope you didn't pay too much attention to his nonsense." Her ladyship fiddled with the narrow gold belt encircling the waist of her black sweater and then let her hands fall limp at her sides. "It was the dementia talking. Sometimes it's worse than others, and today has been one of his bad times. If he were anyone else, living in an ordinary house, he would have had to go into a home months ago. But luckily we have the facilities to keep him here."

"It must be very difficult," I murmured.

"Extremely sad," Daddy agreed with only a tinge of impatience in his voice.

After which neither of us spoke a word until I was backing the Honda Prelude out of the garage. We hadn't even made eye contact as we walked across the red-carpeted area into the narrow corridor leading outdoors. The rain had stopped, and the sky showed patches of blue among the clouds.

Turning the car around in the courtyard took several moments of intense concentration, for I had no wish to go back inside and report that I wrecked it before even reaching the drive. Somehow I didn't think Lady Grizwolde was quite as keen on me as she had been before I witnessed her husband's pathetic antics. And the world is filled with qualified interior designers, although possibly not in Chitterton Fells, where people tend to consider switching a picture from one side of the room to another a major renovation.

I drove at a snail's pace toward the open gates and even when out on the cliff road proceeded with caution until I was well past the spot where we had almost come to grief earlier. Actually that was beginning to seem ages ago. My mind filled with images of Ben, who would have gone on with his life after an interlude of suitable sorrow. I would walk into the house and discover that he had married the lawyer who had helped him have me declared legally dead. She wouldn't be wearing my clothes; they would be too big for her and not sufficiently chic. But she would have taken over every other aspect of my life, including the children, who would have returned from staying with Grandpa and Grandma. They would have been gently informed that Mummy had gone away, but that if they didn't whine for new toys and went to bed when they were told, they would get to see her again one day.

"Woe betide that vicar when I catch up with him, Giselle." Daddy stuck his plummy voice right into the middle of my pathetic daydream. "If I were a less civilized man, I would spin him around by his dog collar and punch his miserable nose into the nearest wall. As it is, I shall give him a tongue-lashing he will never forget. Let him have harmed a blessed inch of that urn and I will...will..." Words failed him.

"I'm sure you will get Harriet back safe and sound." I steered the car around a bend, avoiding the bristling hedgerows that jutted out in places like bearded-faced Peeping Toms, hoping I sounded more convinced than I felt. A man who was as absentminded as Mr. Ambleforth might well not even notice the canvas bag on the front seat of the car he had mistaken for his bicycle. And, unsecured, it could fall on the floor, the lid could come off, and the contents spill all over the rubber mat.

"My dear Giselle." Daddy spoke with what he undoubtedly considered rigid self-control.

"It is my profound hope that you will drive to the vicarage at several miles above this paltry speed before going home. That way we can trap the fellow before he takes off for parts unknown, beard him in his den, and threaten him with a stern letter to be written to his bishop if he does not immediately produce the urn safe and sound."

"But we just telephoned and no one was home," I reasoned, "and we really do need to get back in case Harriet's relatives have arrived early."

"And how, pray tell, am I to explain to them that she is missing?" Daddy's glower burned most of the skin off the side of my face."

To get him off the subject if only for a moment, I said, "It is awkward, but, let's talk about Mr. Jarrow. Do you still think you've seen him before?"

"Alas," he cried, his eyes lifting to the roof of the car, "I have not been in any mood to dwell on the matter,"

"Well, I have...at least thought about it. I remember your mentioning, when talking about one of your outings with Harriet, that there was a man at another table reading a newspaper or a book with a mustache too big for his face. Couldn't that have been Mr. Jarrow?"

"My feeling was that I noticed him at the airport."

"Which one? In Germany or this end?"

"Both. I recall seeing people in flashes, their faces seeming to zoom into close-up range, because in the midst of my agony I marveled that others were going about the business of travel as if God was still in his heaven and all was right with the world."

"Ned said Mr. Jarrow had been in Colchester looking after his old mother," I reminded him.

"Giselle, I am in no mood to rack my brains on the subject of Mr. Jarrow. Until Harriet is restored to me, I shall remain in the depths of despair. I implore you to take me to the vicarage."

"You're right," I said contritely. "It is what we should do. And if no one's there, we can try the church hall and hopefully find Kathleen Ambleforth holding a rehearsal. It's just a day or two until opening night, so she's probably working her cast around the clock."

I was, of course, really praying we would find my car conspicuously parked in front of St. Anselm's with the keys still in the ignition. That way we could steal it back without having to snitch on the vicar to his wife, who must too often find herself at the end of her rope where he was concerned. No such luck! And I was about to find out that there are women in this world with incredible blind spots when it comes to their men. After knocking to no avail on the vicarage door, Daddy and I tracked enough textbook-perfect footprints across the gleaming church-hall floor to have delighted Scotland Yard. As on my last visit, Kathleen didn't appear to notice a presence looming to her rear. Again her eyes were riveted to the stage. This time her niece Ruth, a tall, gangly young woman, was in the process of strangling Freddy.

"Absolutely splendid," Kathleen heralded them. "We're finally seeing the tender passion that binds Clarabelle and Reginald together despite Malicia's cold-blooded attempts to tear them apart. Now let's take the kiss again very slowly. And this time, Freddy, don't pull away until Inspector Allbright taps you on the shoulder and says, 'If it's all right with you, sir, I'll take a closer look to see why there's an arm hanging out of that chest under the window.' "

By now my cousin's face was purple, but Daddy saved him from lapsing into unconsciousness with a loud "Ahem!" which swung Kathleen around to face us.

"Oh, how nice!" Kathleen didn't look or sound tremendously enthusiastic. But then, we were interrupting her directorial flow. Besides which, Daddy's spouting off at her in a wildly lovelorn state last night was probably still fresh in her mind. Still, she made an effort. "Every little bit of audience prepares the actors for looking out and seeing every seat in the house filled on opening night. Helps them shake off the collywobbles. Do sit wherever you like," she said, waving her script at the rows of folding chairs.

"We'd love to stay and watch," I fibbed, "but that's not the reason we're here."

"Something most appalling has occurred...," Daddy began.

"Oh, dear!" Her eyes had shifted back to the stage. "Clarabelle, perhaps you should hug

Reg around the shoulders instead of his throat. But remember, Freddy, I want you to keep that dreamy-eyed expression."

"The thing is," I plowed on, "Mr. Ambleforth went off in my car."

"And he's taken Harriet." Daddy's furious vibrations sent autumn leaves eddying across the floor.

"That isn't right!" Kathleen had finally given us her full attention, or so I thought until I realized she was addressing the gnomelike man with a large magnifying glass hovering on tiptoe behind the footlights as if afraid of inadvertently stomping on Freddy, who had finally collapsed, gasping on the floor.

"Inspector Allbright, you aren't skipping through a meadow with a butterfly net. You have come on official business, devastated by your suspicions that your old friend Major Wagewar has met an untimely death in this house but deeply conflicted because Reg and Clarabelle have always been generous contributors to the Policemen's Widows and Orphans Benefit. One wrong step in this investigation and you may find yourself sitting up at night knitting blankets and hot-water-bottle covers for the annual fund-raiser. Now, let me see the furrowed brow, the intently clenched jaw, the intelligent yet deferential gaze; there's a dear man."

Poor thing! He looked as though he wouldn't mind abandoning his acting career to empty ashtrays and mop up beer spills down at the Dark Horse pub. I knew Tom Tingle from the Hearthside Guild and other local activities, and his diminutive stature and big ears tended to bring out my protective instincts. At any other time I would probably have rushed up onstage, tucked him under my arm, and spirited him off to his house, where he could have got into bed with a hot-water bottle. But Daddy was breathing down my neck like a cyclone. So I tracked after Kathleen and as kindly as possible explained about the Old Abbey, Ned, and the car and hinted that I would rather like to have it back. Sooner, if possible, rather than later."

"Immediately!" stormed Daddy.

"Yes, of course you would! It really is too shockingly bad of Dunstan. And I wish I could assure you that he's an expert driver. But the truth of the matter is that when he's all caught up in St. Ethelwort, he's an absolute menace on the road." Kathleen shook her head. "Still, let's look on the bright side. Maybe he'll run out of petrol. That sometimes brings him round. Especially if it's close to teatime. The poor lamb is so desperately fond of my cheese scones."

"There's only one place for the perpetrator of such a horrible crime, and that's at the end of a rope." I thought it was Daddy speaking, but it was Tom in his role as the inspector. "You're not leaving the scene of the crime," he admonished Reg, otherwise known as Freddy, who plaintively responded that he'd really like to go home to his mum.

"When was she written into the script?" Clarabelle wanted to know.

"I'm talking about my real-life mother."

181

Freddy got up off the floor and dusted himself off. "She's coming to visit, and I need to be home when she arrives."

"Can't you stay just another fifteen minutes?" Kathleen urged him. "It's already next to impossible having a rehearsal without Lady Grizwolde. Such a pity she couldn't come today. Although this could have been the chance for Roxie Malloy to understudy. Had I been able to get hold of her." Heaving sigh. "And then there's always the problem of having to work around the maid's scenes until Dawn gets off school. Temperamental actors!" She rolled up the script and thumped it against a chair.

Afraid I might be the next buffeting block, I tiptoed over to her, asked her to phone as soon as she heard from Mr. Ambleforth, and on receipt of her nod marched Daddy, resisting, all the way out of the church hall. A voice from the rear implored us not to go. Actually, it was Clarabelle in a last-ditch scene with Reg begging him not to abandon their marriage vows to scamper off into Malicia Stillwaters's lethal embrace.

"We've done everything humanly possible," I told Daddy as we climbed into the Honda Prelude. To which he responded with stony silence. In fact, he didn't say a word for the remainder of the short drive. We were within a few yards of Merlin's Court when I saw another car turning in through the gates ahead of us. It was a vehicle I didn't recognize, and I assumed that here again were Harriet's relatives. But suddenly a frothy blond head popped out of the window, and I was looking at Freddy's mother. Aunt Lulu. Far from looking crestfallen at having been dispatched to us by an irate husband fed up with her kleptomania, she had the sunny smile of a schoolgirl intent on causing as much mischief as possible.

CHAPTER 14

FROM PHOTOS I HAD SEEN OF HER AS A CHILD, AUNT Lulu had been a very pretty little girl, and at fifty-something she still looked like Shirley Temple. Which isn't to say that on a good day she didn't show her age. When in the company of her husband, Maurice, not even her dimples or wide eyes could perk up her bewildered expression. But today, in the drawing room at Merlin's Court, she had another man in tow, and she couldn't have been bubblier as she tap-danced her way around the coffee table.

"Ellie, dear, wasn't it just lovely of nice Mr. Price to give me a lift here from the station? We were on the same train, although not in the same carriage." This said in the virtuous, piping voice of one who knew how to comport herself even when away from Mummy's eagle eye. "He heard me asking the ticket collector about the availability of taxis. I really couldn't walk all the way to Merlin's

Court on these short legs. You know how I always tell my life history to everyone, Ellie, when Maurice isn't there to say, 'That's enough, Lulu!' But Mr. Price was so sweet. He very kindly said he would be delighted to take me in his car."

"That was thoughtful," I told the portly man in the pinstriped suit and round spectacles who, through no fault of his own, closely resembled the portentous Maurice.

"No trouble at all." Even the voice was similar.

"Well, just a little." Aunt Lulu giggled. Mr. Price couldn't remember which car was his because it was a rented one, and he had to try lots of doors before finding one that opened. Luckily, that was one thing he did remember—leaving it unlocked. He had been worried about it all the time he'd been gone. And when he tried the key they had given him, it didn't fit, and he had to use a tiny little screwdriver from one of those repair kits, the sort that you sometimes get in a Christmas cracker. I remember the year Freddy got one like it. He wanted the plastic ring that squirted water in people's eyes, but Maurice wouldn't swap with him."

"I shouldn't have dealt with one of those economy-car places." Mr. Price removed his specs and polished them with a handkerchief produced from his breast pocket. "As my dear wife often reminds me, we get what we pay for in this world."

"You have a wife?" Aunt Lulu stopped tap-dancing.

"She's an invalid; has been for many years."

"Oh, how sad," I said.

"Martha is the reason I went back up to London last night." Mr. Price refolded his handkerchief and poked it back into his pocket. "I often have to cut short a business meeting to return home when she has one of her spells."

"What business are you in?" It seemed a good time to be nosy.

"Toothbrushes."

"What fun!" Aunt Lulu perched on the arm of a chair and spread her gathered skirts just a little above her plump knees. "I still have the pink one with the duck handle that I had when I was five. I keep it in a box in my bedroom with all my other childhood treasures. There is nothing like a toothbrush, is there, for bringing back memories."

"I supply them to hotels for complimentary use." Mr. Price paraded over to the windows, took a peek out of them, and returned to the central grouping of sofas and chairs. "And just recently I have begun offering the little travel kits."

"Like the one he used in the car." Aunt Lulu's eyes grew big with admiration.

"Holidaymakers must find them very handy," I said.

"That was Mary's thought."

"Mary?"

"My wife."

"I thought you said her name was Martha?"

"So it is." Mr. Price gave his spectacles another polish. "Mary is my pet name for her.

You know how husbands and wives have these little games they play. All very silly, of course, and making no sense at all to outsiders."

"That sounds so sweet." Aunt Lulu sat on her armchair perch, swinging her short legs. "The only game Maurice plays is watching golf on television. And his pet name for me is Twit."

"How about a drink, Mr. Price?" I suggested. "Or would you rather not as you have to drive?" He had been looking at me with diminished enthusiasm, causing me to reflect sadly that this had not been my day for keeping in people's good graces. But he did smile now. A small, well-tailored sort of smile.

"Perhaps a very small one. Gin, if you have it."

"Tonic water?"

"Just a splash."

"And what about you?" I asked Aunt Lulu.

"Not just now, thank you, Ellie."

"I'm not much of a bartender," I apologized to Mr. Price. "My husband is better, but he's taking Aunt Lulu's suitcase down to her son's cottage."

"What about my handbag?" she asked a shade quickly.

"I expect Ben put it on the trestle table out in the hall."

"Then I'd better go and get it," she said with a breathless little-girl laugh. "I'm one of those silly women who can't bear to be parted from her bag for long. Usually I don't let it get away from me. But in all the excitement of seeing you and Ben again, Ellie, and even more thrillingly your father after all these years, I just put it down without thinking."

Oh, Aunt Lulu! She was typical of a person who cheerfully helped herself to other people's property and lived in fear of having the nose pinched off her face.

"I think I should get it," she was telling Mr. Price as one of the latticed windows opened, a long leg descended over the sill, and a moment later the rest of Freddy entered the room. Upon spotting his mother, however, he appeared ready to beat a hasty retreat.

"No you don't," I told him.

"Hello, Mumsie." He stood looking like every mother's nightmare, with his ponytail and earring and his knees out of his jeans. "Had a good journey down? Pigged out in the buffet car on the train, I hope, because there's not a thing to eat at the cottage. Where's the pater?"

"He decided at the last moment not to bring me down. He said his secretary had complained that he had been taking too many days off lately. Apparently she burst into tears and said that life in the office was meaningless without him. And you know how he can't bear to have a young girl sob in his arms." There was not a trace of sarcasm in Aunt Lulu's voice. "But Freddy, dear, you must let me introduce you to nice Mr. Price. He picked me up at the station. And we've been having such a fun time."

"Hello." My cousin eyed the portly man in the pinstriped suit without exuberance.

"Freddy was born when I was little more than a schoolgirl, Mr. Price." Another of Auntie's giggles. "Isn't he a big boy for fourteen?"

"A credit to you, I'm sure."

"When I was pregnant, his father and I were sure he was going to be a girl. We had our hearts set on the name Frederica. So when he was born, we had to rack our brains for a masculine equivalent."

Freddy looked from me to the yellow Chinese vases on the mantelpiece. "If I threw something, something very expensive and easily breakable, do you think she would behave like a normal mother and send me to my room?"

"How about a drink?" I asked while walking over to hand Mr. Price his gin and tonic. Ben and Daddy will be here in a minute, and even though it's a little early in the day, we could probably make it into a real cocktail hour and open a tin of peanuts."

"Yes, isn't it wonderful about Morley?" Aunt Lulu enthused. "Home after all these years of traveling the world."

"His job kept him on the move?" Mr. Price sipped his drink.

"Not really," I hedged.

"Morley has made a successful career out of not working. Such a credit to him." Aunt Lulu's voice held sincere admiration. "After all, that's something most men can't claim in this day and age. And it's not as though that trust fund of his can be all that big. At least that's what Maurice says. He's always believed that Morley must have had other irons in the fire. But I think that's unkind. Your father is just awfully good at doing nothing, Ellie."

"Does he plan to make a long visit with you?" Mr. Price asked me as he went to sit down on the sofa facing the window, only to find that Freddy had already accommodated himself full-length and appeared unlikely to budge.

"He hasn't said," I replied coolly.

"Uncle Morley is here on a sad errand." My cousin obviously felt compelled, despite his lethargic appearance, to spill the beans about things that could surely be of no interest to a total stranger. "Harriet Brown, the woman he loved, was killed recently in a car accident."

"Driving in this country has become a nightmare." Mr. Price shook his head sadly, and Freddy quickly put him right on one point.

"This accident occurred in Germany. And poor Uncle got stuck with the rotten task of bringing her ashes home to her family."

"He has my deepest sympathy, living as I do in daily dread of something happening to Mary Martha." Mr. Price studied his drink as if seeing in its depths the bitterest of eventualities. "Naturally, the subject comes up every now and then about the choices to be made when she does pass away, and she says she would prefer cremation. The dear woman believes it might bring me some small comfort if I were to have her scattered among the rosebushes in the garden. And I think she's right. I'm sure I don't know how your father"— the widower-to-be was now looking at me— "your poor father, got through the business

190

of handing over those ashes. Was he able to stay composed in the presence of his lady love's family?"

I wanted to say: Aren't we inquisitive? But Freddy, still lying flat on the sofa with his eyes closed, got his jaw working first.

"Uncle Morley hasn't performed his promised task yet. The relatives will be here any minute. But there's been a hitch. Someone's made off with the urn."

"It wasn't me," protested Aunt Lulu as my mouth dropped.

"Mrs. Ambleforth told you?" I looked at Freddy.

"As I was trying to escape the church hall before her pie-faced niece could ask me if kissing her in the third act had meant as much to her as it had to me. And should her uncle Dunstie post the banns next Sunday."

Mr. Price had been looking up at the ceiling during most of this pathetic confession, but the moment Freddy flopped back on the sofa, he fixed spectacled eyes on me.

"Your father must be beside himself. Does he know who stole the urn? Has he set about getting it back?"

"It wasn't stolen." My reply was curt. "It was all an unfortunate mistake. I'm sure the person who inadvertently went off with it will return it very soon, safe and sound in its canvas bag. Either this afternoon or later in the evening."

"And who is this person?"

"I'd rather not say, Mr. Price." Perhaps some of the ill-concealed irritation in my voice got through to him, because his faced flushed. And I couldn't see any reason for him to be annoyed. Not unless he was terribly thin-skinned.

"Do you know, I really believe I should be going." He swallowed what was left of his gin and tonic and set the glass down.

"Must you really rush off?" Aunt Lulu pouted—something my mother once said a woman of a certain age should avoid doing at all costs. "I was hoping you could stay for tea, Mr. Price. Ellie's husband is a chef, and Freddy works with him, so I'm sure they could rustle up something quite wonderful between the two of them." Her demure gaze hinted at the possibility that she herself could rustle up something even more tempting. But perhaps with thoughts of his invalid wife prevalent in his mind, Mr. Price was bidding us a firm good-bye when Ben walked into the sitting room.

My one and only husband was wearing his navy blue sweater and looked both handsome and admirably domestic carrying a tray loaded with cups and saucers, a milk jug, sugar bowl, and teapot. Strangely, something about Mr. Price's bearing immediately changed. He stood straighter; even his features seemed to alter, his expression becoming at once austere and deferential.

"Allow me to take that, sir!" Gliding forward, he removed the tray from Ben's hands and bore it away to a side table, where he deposited it as if it were the coronation crown being lowered onto the royal head. Whereupon he adjusted a couple of cup handles, lifted the teapot lid to inspect the brew, and with an inclination of his head, said: "If that will be all, sir, I will leave you and your family to your afternoon tea."

"Thank you." Ben's black brows went up, and by the time they had come down again and I had stopped blinking, Mr. Price had padded across the room and out the door.

"We'll have to see him off," I exclaimed, and latching on to my husband's sweater sleeve, headed out into the hall. But it was too late for adieus. We were barely in time to see the front door close. Then we proceeded to waste time eyeing each other like two people who had just been redeposited on earth by a Martian man in a spaceship. A moment later, we heard a car being driven off in a flurry of gravel.

"Just who was that man?" Ben leaned against the trestle table and folded his arms.

"The one who brought Aunt Lulu up from the station."

"I know that, but what else did you find out about him?"

"He's a toothbrush salesman."

"Is that what he told you?"

"Why would he lie about it?"

"I don't know." Ben plucked a chrysanthemum from the bronze vase and began depleting it of leaves, just as I had with a similar bloom when we had been in the hall the previous afternoon. "But that business of his taking the tea tray... Surely you thought the same thing I did, Ellie."

"What?"

"The man has to be a butler."

"Now you mention it, he did have the manner. But he could have recently changed jobs."

"Where's Daddy?" I asked.

"Upstairs in his room. He's very upset about the missing urn. It could be making him paranoid. He said he recognized that man."

"Mr. Price?"

"Morley thinks he was one of the men on the escalator at the underground."

"The one who pushed him?"

"No, the one who picked up his suitcase."

"I wonder if Daddy is cracking." I stood hugging my arms. "He also thought he recognized Mr. Jarrow, Sir Casper's secretary. But what if he's right. Aunt Lulu blabbed that Mr. Price couldn't find his car parked outside the station. It was a rented one, or so he said, and he had to hunt around for one with an open door; some story about remembering he had left it unlocked. And then, because he didn't have the right key, he had to start the ignition with a little screwdriver."

"You listened to that with a straight face?"

"No." I walked up and down the Turkish rug. "But it could have been true, I suppose. Getting to know our new vicar has caused me to take wackiness somewhat more in stride. "But I might have smelled a rat if"—being a wife I had to point the finger of blame at the ever readily available source—"you hadn't done such a good job last night of convincing me that I was letting my imagination run riot."

"That was when you were harping on about the Gypsies."

"I still say they have to fit into what's going on somewhere. But let's not squabble, darling." I sat down on the bottom stair. "If we take the appearance of Mr. Price on the scene as too big a coincidence to be ignored, we have to figure out just what Daddy has got himself mixed up in."

"And what was Harriet's role before she got herself killed?" Ben was now the one pacing the carpet.

I sat looking wishfully up at him. "Wouldn't it be wonderful Ben, if the whole thing was my stupid imagination? That way we could hand Harriet over to her kith and kin with clear consciences, and Daddy could get on with his life without additional turmoil. But somehow I didn't think things are about to get that simple." It was on the tip of my tongue to tell him that Mr. Jarrow was supposed to have been in Colchester in recent weeks and that the atmosphere at the Old Abbey had been decidedly murky. But, there went the doorbell! It would be Harriet's relatives, and I dreaded to think what we would tell them!

CHAPTER 15

"I'LL LET YOU ANSWER IT. A GOOD WIFE DOESN'T HOG all the unpleasant tasks," I was telling Ben when Freddy came out of the drawing room.

"You're angry with me, aren't you?" Freddy looked at me with mournful eyes. "For running off at the mouth to that bloke Price."

"I wasn't thrilled," I told him.

"This whole business of Mumsie and how to get her back on the straight and narrow has me hopelessly rattled, Coz."

"Sorry, now isn't the time for me to cradle you in my arms. I have to save my strength to calm down Harriet's people when they go into hysterics."

"That's them?" He watched Ben head for the front door.

"I've got that sinking feeling." I grabbed hold of his arm and fast-trotted us across the hall.

"At least the children are gone, so Mumsie can't stuff them in her handbag."

"Very true," I agreed as I dragged him back into the sitting room, only to have him wiggle free, duck back around the door, to then reappear seconds later with Aunt Lulu's bag, an innocuous-looking brown one. Not big enough to hold more than a lipstick and a packet of gum, or so I would have thought.

"That's why I came out," Freddy whispered to me. "Mumsie would have gone and fetched it herself, but I didn't want her interrupting you and Ben while you were having a heart-to-heart." His spirits had recovered sufficiently for him to produce a virtuous look with impish overtones. Sad to say, I really wasn't all that interested in his state of mind.

My ears were pricked for the sound of voices out in the hall. I could hear Ben without being able to make out the words and caught fragmented murmurs from a woman— or women—and then a man speaking. Other than that, all I could be sure of was that Kathleen Ambleforth was not among our visitors. She wasn't the sort to take a backseat in any conversation. And hers was a voice that carried. Even standing as I now did between the two sofas, I would have been able to make out every word of what she was saying. Not so her husband. His voice was soft, in the manner of one who doesn't like to disturb his train of thought by his own noisy interruptions. And it tended to fade even lower when he retreated to the eleventh century. Could it be he out there, accompanied by his niece Ruth, come to return our car and apologize for the inconvenience?

I was torn between hoping this might be the case, for I was eager to take a look inside the urn before meeting Harriet's relatives. The clock on the mantelpiece ticked like a bomb about to go off. I flinched when Aunt Lulu piped up within inches of me.

"Freddy, why are you holding my bag?"

"Because I said I would fetch it for you, Mumsie." My cousin sounded like an increasingly recalcitrant child.

"Do give it to me." His mother could also have passed for six. "If anyone should walk in and see you holding it, they'd very likely take you for a cross-dresser, and that would be something else for your father to blame on me. Ellie, make him give it to me right now."

"Oh, for heaven sake!" I moved to take the bag from Freddy, but he scooted away from me with a swish of his ponytail and a twitch of the skull and crossbones earring. Meanwhile, the voices out in the hall were coming closer. The ticking clock sounded ready to explode.

"Just what are you hiding in here?" Freddy jiggled the brown leather strap as he bore down on his little Shirley Temple mother, who retreated behind one of the Queen Anne chairs.

"Nothing!" Her pout was as adorable as it was irritating.

"I don't believe you." Freddy tossed the bag down on the chair. "Do you really think I don't know when you've been up to something? That little stay at Oaklands didn't teach you a thing, did it, Mumsie."

"There you're wrong, dear." Aunt Lulu

smiled in a dreamy-eyed way as she stood touching the tightly fitted cuffs of her wide-sleeved pink sweater. "It was a marvelous educational experience, so emotionally stimulating and mind expanding. Honestly, I can't thank your father enough for making me go." She was curtailed from further enthusiasm when Ben entered the room, with Harriet's relatives clustering along behind him.

"There you are, sweetheart." He beamed a smile my way as if suddenly spotting me paddling upriver in a canoe. "The Hoppers are back and eager to meet your father." He stepped sideways, and the man and two women emerged into full view.

"We're so sorry you've had to make a second trip." I moved forward and extended my hand.

Ben completed the introductions, growing in handsome, debonair charm with every syllable—in such contrast to the Hoppers, whose responses were produced in wooden tones. Fittingly so, because they still reminded me strongly of dolls—those brightly painted Russian dolls, without arms and legs, that come in descending sizes and fit one inside the other. Cyril, the man, and the two women, Enid and Doris, weren't missing any limbs, but they stood so stiffly that they each appeared to have been manufactured in one piece. All three had very flat black hair, cut in the same rounded shape, and identical blank-eyed stares.

"Do please sit down." I waved a hand that felt as though it belonged to someone else while avoiding Freddy's wicked grin.

"Oh, yes, do make yourselves comfortable." Aunt Lulu disported herself little-girl fashion on the chair where her handbag reposed like a brown leather cushion. Reaching out a hand, she patted the arm of the sofa. "Why don't you come and sit next to me, Edith." Actually she was talking to Doris; at least I think she was, but it didn't matter. The woman in the red blouse atop the black skirt meekly did as she was bidden and placed her bag, which wasn't dissimilar to Aunt Lulu's, on the floor. The woman in the yellow blouse and black skirt (who I thought was Edith) and Cyril, in the royal blue shirt and black trousers, took their seats.

"Well! Well! Here we all are!" Freddy clapped me on the shoulder; no doubt hoping to provide some desperately needed moral support and causing my knees to buckle in the process. His voice was so falsely jocular that it wasn't surprising that his mother leaped to an erroneous and, to her mind, ghastly possibility.

"Who are these Hoppers?" Her eyes grew big with horror, and she recoiled into the depths of her chair as if about to cross herself. "They aren't social workers, are they?"

"Of course not. They are here to see Daddy," I said firmly. "They've come on a distressing errand, and we don't want to make it any harder for them than necessary, now do we?"

"Would you like Mumsie and me to clear off?" Freddy made this offer with all the fortitude of a man offering to reboard the Titanic. But given the awkwardness of the missing urn,

I wasn't averse to the occasional distraction of Freddy or Aunt Lulu.

"Do you mind my aunt and cousin staying?" I asked the Hoppers.

"No, I don't mind," responded Cyril. "Do you mind, Edith?" he said, turning his round black head an inch to the right.

"No, I don't mind; do you, Doris?" Yellow blouse addressing the red blouse.

"Not if you don't mind, Edith."

They all spoke, without moving their lips, in identical wooden voices, and I could not prevent the thought that it would be a kindness to reassemble them into one doll and drop it into the children's toy box.

"Would you like me to fetch Uncle Morley?" Freddy whispered to me.

"There's no getting around it," I murmured back. "He has to be here. Try and fortify him with a glass of brandy; the decanter should still be in his room."

"Righty-ho!" He went out the door, and before he could close it behind him, Tobias came stalking in, his tail sticking straight up as if daring anyone to meow at him the wrong way. Ben and I both went to pick him up, and under cover of this momentary confusion I was able to ask the big question.

"Did you tell them that we don't have Harriet?"

Ben talked into the cat's fur. "I thought we should soften them up first; let them think we're salt-of-the-earth people." His eyes met mine with rueful tenderness. "Sorry. I know you're not fond of that phrase."

For a couple of seconds I couldn't think what he meant, and when I remembered Daddy's reference to my adored mother, I couldn't reconnect to my wounded anger of last night. Too much had happened, including that moment at the Old Abbey when I had looked at him and found him the most comforting thing in the room simply because he was my father.

"I'm sure my husband has offered you his condolences, and I'd like to add mine on your sad loss," I told the Hoppers while taking the chair next to Aunt Lulu, who was bent down picking up her handbag, which she must have dropped while I was engaged in my rude, whispered conversation with Ben. "How, if you don't mind my asking, were you related to Harriet?" I was growing a little flustered at getting no response from the Russian dolls.

"She was our cousin," said Cyril.

"That's right, our cousin," put in one of the female dolls.

"Our very dear cousin," offered the other.

"The Hoppers are brother and sisters." Ben tossed me a lifeline.

"Did you have a long journey getting here?" I asked them.

"We're staying at Cliffside House." Cyril fixed his polished black eyes on my face.

"You know it, Ellie." Ben stood behind the drinks table, with Tobias draped over his shoulder. "It's the B and B run by Mrs. Blum."

"Yes, it's at the bend in the road just before

you come to the Old Abbey. Mrs. Blum is Mrs. Potter's sister." I could feel myself turning into a parrot. Any moment now I would start sprouting green and red feathers.

"Is that so?" Ben raised a convincingly interested eyebrow.

"Did someone from Cliffside give you a lift here?"

"We came by taxi. Like this morning." Doris gave up this information after looking down at her black lace-up, patent-leather shoes, which matched the ones worn by Doris and Cyril.

"What a pity you didn't have a Mr. Price to rescue you!" Aunt Lulu, who had been sitting looking smug for no apparent reason, gave one of her infantile giggles. The Hoppers responded with blank faces; but as blankness had heretofore been their collective expression, it was impossible to tell if they were puzzled by her remark.

"Mr. Price is a traveling salesman who gave Aunt Lulu a lift here from the station." I tugged at my camel cardigan, wishing that Freddy would appear with Daddy in tow. It should have surprised me that the Hoppers hadn't asked about him, but it had crept in upon me that they were incapable of initiating any part of this trying conversation. Or, for reasons of their own, were being intentionally guarded. Had Cyril misunderstood my question about how far they had traveled to reach Merlin's Court? Or were he, Doris, and Edith disinclined to say where they lived for fear that Daddy would attach himself to them as a means of keeping Harriet's memory alive in his heart? If so, they had a point, but somehow I didn't think any of this was simple. Could we even be sure that the Hoppers were who they claimed to be? Harriet's bereaved relatives intent on fulfilling her final wishes?

"Such a lovely man, Mr. Price!" Aunt Lulu smiled dreamily. "And so clever at breaking into his own car. How I wish my new friends from Oaklands could meet him. That's what Maurice doesn't understand. The fun of sitting around with people who share the same hobby, dishing out little tips and analyzing intriguing problems. I don't see why he can't see that he would be worse off married to one of those obsessive bridge players. We all know how vicious they can be. Harping on forever about how someone false carded one Tuesday afternoon in 1954 at Mrs. so-and-so's house and to make matters worse her luncheon was pitiful. A total embarrassment to the club."

Thank goodness Freddy hadn't returned in time to hear this brazen speech and realize that if ever a mother was sorely in need of a son's moral guidance, it was Aunt Lulu. I even went so far as to hope my cousin had shared a swig or two with Daddy from the brandy decanter, which brought my mind around again to my hostess duties.

"My father will be down in a moment," I assured the Hoppers, having delayed making this statement until I thought there was at least a likelihood of its proving true. "Would you like something to drink. Tea, perhaps, or a sherry?" Somehow I couldn't picture any of them downing a martini, even at what was approaching the reasonably civilized hour of four o'clock.

"No, thank you," said Cyril.

"Not for me," said Edith.

"Nor me," said Doris.

"Then how about something to eat?" Ben rose valiantly to the occasion after putting Tobias down on the floor. "I have some sandwiches made and a sponge cake ready to cut."

"We never eat between meals." Edith spoke first this time.

"Never," agreed Cyril.

"Not ever," concluded Doris.

Where, oh, where, I thought wildly, was my father? When I was a child, he had been rather good at appearing when desperately needed, even abandoning the book he was reading, probably Tolstoy, to come and sit on my bed during a thunderstorm. It was only after I was in my teens that he got the idea that it was only my mother I needed and that he was more hindrance than help to me in my aspiring role as a woman. Tobias jolted me back into focus by landing on my lap. Cyril was talking about ice cream.

"That's the only exception to our eating habits. On a very hot day we sometimes treat ourselves to a small vanilla cone each." For the first time I saw a flicker of expression in his eyes. Was he instantly regretting this outburst? Had he unleashed in his sisters a wild urge to offer further glimpses into the lives of the Hopper family?

"Oaklands," said Doris.

"You were speaking of it," Edith reminded Aunt Lulu.

"So, I was." Auntie dimpled prettily. "It's hard not to, because I had such a wonderful time there. It was partly like going to a business convention and having your mind constantly stimulated by new concepts and the reworking of old ones. And also like being on holiday. Getting up when I wanted. Going to bed without being told to do so by Maurice. They are very forward thinking at Oaklands."

"Harriet was at a place of that name," said Doris.

"Years ago." Edith actually nodded her head.

"Was she in treatment?" Aunt Lulu leaned forward in her chair with hands clasped.

"No." Cyril fixed his black eyes on each sister in turn.

"She wasn't a...a therapist?" Auntie no longer looked quite so eager to bond.

"She worked in the cafeteria. Isn't that right, Edith?" Doris looked to her sister for confirmation.

"And helped with the cleaning. Harriet said it was hard work, but worth it because of all she learned along the way."

"About making beds," interposed Cyril, "with hospital corners."

"Harriet is...was a wonderful person." This was Edith talking now, and for the first time I saw something real in her face. "We grew up together on the same street. It was a rough neighborhood, and she always took care of us. Stopped the other kids from making fun of Cyril, Doris, and me. And we've never let anyone say a word against her. Have we, Doris?"

"Not ever."

"She was always clever. Ever so good at sums. And popular, too. She was always chosen to be in the school plays." It seemed Edith might keep going until someone removed her batteries. I got the feeling that Cyril would have liked to have done so. What was he afraid of? I wondered as I caught Ben looking at the clock.

Just at that moment, the door opened, and in came Daddy, followed by Freddy. Instantly, all animation, such as it was, left Edith's face.

"Those are Harriet's relations?" My father, apparently having taken Freddy up on his offer of brandy, directed a zigzagging finger at the Hoppers before advancing toward them in a series of narrowing circles that brought a couple of side tables and their lamps into peril. Tobias very sensibly got off my lap and retreated behind the curtains.

"Yes, Morley." Ben rescued him before he could send the coffee table into the fireplace. "These are Harriet's cousins, Cyril, Edith, and Doris Hopper. Ellie and I have been waiting for you to tell them about the situation regarding the urn."

"You left me to do it?" Daddy ignored the extended wooden hands and tottered back to

Freddy, using him as a lamppost to cling to while looking understandably aggrieved.

"To do what?" Aunt Lulu asked, her feet tap-dancing on the floor.

"To explain." I looked around as if hoping the words would drop into my hand. "To explain that he isn't able to give them Harriet's ashes at this moment. Because...he can't" was the very best I could do with the Hoppers looking at me as though they might suddenly come to life.

"We feel dreadful about this." Ben disconnected Daddy from Freddy, marched him forward, and lowered him into the nearest chair. "But the truth is"—so often the words of someone telling anything but—"Morley is in such a precarious emotional state, we're afraid that he might go right over the edge if we forced him to give you the urn today."

"But we must have it. Harriet is..." Edith's voice went from a whisper to a whimper.

"Harriet is our cousin," Cyril finished for her.

"Our very dear cousin," contributed Doris.

"In death as in life!" Her brother added the exclamation point.

"I understand your feelings, but my father-in-law was deeply in love with her, and her tragic death has left him heartbroken." Ben gripped Daddy's shoulder, and I knew he was daring him to speak. "You only have to look at him to see that he's extraordinarily fragile."

"He looks drunk to me." Aunt Lulu tiptoed over to take a peek.

"Don't be daft, Mumsie," Freddy flared at her, and she sat back down. "I only gave him a drop of brandy when he turned violent and tried to shove me out a second-floor window after I tried to persuade him to give up the urn. I've spent nearly half an hour calming him down, and I don't want anyone, especially my own mother, putting themselves at risk by setting him off again."

"Sound thinking." Ben maintained his restraining hold on Daddy, who did look as if he were about to lunge out of his chair.

"I don't like violence." Cyril trod back into line with his sisters.

"He always cried when the other boys hit him," said Doris.

"And then Harriet had to go and beat them up." Edith nodded her wooden head.

"It would be terrible if my father did get physical and we had to ring for the police." I sent him a look that dared him to speak.

"Terrible, indeed! The last thing Harriet would"—Cyril's voice cracked—"would have wanted."

"I'm sure Daddy will be better in the morning," I said bracingly as the brother and sister edged toward the door. "And the good thing is that you are staying close by. You hadn't planned on going home tonight?"

"No, not till tomorrow." It might have been one or all three of them talking.

I followed them out into the hall. "Then why don't we leave it that either my husband or I will bring the urn to you tomorrow morning? Daddy can come, too, if he's again in his right mind. I know he would love to talk to you about Harriet. And now, if you really think it best to leave, I'll drive you back to Cliffside House."

A needless gesture, because they insisted that they had arranged for a taxi to pick them up just about this time and they would walk down the drive to meet it. From the looks on their faces as they sidled out the front door, I was pretty sure that the Hoppers would have preferred no further encounters with any members of my family. And as I watched them toddle away, I couldn't find it in my heart to blame them for wondering just what sort of people their Harriet had got herself mixed up with.

CHAPTER 16

"THANK GOD! I WAS SPARED FROM EMBARRASSING myself!" my father wended his inebriated way across the hall to the stairs. It was clear to me that despite his acknowledgment of heavenly intervention, he was wallowing in self-congratulation. "Had I not brilliantly followed your lead, my dear Giselle, as a lesser man might have done," he proclaimed, "the vicar's theft of your car would have been revealed. And those strange little people would have spent an agonizing night wondering when, if ever, Harriet would be returned to those of us who worship the ground she once so gladsomely trod."

I took it as an encouraging sign that he did not seem bent on doing any immediate agonizing himself. Indeed, he struck quite a jovial pose as he lolled against the banisters. In all likelihood, the reprieve would be short-lived. The effects of the brandy would dissipate,

211

and gloom would reclaim him. But every step he took back to life and hope must surely do him some good. Or so I told myself as I helped him up the stairs to his bedroom.

His suitcase was on the floor by the wardrobe, and a pair of his shoes protruded from under a chair. But it didn't yet feel like his room. That wasn't to be expected. But neither should I have felt Harriet's presence so strongly, especially with the urn being gone. Did her perfume linger on the shirt Daddy had laid over the foot rail of the bed? Or was I imagining that dusky summer evening fragrance? No, she was here, I decided while walking around him to turn back the coverlet. I could feel her. Did that mean her love for my father and his for her had truly made them one in spirit?

Rubbish! I gave the pillow an unnecessary thump. That a love affair ended tragically did not make it Romeo and Juliet. Daddy dropped with a wallop onto the bed, and something other than annoyance fueled me as I heaved his feet up with the rest of him. It was my mother's voice inside my head: "It's been a long day, with no time to sort anything out in your head. No wonder you're cross, darling. Why don't you go for a nice long walk to blow away the cobwebs?" For a moment I was sure I felt her hand on my shoulder, until I realized I had backed into the edge of the door that I'd left open. But then I had let out a yelp.

"Did you speak, Giselle?" Daddy inquired in a drowsy voice from the bed.

"No, I just screamed."

"Ah, well, that's good!"

Much he cared. I sighed as I spread the coverlet back over him. But I didn't nurse a sense of ill usage. Suddenly my mind filled with a picture of Harriet working at Oaklands. Was it the same Oaklands where Aunt Lulu had so recently gone for treatment? A little bell went off inside my head. Something Daddy had said about his time with Harriet. The memory wiggled around like a tadpole, slippery and elusive. Never mind, I decided as it disappeared back into the pond. And instantly I remembered. Harriet had talked to Daddy about an aunt who she thought might have lived in, or near, Chitterton Fells and how her married name had been Oaklands. Or maybe that's what her house had been called. If Daddy's retelling was accurate, Harriet's reminiscences had been a bit of a rigmarole.

"They were very strange people," he murmured as I reached under the coverlet for his feet to remove his shoes.

"Who?"

"Harriet's relations."

"Most peculiar." I did battle with a knotted lace.

Had Harriet been thinking of the time she worked at Oaklands when she spoke of the aunt? Was there even an aunt? Or had Harriet made her up on the spur of the moment when Daddy mentioned that I lived in Chitterton Fells? Had she used the name Oaklands because the inclusion of pieces of the truth made her conversation more believable to her own ears?

"What were they called, Giselle?"

"What were what called, Daddy?" I was now wrestling with the second shoelace.

"Those people who came for Harriet."

"The Hoppers. Cyril, Doris, and Edith."

"I have vast difficulty, Giselle, believing that the Hobbits, if that's what you called them, could be even distantly related to my wondrous Harriet." Perhaps not. Were they instead her accomplices? It was the first time I had considered Harriet's knowing involvement in whatever Daddy had got mixed up in. He had closed his eyes, and after placing his shoes under the chair alongside his other pair, I bent and kissed his cheek and slipped from the room. Let him have a good long sleep. Maybe by the time he woke up, the urn would have been returned.

I stopped to use the phone in the gallery and got my mother-in-law on the first ring. If she sounded harassed, it was in a happily important sort of way. I knew, without having to be told, that the twins were hanging on her skirts and she had baby Rose in the crook of one arm. Grandpa was cooking supper, she told me. Sausages for the second night in a row, but with chips this time and baked beans. She had made a steamed pudding with lots of treacle and was about to make a big jug of custard. At this point, Tam got hold of the phone. He'd seen five cats on a wall while out taking a walk with Grandpa, and Abbey hadn't been good. Whereupon his twin seized the phone. Having explained why she had thrown her doll out the window, she spilled the exciting news that Grandma had done her hair in plaits and was going to buy some pink ribbons tomorrow. And now she had to go and play. But Rose wanted to talk to me.

I went downstairs into the kitchen, where I found my husband. A few moments later, Ben was putting a cup and saucer into my hands. I knew I could count on him for some much-needed pampering. But what I hadn't counted on was seeing Freddy and Aunt Lulu. He did have his cottage, and surely there were at least a few things there for her to pinch. Such as that awful photo of me in the hall.

"Hello, Ellie." My cousin turned a woebegone face in my direction. "You wouldn't happen to have room in the fridge for Mumsie, would you?"

I looked at Ben, who shifted Tobias off the rocking chair and sat down before breaking the news: "Freddy and Aunt Lulu have been having an altercation."

"Couldn't they have it somewhere else?"

"That's not very hospitable, dear." Auntie helped herself to a ham-and-tongue sandwich from the plate on the table. "There's no fun in having a quarrel without people to cheer on one side or the other."

"But Freddy would be listening," I pointed out.

"No, he wouldn't. He only talks. What I say goes in one ear and out the other." She took a contemplative bite of the sandwich. "This is delicious. You'll have to give me the recipe, Ben."

"She says that sort of stupid thing, hoping I'll decide she's too daft to merit any effort to get through to her." Freddy looked ready to strangle himself with his ponytail. "But it won't work. There will be no more accepting rides from strange men and no more bragging about what fun it is to be a kleptomaniac."

His mother looked at him sadly. "Sometimes I wonder if I brought the wrong baby home from the hospital."

"Do you really?" My cousin suddenly radiated hope. "Think, Mumsie, and this time I won't be cross. Did you pretend to go in to have your tonsils out and sneak off with me while the doctors and nurses weren't looking?"

"I don't think so." Aunt Lulu pursed her little-girl lips. "No, dear, it couldn't have happened that way. I gave birth to you at home. Afterwards I could never think what to do with those big sugar tongs I took out of the midwife's bag."

"How about dinner?" Ben stood up, smothered a yawn, and stretched so that the rib of his navy blue sweater rode halfway up to his chest.

"Not for Freddy and Aunt Lulu," I said. "And not for me just now, darling. I think I'd like to take a walk down to the vicarage to see if Mr. Ambleforth has returned home."

"Why not phone?"

"I could use a breath of air to blow away the cobwebs."

"Let me go with you."

"I'd rather you stayed in case Daddy wakes up."

"I'll walk her down," said Freddy.

"There's no need." I really wanted time alone to think.

"Yes, there is," Ben disagreed. And I could hardly argue with him when I was the one who had put it into his head that evildoers had placed Chitterton Fells on the map. Where once there had been a dot, there would now be a blot. Besides, Freddy needed to walk off some of his irritation with Aunt Lulu. Hostility was too strong a word. I knew he was fond of his mother despite her foibles and would have done anything for her short of cutting his hair, shaving off his scraggly beard, or moving home. And that landed us in the same boat. My father was no longer the stranger who had walked through the door last night. He seemed to have been back for years, and I had rediscovered that love is a very mixed bag.

"You should have worn a jacket," Freddy said as we went through the iron gates and turned left toward the vicarage. The afternoon was misting into twilight. There was a sharp wind coming in off the sea, and he must have noticed that I was shivering, although not as badly as the trees that stood in clumps on the rocky rise beyond the hedgerows. One group in particular appeared to be shaking all the way down to their roots. Brown, yellow, and russet leaves came flying our way, and I had to pluck a couple out of my hair.

"My cardigan's warm enough," I lied.

"You could have fooled me." Freddy broke stride to eye me askance. "You're shivering." He wrapped an arm around my shoulders.

"You're not exactly dressed for the weather." I looked pointedly at his ripped sweatshirt and jeans.

"I've always liked my clothes well ventilated." His grin lasted a split second before edging into a scowl. "Besides, if I'd got myself done up in a sports jacket and, God forbid, a tie, Ruth might get the wrong idea."

"That I had marched you down to propose?"

"There's no need to sneer, Ellie." Now it was Freddy's steps that faltered. "I tell you, that girl seriously wants me."

"And whose fault is that?" I asked him as we passed the bus stop. "You can't go through life being an irresponsible charmer and not expect impressionable females to fall all over you."

"Sometimes I feel like a pound of bacon during wartime rationing," he said with a deep sigh.

"Then you must only be nice to Jewish girls and vegetarians."

Freddy walked on for a few moments in silence and then confessed: "Actually, Ellie, I think almost any man would do in this situation."

"Ruth is pregnant by the verger?"

"Nothing that simple. She's desperately afraid she may shortly be forced into getting a job."

"I thought she had one, typing the vicar's manuscripts."

"So she does, but that's hardly employment as most people know it. And she confided in me during a weak moment—"

"I don't think I need to hear this," I told him sternly as we crossed the top of Hawthorn Lane and came to the iron fence with its sign reading St. Anselm's Church and in smaller lettering the times of services.

"After I knelt dripping tears over her lifeless body."

"As Clarabelle in the play?"

"The trouble is, I'm just too good an actor." Freddy shook his head, or it could be that the wind did it for him. It had already spun mine around a couple of times. "But to get back to Ruth's problem," he said. "The vicar's close to finishing up the latest volume of his life of St. Ethelwort, and he's been making noises to the effect that if the final chapter comes out the way he hopes, he'll have written the final definitive word. At which time he and Kathleen will tip Ruth out of the nest. It seems they've got the loony idea that she's itching to get out in the world and make a name for herself typing on a word processor."

"But she's an old-fashioned girl?"

"And in this modern world, Coz, there just aren't enough curates or chaps in boaters showing up to play croquet on the vicarage lawn. So the likes of Ruth now have to scramble for the prize catch." Freddy tried without success to grimace away a smug smirk. "So where does that leave me?"

"Running away with your tail between your legs?" I suggested as we went through the litch-gate.

Freddy stopped in his tracks when we were within a few yards of the Victorian house. "A man is never a hero to his cousin, so I know you won't be disappointed, Ellie, if I lurk out here while you go in."

"Suit yourself." I waved a dismissive hand and watched him dodge behind a fir tree as I mounted the step and pressed the doorbell. It would serve him right, I thought crossly, if it started to rain. But I didn't get to indulge myself in picturing him being nursed through pneumonia by his mother, who would realize how much she loved him and promise never to leave his bedside. A dreadful howling pierced my eardrums, and when the door opened a crack, a black bundle of terror unleashed itself into the twilight.

"Bad dog," said a plaintive voice, followed by a sigh. I saw a shoulder shrug before a face appeared in the widening wedge, and somehow I found myself in the vicarage hall.

"We met, but you may not remember. I'm Ellie Haskell," I told Ruth. Freddy had described her as a pie-faced creature, and it was true that Mother Nature had not been particularly generous in her case. She was pale and bleary-eyed, with too much hair and not enough eyelashes.

"He'll be gone for hours." She closed the door with a snap.

"Oh, no!" I couldn't hide my distress.

"He'll race around in circles like a mad thing

until he finds something to chase up a tree."

"You're talking about the dog." My relief was such that I was able to spare a pitying thought for Freddy's trying to escape with both ankles intact. "I thought you meant the vicar."

"You came to see Uncle Dunstan?"

"Is he here?"

"No, he's been gone most of the day, and Aunt Kathleen left after rehearsal to go to her gardening club. Did you say your name's Ellie?" The pale face became a little less blank in response to my nod. "Mrs. Potter told me about Uncle Dunstan making off with your car. I met her when I was out walking Blackie. You can wait if you like." The offer was accompanied by a glance at her watch. "There's no telling when Uncle will be back, but Auntie shouldn't be too much longer."

I hesitated. "Perhaps for ten minutes."

"Come on, then; we'll go into the study." Ruth pushed open a door to our left. "The sitting room is kept for tea parties and visits from church bigwigs. I suppose you've noticed already that Auntie has rules for everything. It's how she keeps sane, I suppose, being married to Uncle Dunstan. But I guess you know all there is to know about living with someone who's a little off."

"What do you mean?" I walked smack into a leather armchair.

Ruth blinked her pale lashes. "Auntie told me about your father coming downstairs last night babbling away about tortured love, with his arms outstretched and eyes all glassy, and how she was so startled when he went to grab her that she jumped on Uncle Dunstan's knee."

"She said that?"

"Yes."

"And did you tell anyone?" I now collided with the desk, and a pen rolled off a pile of papers onto the floor.

"Only Mrs. Potter. She's such a talker that you have to say something back. And I'm sure she brought your name up first. Something about seeing your children being driven off in a car with an elderly couple. And how she wondered where they were going and why."

"Why don't you tell her next time you see her that I had to give them away because they were impossible to house-train and kept chewing on the furniture?" I tried to put a laugh in my voice but clearly failed.

"I don't know much about children," said Ruth. "And I probably never will. I'll end up in an office with hard seats and a water cooler outside the door. But I'd rather that than to be like Lady Grizwolde, married to a dreadful old man of sixty-five just for the security."

"Oh, I think you have to be wrong about his age!" I knocked another pen off the desk. "I saw Sir Casper today, and he has to be at least eighty."

"He isn't." Ruth shook her head vehemently. "I've got to know Sarah, who works as a maid at the Old Abbey, and she told me he's sixty-five. He looks like he does because his health is shot as a result of smoking his whole life."

"I can't believe it." I sat down on the edge of the desk. And an envelope dropped to the floor to join the pen.

"Unfiltered cigarettes."

"Even so..." Sir Casper's cadaverous face and octopus gait rose up before my mind's eye.

"Sixty to eighty a day."

"His face should be on every packet sold!"

"Sarah says that his mother caught him smoking when he was nine years old and made him kneel in the chapel all day praying for forgiveness. She was a very religious woman." Ruth was warming to her story. "She was German, and she never adjusted to living in England. It made her bitter. That's according to Sarah's grandfather Ned. He's still the gardener at the Old Abbey. And he's over eighty."

"You don't happen to know whereabouts in Germany?" I asked, staring down at the envelope I had picked up with the pen.

"That Sir Casper's mother came from?" Ruth opened her eyes wide under her pale brows. "Yes, I do. I've a good memory. Aunt Kathleen didn't pick me to play Clarabelle in Murder Most Fowl because I'm her niece or because I have the range to play a down-trodden woman. Auntie knew I would only have to read my lines a few times to have them down pat, even though it's a big part. Sir Casper's mother came from a small town in the southern part of Germany called Schönbrunn."

CHAPTER 17

BEN MET FREDDY AND ME IN THE HALL WHEN WE GOT back.

"What's wrong?" Freddy eyed my husband with concern while jogging in place on the flagstones. "Did the mater walk off with the grandfather clock?"

"Don't be silly," I said. "You can see it's still there."

Ben took hold of my hand. "Your father's got himself worked up, that's all. He came downstairs about ten minutes ago, and when I asked if he felt better after his nap, he railed against fate and said he was a worm and should be tossed out to the birds. Since then, all he's done is sit with his head in his hands."

"In there?" I pointed to the drawing room.

Ben nodded. "Aunt Lulu's with him."

"Isn't that great?" Freddy tugged at his beard. "She can pick his pocket while patting

224

his arm and saying: 'Cry it all out. You'll feel as though a weight has been lifted.' "

I pushed open the door and saw my father seated in a chair that was too small for him, his jaunty bow tie at pathetic variance with his reddened eyes and wet cheeks.

"Ah, there you are, Giselle." He signaled to me with his handkerchief as if flagging a train without much hope of staving off its deadly rush. "I am glad you went out for a breath of fresh air, but perhaps I would have been better able to control my anguish if you had been here to offer a daughterly word of counsel."

"He's been trying so hard to be brave." Aunt Lulu stopped tap-dancing around him and looked at us with misty baby-blue eyes. "And I've been trying to think up ways to cheer him up. But when I was telling him about the marvelous time I had at Oaklands and mentioned that the Hoppers had said Harriet worked there years ago, he burst into more sobs."

Daddy groaned, and his chair did one of its marvelous imitations. "There's so much I didn't know about her!"

"I think you may be right about that." My heart ached for him.

"She concealed her light under a bushel!"

"A marvelous attribute in a woman." Freddy ignored my disgusted look. "Come on, Uncle Morley, old cock, tell us what's set you off again."

"You had seemed to be doing better today, even with the urn going missing." Ben pressed a glass of brandy into my father's hand.

"I have failed her."

"That's nonsense, Daddy." I knelt by his chair and patted his knee. "It's not your fault Mr. Ambleforth is an absentminded clergyman who wouldn't know his own car if it ran over him."

"I should have gone after him, chased him down like the dog he is, cornered him in a field if necessary, and not offered him a choice of weapons. I should have fought it out with him man to man, with balled-up fists and fire in my eyes."

"A lovely fantasy," I said soothingly, "but how could you have gone after him? On his rickety old bicycle? Oh, I know Lady Grizwolde lent us the Honda, but by then he was probably in the next county, if not back in the eleventh century with St. Ethelwort. And we couldn't notify the police. They might have arrested him."

"Please!" Aunt Lulu covered her ears. "You know how I hate that word!"

"Ellie's right, Uncle Morley." Freddy stepped up to the hearth rug. "It wouldn't have been right to set the law on the vicar. He's a crackpot, not a crook."

"I fear I have failed properly to express myself." Daddy tucked his hanky into his shirt neck like a bib and sipped his brandy. "The brutal truth is that I was torn between alarm at Reverend Ambleforth's misappropriation of the urn and relief that in doing so he had prevented me from handing it over to the Hoppits."

"And now it looks as though the vicar may have done a bunk." Aunt Lulu's lips quivered.

Freddy scowled at her. "Don't talk rot, Mumsie."

"You can't always think the best of people, dear." She looked tenderly back at him. "It's naive."

"I don't believe what I'm hearing!" Her son tugged wildly at his beard. "Who was it making goo-goo eyes at that Mr. Price? A man who is probably the genuine article when it comes to car thieves? Do you really think that anyone but you bought that story about the wrong key?"

"Darling, of course I realized he was a bad lot." Auntie tried to hide a smirk behind her fingertips. "That's why I found him charming. Especially so," she mused aloud, "because he really was rather sweetly inept. Not even able to keep his wife's name straight. My guess is that he's new to the criminal life or has been forced to take a more active role than is usual for him. No wonder it was such a piece of cake...." She squinted a look at Freddy and shut up.

"Ben told me you recognized Mr. Price, if that's his real name, as one of the two men on the escalator." I removed the brandy glass from my father's drooping hand.

"Did I say that?" He shook his head and stared dolefully into space.

"You also asked Sir Casper's secretary, Mr. Jarrow, if he had been in Germany lately."

"Did I?"

My eyes met Ben's, and I knew what he was

thinking. My father wasn't sure what he remembered.

"What did you mean about a piece of cake?" Freddy stood with his arms folded, eyeing his mother.

"I don't remember." She was taking a leaf out of Daddy's book.

"Yes, you do, Mumsie."

"You're going to be cross. But if you insist, dear, I'll show you." Aunt Lulu lifted a cushion off one of the Queen Anne chairs and produced her handbag. "It really was a piece of cake." She was now unsnapping the catch. "I learned so many new tips at Oaklands, the kind that make all the difference between being an amateur and a professional. But I have to admit"—she included me and Ben in her frank gaze—"that I did feel a little quiver of alarm when I slid my hand into Mr. Price's jacket pocket when he was starting the car with the screwdriver."

"I can understand that," I said.

"Ellie, dear." Auntie had her bag open. "I wasn't afraid Mr. Price would realize and turn impolite. I learned a lot in all those late-night practice sessions at Oaklands. It was what I found in his pocket that took me by surprise."

"Mumsie!" Freddy backed into me, sending Daddy's brandy glass, which I was still holding, into a downward spiral that ended in a surprisingly gentle bounce on the turquoise-and-rose carpet.

"Sorry dear! I didn't realize that I was pointing it at you." Aunt Lulu's eyes went to the gun she was holding. "It's really rather sweet, isn't it? Small and nicely balanced. Just right for a pocket. But perhaps Mr. Price has bigger ones in his suitcase."

"You're cheering me up no end." Ben spoke in the bemused voice of one who feels his brain turning full circle.

"I suppose we should take it straight down to the police station," I said.

Freddy stooped like a blind man to pick up the brandy glass. "If we do, Mumsie will have to admit she stole the gun. That's not likely to win her any medals. And should the police catch up with Mr. Price, he may retaliate by trying to involve her. He could even say they had a row and she turned against him. Maybe they'd go light on her, but quite honestly"— he looked appealingly to me—"I don't want to risk it."

Ben took the brandy glass that somehow I was holding again and deposited it on the drinks table. "If only we had that damn urn and could figure out where it fits into all this."

I expected my father to come out of his fog in response to this blasphemous reference to Harriet, but he continued to sit without a hair stirring on his head.

Squaring my shoulders, I looked at Aunt Lulu. "I wish we knew more about the Hoppers," I said.

"In what way, Ellie?" inquired Aunt Lulu.

"In the way of your acquiring something of interest from Doris or Edith's handbag."

"You saw me?" Her little-girl face fell.

"No, but I noticed how alike your bag was to the one on the floor close to your chair. And I also thought the sweater you were wearing was not only pretty but also serviceable, with its baggy sleeves and fitted cuffs."

Ben raised an eyebrow at Freddy, who shook his head, saying: "It's a fact of life, mate. The reason men can't cut it as detectives is that we don't understand women's clothes." Meanwhile, Aunt Lulu had reopened her handbag.

"Here." She held out her hand. "It's not much, but it's all there was apart from a change purse. And I wasn't about to take that." She beamed proudly. "It might have contained the only money the Hoppers had brought with them."

I looked at what she had given me: A snapshot of a reasonably attractive middle-aged woman with platinum-blond hair. And a button.

I went over to Daddy and held out the snapshot. "Is this

Harriet?"

"My angel!" He clearly didn't mean me as he clutched, as if at a lifeline, at the image of the woman he had loved and lost. "Where, oh, where, did you get this, Giselle?"

"From the Hoppers," I hedged.

"How very generous of them. Would you believe that Harriet would never let me take a photo of her or give me one she already had?"

"Yes, I think I can believe that quite easily. Daddy, I think it's time you took a good hard look at your relationship with Harriet. You need to ask yourself why she never gave you the number of the Voelkels' house on Glatzerstrasse, let alone ever allowed you to visit her there, and whether it really seems credible that they were not on the telephone. Surely even a pair of eccentrics would have had one put in when they had a person staying with them who supposedly had come to Germany for medical treatment in case she needed to get hold of her doctor in a hurry."

"Just what are you suggesting, Giselle?" He made my name sound like an indictment as he turned his Roman nose on me like a sword designed to slay dragons and undutiful daughters.

"Morley"—Ben moved over to stand in front of the fireplace—"I know the idea has to be devastating, but what if Harriet latched on to you that first evening in the biergarten because she needed someone she could con into bringing something illegal into England?"

"Perhaps because she was known to the authorities and couldn't risk bringing that urn through herself." I hated seeing the pain in my father's eyes and wished desperately that my mother could have been here to put her arms around him. Freddy, bless him, squeezed his shoulder.

"You have to admit, Uncle Morely"—he spoke with none of his usual flippancy—"that something here smells like week-old fish. That business with your luggage on the escalator and Mr. Price showing up armed and dangerous in Chitterton Fells, although where he fits in with the Hoppers is a puzzler."

"And then there's Mr. Jarrow," I pointed out.

Daddy's cheeks swelled into purple balloons, and his full lips flapped with wounded fury. "I am at a loss to understand how you can all stand there maligning one who never had an unkind word to say about anyone. When I think, Giselle, of how admiring Harriet was when I showed her the photo you had recently sent me and how she so sweetly asked if she might be allowed to keep it, your betrayal stabs me through the heart."

"Which photo was that, Daddy?"

"One of you and Bentwick and the children."

"And yet she would not give you one of herself." There had to be some way of getting through to him.

"What I want to know, Ellie"—Aunt Lulu's face was flushed with eagerness—"is what you think Morley was enticed into smuggling into this country. Was it the urn itself? Does it look valuable?"

"It's a clay pot, not a thing of beauty or a joy forever." Freddy, with one of his bursts of sensitivity, added, "No offense Uncle Morley, old cock."

"Oh, you know how nutty people can be." Aunt Lulu flashed us a knowledgeable smile. "They'll pay the earth for a Rembrandt they have to hide in a safe. And it's not always about material value. A nice gentleman I met at Oaklands told me he once paid an astonishing sum to steal an ordinary teacup. Because it had sentimental value to the purchaser."

"But it may not be the urn itself, but what's

inside, that's important." I sat down on the footstool in front of Daddy's chair.

Freddy looked down at me from his lanky height. "Damn! I'm itching to take a look to find out. Meanwhile, do we conclude that the purchaser is living in this area?"

"But it's a possibility if we accept the premise that Harriet zeroed in on Daddy because he told her he had a daughter living in Chitterton Fells. Maybe she was a woman who believed in omens. She mentioned the Gypsy, didn't she?" I opened my hand and saw that I was still holding the button, along with the photo of Harriet, Aunt Lulu had given me. A brown button that looked as if it might have come off a coat. And I was remembering the one my Gypsy had pulled off a loose thread and told me to keep as a good-luck charm.

My father rose from his chair with a look on his face I had not seen before. I wouldn't have been surprised if he had let out a roar bringing down on our heads not only the ceiling but the entire roof.

"I will not remain in this room listening to these vile aspersions against the memory of the woman I hold most dear." He had brought the seat cushion up with him and now shook it off like an infuriated hound before heading with a thunderous stride for the door.

"But Daddy!" I stumbled up from the footstool and went after him. "What if Harriet is more than a memory? What if she is still very much alive?"

CHAPTER 18

"WHEN DID YOU GET TO THINKING THAT HARRIET is alive?" Ben asked when the drawing door closed on a final glimpse of my father's wounded back.

"It took me longer than it should have. I can't talk about it now." I was close to tears. "I've done this all wrong, left Daddy thinking he's alone in the world, betrayed on all sides. Why would he believe anything I have to say when he has to know deep down, inside that cocoon of his, that I've resented Harriet from the word go? I'm not even sure that my motives are pure. Maybe I'm a horrible, vindictive person leaping at the chance to punish him for walking out on me when I was seventeen." I went to brush past Freddy, but he wrapped an arm around me and tickled my face with a bearded kiss.

"I'll go up to him, Coz. You won't get any-where like this. You'll fall all over yourself apologizing, retract everything, and be back to square one."

"My little boy is right for once, Ellie." Aunt Lulu appeared at my other shoulder. "He and Morley can have a man-to-man talk while you sit down and pour your heart out to Ben and me. Unless," she added, sounding supremely self-sacrificing, "you would rather I got us something to eat."

"Thanks, Aunt Lulu. You're a rock." Ben guided her toward the door in Freddy's wake. "There's a chicken-and-wild-rice casserole in the fridge that only needs the aluminum foil removed before being put in the oven for half an hour. And if you'd like to make a salad, there are lettuce and tomatoes in the crisper."

"Are you sure you don't want me to make a loaf of bread as well?" I could hear the petulance in her voice as she disappeared into the hall. At any other time I would have felt sorry for her and the doors that were about to get slammed in the kitchen. Or, in the case of the fridge, left open.

"We could still run away to France." Ben held me in his arms, and I could feel him smiling against my hair.

"I hate being an adult." I stepped reluctantly away from him. "It must be great to be Aunt Lulu. A child in a woman's body."

"While you, Ellie, take on responsibility for everything that goes wrong in the world, whether it's war in Afghanistan or high winds over the English Channel."

"That's not true," I protested, "but I did go at Daddy all wrong."

"He was going to be hurt whenever he was faced with the truth."

"Does that mean, then, that you really have set aside all your doubts?" I sat looking tearily up at him from the arm of the sofa.

He stood with his hands in his jean pockets. "Call it deductive reasoning or plain old male intuition, but I'm sure Harriet made a prize chump out of Morley. I'm not sure what his role is, but it's clear to me that Mr. Price offered Aunt Lulu a lift here because he heard her telling the railway-station employee that she had to get to Merlin's Court and he knew that's where your father was staying. He needed to find out if Morley still had the urn."

"Wait a minute," I interrupted, feeling suddenly more resolute and less wobbly. "Isn't that saying someone didn't trust Daddy to fulfill his promise to Harriet and hand over her ashes to the Hoppers?"

"It looks that way."

"Even so, why tip us off that there's something fishy going on?" I plucked at a loose thread in the sofa's ivory damask. "Wouldn't it have made a lot more sense to get in touch with the Hoppers first to find out from them where the situation stood?"

"Of course." Ben shifted me from the arm of the sofa onto one of the seat cushions and sat down beside me. "But I've got Mr. Price sized up as a bungler. He shows up in Chitterton Fells a day late. Your father arrived yesterday. Perhaps he had to go back to headquarters because he had forgotten his gun or had lost his list of laboriously written out instructions. Equally stupidly, he probably thought a change of clothes and a pair of glasses enough of a disguise to prevent your father from recognizing him from the airport." Ben leaned his head back. "I remember talking to a detective inspector once when I was working in a London restaurant, and he told me, 'We at the Yard may not all be Sherlock Holmeses, but we certainly beat most of the competition.' "

"There could be the psychological factor." I had to raise my voice because the grandfather clock was striking seven. It might have been the reverberations, but for a moment I thought I heard a car engine."

"What do you mean, Ellie."

"Well"—setting aside auditory distractions—"if you're right about Mr. Price's real profession, maybe he thinks of himself as invisible much of the time. Isn't it supposed to be the mark of a good butler to fade into the background during the performance of his duties? To be just a voice granting admittance to his employer's presence or a pair of hands carrying in the tea tray? And if the other man at the airport, the one who tried to push Daddy down the escalator, was his boss, Mr. Price would have considered himself on the job at the time."

"Then let's say the boss was injured to the point of incapacitation after falling down the escalator. He might have been embarrassed, not to say nervous, about notifying whoever hired him to snatch your father's suitcase

237

that he'd botched things. What to do? He instructs his butler to stop polishing the silver or inventorying the bed linen and toddle down to Chitterton Fells."

"That could explain Mr. Price showing up here a day late.

The boss could have been out of it at first with a concussion or frantically trying to find someone more reliable to take over." I nestled comfortably into the best cushion of all, my husband's shoulder. "But even if we're right about Mr. Price and his boss, there's something that doesn't make any sense. Why try to snatch Daddy's suitcase after Harriet had set up her scheme to have him deliver the urn to the Hoppers?"

"Maybe the boss is as much a burglar as Mr. Price." Ben gave me a rueful smile. "Could we be dealing with rival gangs both after the same pot of gold?"

"The clay pot," I reminded him.

"Or what's inside."

"Whatever," I said. "Harriet was afraid to bring it through herself for fear of being recognized by the authorities. But she could be reasonably confident of Daddy getting the goods out of Germany and into England without incident. Even his loquaciousness on the subject of Harriet and her final wishes had the potential of being more beneficial than risky. He would be so blatantly genuine and so clearly capable of waffling on indefinitely that the customs people would be eager to push him along and shout: 'Next!' "

"We could drive ourselves up the wall

trying to fill in all the pieces." Ben got up and started to pace. "What we should probably be focusing on is how to convince your father that Harriet is indeed alive."

"Then you believe me?" I would have jumped up and thrown my arms around him if the sofa hadn't held me down, as if having grown a little possessive about having me on its lap.

"It's so obvious, isn't it?"

"I love it when you give me credit for being brilliant."

"And I'm grateful when you don't ask me how I could have been so thick as not to have seen it for myself. I suppose you wouldn't consider taking this mutual admiration upstairs and making an evening of it?" He raised an enticing eyebrow. "That wouldn't be fair to Aunt Lulu, would it? Not after she's gone to all the trouble of hefting that casserole out of the fridge and putting it in the oven."

"Don't count on it," I said. "She's probably put it in the washing machine."

"Then I guess we'll have chicken-and-wild-rice soup. But back to Harriet." Ben resumed his pacing. "Your father only had Ingo Voelkel's word for it that she was killed in that car accident. If she had died of natural causes Morley would very likely have asked to see the body. This way he could be persuaded her injuries were so severe she was unrecognizable. It was clever to have set him up with the talk about her mysterious illness so that he was programmed to believe, however much he might rant and rave, in the tragic inevitability of her death. But there could have been another problem in Voelkel telling him that she had succumbed after fighting the good fight. Morley might have insisted on talking to her doctor to reassure himself that nothing could have been done to save her."

"The accident story was definitely better." I hugged my arms around myself because I had grown cold. "And the delay in notifying him would throw Daddy sufficiently off balance so that he would be even less likely to make any difficulties. Saying that Harriet had gone to get the car as a surprise for him was also a nice touch. Pile on the emotions. Turn him into a zombie with only one thought lodged in his head. To get that urn to England and the Hoppers."

"I wonder if Harriet and Ingo Voelkel were lovers as well as accomplices and whether there was even a Mrs. Voekel. She was conspicuous by her absence, wasn't she? And what about the elderly housekeeper? Was she an accomplice?" Ben had completed his ramblings around the room and returned to place a glass in my hand. "I do seem to keep administering brandy." He leaned forward to kiss me. "But you look like you need to get a little fire going inside you."

"I've been wondering about something else." I answered him after taking a few dutiful sips of what the husband ordered. "It's about that button."

"What button?"

"The one Aunt Lulu took from Doris or

Edith's handbag." Putting down the glass on the lamp table, I got up and went over to the mantelpiece. Then, without saying another word, I left the room and crossed the hall to the cupboard under the stairs, where I usually hung my handbag upon returning to the house. A few moments later, I was back, standing in front of Ben with a button in each hand.

"Do these look alike to you?"

He bent his head for a closer look. "Yes."

"Would you say that they are a match?" I persisted.

"If you're asking me, Ellie, if they look as though they came from the same garment, my answer stands. Yes."

"What will you say if I tell you that one of them was given to me by the Gypsy who stopped me in the town square yesterday to tell my fortune?"

"Why did she do that?" Both Ben's eyebrows went up.

"She tugged it off a loose thread and told me to keep it as a lucky charm. I think she wanted to drive home the point that it would be a big mistake for us to go to France. She may have been afraid that if Daddy showed up all brokenhearted, we might persuade him to come with us on holiday and that would have delayed things."

"And how do you think the Hoppers came by the other button?"

"From Harriet."

"You're thinking...?"

"That she was the Gypsy?"

"It fits, doesn't it? Harriet arrived in Chitterton Fells ahead of Daddy. When she spotted me crossing the square, recognizing me from that photo he had given her, she jumped at the chance to size up whether I was as gullible as my father or to have a bit of malicious fun with me."

"Did she—the Gypsy—look anything like that photo of Harriet; the one Aunt Lulu stole from the Hoppers?"

"I can't say I spotted any resemblance." I stood fingering the buttons. "But I didn't have a chance to study the photo, and now Daddy has taken it up to his room. Anyway, there's a big difference from looking at a snapshot to seeing someone in person. Also, hair and clothing make an enormous difference. Harriet was a platinum blonde, although that could have been a wig, and I'm sure she was always exquisitely made up for her meetings with Daddy. The Gypsy's hair was in need of a good wash, and her complexion wasn't anything to write home about." I could suddenly see her so clearly. "But she did have brown eyes. As did Harriet, although sometimes Daddy described them as hazel. And there's something else. The Gypsy was puffing away on a cigarette the whole time she was talking to me."

"I don't remember your father saying that Harriet smoked." Ben looked as though I had lost him a mile and a half back.

"No, he didn't." I slipped the buttons into my shirt pocket.

"I'm missing something here." Ben was now rubbing his forehead.

"That's because you've forgotten what Daddy told us about that depressing room in Ingo Voelkel's house."

His blue-green eyes narrowed. "Was something said about the dead cat in the picture having died of secondhand smoke?"

"It's not likely you would remember." I reached up to smooth the curls back from his furrowed brow. "The only reason I do is because houses and how they are decorated is my business. I can see that room as clearly as if I had been in it. I can sense the dark weight of the furniture and the carved wooden ceiling, feel the gloom of that horrible picture, and smell the stale fireplace ash and the stink of cigarette butts in the ashtrays." I shuddered. "It's unpleasant, isn't it, to think of Harriet coming back to that house after an evening with my poor, besotted Daddy and sitting smoking one cigarette after the other while gloating to her real lover about how well things were progressing?"

The telephone rang out in the hall, but before Ben got halfway across the room, it stopped. Whoever had answered it would either take a message or come to tell us who was calling. I didn't go into a panic that it was bad news about one or all of the children. At least I was getting more realistic in that regard. My in-laws might be in their seventies, but they still had remarkable energy and would not be dozing in their easy chairs while Tam and Abbey got up to dangerous tricks or Rose decided to crawl off home.

I reached for Ben's hand, and we were about to go into the hall together when the door bounced open and Mrs. Malloy stood eyeing us balefully from the threshold. And I'd thought she'd gone home hours ago.

"Well, if this isn't a pretty state of affairs, both of you here and neither one could get your legs moving to answer the phone. "There I was just about to take a break from studying me script when I smelled the lovely aroma of burning chicken and fancied I could just about swallow a mouthful. If it went down quick with a glass of gin. Then there it goes— that bloody ting-a-ling-a-ling. And not another soul in the hall to say, Mrs. M. you didn't ought to go straining yourself lifting that receiver."

"Who was it?" I asked.

"Oh, now you want to know!" Mrs. Malloy teetered forward on her ridiculously high heels and encamped in the nearest chair. "And never a word said about it being written all over my face that I've just suffered the most terrible shock." Ben and I both opened our mouths, but she steamed ahead. "Some of us is more sensitive than others, Mrs. H., and being who I am, I'm going to fall right to pieces if someone don't put a drink in my hand this minute."

"Give her the gin bottle, forget the glass," I told Ben.

"I'll do nothing of the sort," he countered. "Mrs. Malloy, pull yourself together and tell us about that phone call."

"You're wonderful when you're being masterful." She smiled dreamily for a split second before pulling her frown back together. "Well, if you're going to drag it out of me without a thought to how I'm feeling, I'll tell you. It was Mrs. Potter ringing up to say she'd just been talking to her sister, Mrs. Blum, that runs Cliffside House, that B and B right near the Old Abbey. And there's been a terrible accident. A car went off the road. Right down to the beach. That's not something anyone walks away from with a sprained wrist." Mrs. Malloy looked at me with real terror in her eyes. "It's a terrible thing, and don't think I'm not sorry for whoever was in that car. But, Mrs. H., what if it was Lady Grizwolde and I have to take over the role of Malicia Stillwaters for the entire run of Murder Most Fowl. Could be I'm just feeling peaky, but what if I'm coming down with a bad attack of stage fright?"

Poor Mrs. M.! She wasn't destined to receive our undivided sympathy, for the moment was shattered by a blood-curdling scream from outside the house.

CHAPTER 19

BEN DREW A WOMAN INTO THE HALL AND CLOSED
the door.

"Ellie, this is Frau Grundman, and she's
urgently in need of a glass of brandy." He had
insisted I stay inside while he went to investigate.

"I'll get it," I said, and moved like a robot.
"Bring her into the sitting room."

"Who did he say she was?" Mrs. Malloy
stage-whispered in my ear.

"I think she's my father's German landlady.
Would you please go into the kitchen and try
to prevent Aunt Lulu from burning the
chicken casserole to a turn? It looks as though
we could be having one more for dinner."

"That's how it always is, Mrs. H. Just when
things start to get interesting, I'm got out of
the way like one of the kiddies."

"Oh, for heaven's sake!" I was now at the

drinks table, trying to find a glass that didn't appear to have been drunk from and not washed up. "You can listen at the keyhole the way you always do. And take notes if you like."

"It's just that I've got me pride, Mrs. H.!"

"Well, chug it down with a G and T."

"I should be in a white pinny." Mrs. Malloy tilted her chin and risked scraping her nose on the ceiling. "I should be weaving me way round the room with a plate of nibbles. That's the way things is meant to be done in proper run houses when the Mr. and Mrs. is receiving guests."

"Well, most people's guests don't look as though they've had someone jump out of the bushes at them shouting, 'Boo!'"

"I'll give you that," Mrs. M. admitted, "but then again, there is that old saying about sticks and stones. Still, not everyone is as tough as you and me." An acknowledgment that all was forgiven and we were back to being friends. "And foreigners are a funny lot. Taking offense where none's intended. Of course, a conk on the head's the same in any language. There's no parlais-vousing your way around that. But she didn't look like she was hurt, did she? On the other hand, you and I aren't doctors, Mrs. H...."

"No, but you're going to be needing one in a minute." The words slipped out before I could bite them back, and she stalked to the door just as Ben came in with our visitor. A collision was narrowly avoided, and I hurried forward to press a glass of sherry (we seemed to be out of brandy) into Daddy's former landlady's hand. "Please sit down," I begged her. "My husband can tell me what happened."

"Fau Grundman glimpsed a man lurking in the shrubbery." Ben helped her over to one of the sofas and shifted a table forward for her drink. "She thought he was about to jump out at her, so she screamed."

"As loud as my lungs could do it, to scare him away." Frau Grundman sat nodding her head at me. "But now I think I have been making nonsense. Herr Haskell tells me you have a male cousin staying here at your house."

"Actually he lives in the cottage at the gates, but I can't think of any reason for him to be crawling around the garden at this hour." I looked from her to Ben and back again. "Unless he was trying to catch our cat, Tobias, and bring him in for the night. We don't like him out if it looks like rain. And then, of course"—I wrinkled my brow—"my father is here."

"But I would have known if it was Herr Simons." Frau Grundman lowered her head to her drink. She was very much the way I had pictured her, with blue eyes, graying hair, and a matronly figure. But she was also prettier. Her complexion was one that a girl might have envied, and when she smiled, as she did now, her face lit up like a lamp. "Your father is so big, there would be no hiding him under a bush. Such a good, dear man. It was terrible what happened to break his heart. He so much loved his Harriet Brown, who was too soon to die."

"I upset him tonight." I sat down on the sofa opposite. "He went up to his room, but maybe he came down again and went outside to clear his head."

"Or to scare you into thinking he'd walked out." Ben stood behind me, his fingertips kneading my shoulders. "You're right about Morley being a decent bloke, Frau Grundman, but he does tend to be a shade theatrical."

"It is what gives him his charm and softens a woman's heart to him. He is the enormous teddy bear that needs to be told he is strongest and bravest of all the other teddies. The first time he is in my house I want to put a ribbon around his neck. When we get to know each other a little more better, I tell him he would look good in the bow tie. The other kind sit too short on him. So I give him a blue-and-white bow tie that was once belonging to my husband that died long years ago. And Mr. Simons, he was very pleased!"

"And I thought the bow ties were Harriet's influence," I said.

"It was for her he want to make himself the handsome man." Frau Grundman drank her sherry. "But I think he liked for me to give him the words of advice. It was good that we had become friends, because when the bad days come, he needs a shoulder to hold. When he leaves my house to come to England, I cannot keep the worry of him out of my head. What if this daughter he speaks about is gone from her home when he comes to the door? This is what keeps going around my thoughts, until I think, I will go after Herr Simons to make sure he is safe with his family. I have the address. It is written out in the book for guests that stays in my hall. I bring him a jar of my pickled cabbage that he likes so much. I don't put it in my case. I carry it in the bag I use to bring home the shopping. And when I hear the noise and think I see a man in that bush, I make up my mind I will hit him with it if he comes for me."

"Is the bag canvas?" I asked.

"I am sorry." Frau Haskell looked puzzled. "I do not know the meaning."

"Cloth..." I floundered for a more precise word.

"Yes, it is." Ben stopped massaging my shoulders. "And I know what you are getting at, Ellie. Your father had the urn wrapped in a similar bag when he arrived."

"And this morning, when we went to the Old Abbey."

"So if it was Mr. Price in the bushes and he saw Frau Grundman coming up the drive, he could have jumped to the wrong conclusion." I twisted around to face him. "He would think she was the person who had gone off with the urn by mistake and was returning it to us. Imagine how he would have felt if he had snatched the bag and had found himself with a jar of pickled cabbage!"

"But he hadn't seen your father's bag," Ben pointed out.

"We don't know that," I said, "Daddy might have taken it on the plane with him and only put it in his case when he got to Heathrow and needed to steady himself going down the escalator to the underground. In fact, I'm sure that's what he would have done. Besides, I seem to remember saying to Mr. Price this afternoon something about hoping the urn would be returned safe and sound in its canvas bag."

Ben emerged from the back of the sofa with his hands in his jeans pockets. His stance when he was seriously contemplative. Frau Grundman had faded into the cushions, but I quickly brought her back into focus and apologized.

"I'm sorry. That was very rude of us talking as if you weren't here, but some odd things have been happening since my father arrived last night. And now there's this scare you've had. Goodness only knows what would have happened if you hadn't caught sight of the man and scared him off by screaming before he could attack you. We'll have to phone the police. Or did you do that already, Ben?"

"Sorry"—he grimaced—"I should have. But I was concerned with making sure Frau Grundman was all right."

"I am," she said quickly, and set her glass down with deliberate care. "I am not hurt or any more worried. I think now maybe I make a mistake and that there was no man in the bushes. I am just tired from taking the trip. The police they will not think much of my story, and I will make a nuisance for nothing. It is better, Frau Haskell, not to telephone them."

"I don't know." I looked to Ben.

"It will be upsetting to your father." Her color rose as she spoke. "And I did not come to make more trouble for him."

Was concern for Herr Simons the only reason for her reluctance? I wondered.

"If you'd rather forget about it, Frau Grundman, we will, of course, do as you wish." Ben was studying her closely as he spoke, and I decided to test the waters.

"I do understand what you mean." I smiled at her. "I often wonder if I'm allowing my imagination to get the better of me. Even now I'm asking myself if I haven't fabricated the idea that there's something fishy about Harriet asking my father to bring her ashes home if she died, then driving her car into the river a short time later. Perhaps I'm making too much out of the fact that two men tried to snatch his case at the airport? And then, lo and behold, one of them shows up here this afternoon with a gun. Well, not actually in his possession," I amended. "My aunt took it without his knowledge when he was giving her a lift in his car." I waited expectantly for Frau Grundman to look at me as though I were mad and start easing off the sofa, but she stayed put and appeared more interested than alarmed.

"Why did this aunt take the gun?"

"She's a kleptomaniac," Ben informed her.

"That is sad. One lady who comes often to my guest house has the same problem. It is no big trouble to me. I hide the silver saltcellars, that is all. But her family has tried everything to make the cure—from the psychiatrists to

252

water therapy. These are not well people, but in the case of your aunt, it was useful what she did getting the gun from this Herr...?"

"He said his name was Price."

"Why do you think he comes this afternoon to your house?"

"We can only guess," I said, "but we think he may be connected to a rival gang that wants what's in that urn instead of Harriet's ashes."

"Ah, so that is what fits together inside your heads." Frau Grundman looked intrigued. I also sensed that she was relieved. Could it be that she had come here prepared to risk sounding like a lunatic or, even more embarrassingly, like a jealous shrew by voicing her own suspicions that Harriet had not been, pure and simply, a woman in love?"

"Maybe we should ring the police." Ben was pacing the carpet as if intent on wearing it threadbare. I understood his feelings completely. I would have given anything to have been sitting on a kindly detective inspector's knee, explaining to him that while we didn't have any evidence to back up all the suspicions, my husband and I wanted to cooperate.

"You know they wouldn't buy a word of this," I heard myself say. "I'm just relieved that Frau Grundman doesn't seem to think we are totally out of our minds. Or are you just being kind?" I looked anxiously into her pleasantly open face.

"I have been worried also." Her blue gaze was unusually comforting. "But, like, you, I did not know if I was making a molehill out

253

of the mountain. I must tell you that when first I met Harriet Brown, I did not like her. I said so to my sister Hilde, who is housekeeper to Father Bergdorff at the Christ Kirche in Loetzinn. But then I ask myself if it was that I did not like that Herr Simons was in love with her. I am old enough to look into my own heart. When I saw what was there, I told myself: Ursel, you meet a man who makes you smile like you haven't done since your Heiko died, but Herr Simons does not look at you. He wants this other woman. So do you make hurt for yourself by thinking the unkind thoughts about her, or do you look to see what makes him love her?"

"Was she beautiful?" I asked.

"I think not so much." Frau Grundman thought for a moment. "It was the silver-blond hair and the makeup that would make you think she was. That, and she had the excellent figure. She is my dress size, but so different; hers is a very womanly shape. It is no wonder she bewitches Herr Simons. It is the physical attraction, I want to believe. When he knows her better, he will see she is not so special. So I insist to myself, but what happens is that I begin to like her. She is nice to me. Always the warm greeting when she comes with him to the guest house. Always the smiling thank you for anything I do for her. I no longer think she has the hard face. Perhaps I am looking at her with different eyes. Or it could be that love brought out the person she had put into hiding. Of this I am sure: She did love your father, Frau Haskell."

"Please call me Ellie." I didn't have any other answer.

"It is a good name." She gave me the sort of smile that found its way to my face when I wanted to boost the children's spirits. "And you must please call me Ursel."

"And I'm Ben." I could tell that he liked her. "You were saying that you also have been worried that there was something wrong with the situation."

She nodded. "The day after Herr Simons came back with the dreadful news that Harriet had been killed, I find a gold-and-sapphire earring she had dropped on my stairs. I know it is hers because she was upset about losing it. And I think I will not say anything to the dear, heartbroken man about it. Why make more hurt for him? He will look at it and cry. The next time I go to see Hilde, I will take the earring to Harriet's friends the Voelkels on Glatzerstrasse. They will put it with the other one, and someone will get to inherit a pretty keepsake. But when I go to the house and ring the bell, there is no answer, and as I am going away, a woman walking with her little girl speaks to me. She asks who I am wanting, and when I tell her, she says I must have the wrong address. That house has been empty for over a year."

"Could you have had the wrong number?" Ben did some more prowling around the carpet.

"No, that is not, I think, possible." Frau Grundman shook her head. "It is the same I write down and give to Herr Simons the day

255

Herr Voelkel telephones to tell him to go to Glatzerstrasse. Also I forget to tell you that on my way to the door I look through a window into the room where there is a picture of a very long, very stiff cat hanging over the mantelpiece. The woman with the little girl who speaks to me tells me that a taxidermist lived in that house until he died at a hundred and one. No one will buy it because they think it gives the creeps and is haunted by the ghosts of many very angry animals."

I was glad that Tobias wasn't around to hear this and get any ideas about how to handle eternity when his time came. Otherwise I couldn't find anything to cheer about. Harriet and Herr Voelkel had not been foolish enough to leave a forwarding address. He had used the house for his interview with Daddy and had possibly never been in the place before or since. Again I wondered about the housekeeper, the old woman in black who had answered the door. What was her role? How important was she to the scheme? Herr Voelkel probably got the key from the estate agent, all very simple and seemingly aboveboard.

"If there was a plot," Ben said, "Harriet has to be alive. At least that's the conclusion Ellie and I have reached. What do you think, Ursel?"

"I think she'd like to see Daddy," I told him.

"But he has gone to bed." Ursel got to her feet. "I will come back, if I may, in the morning. I am booked in at a guest house near the train station. Very nice and clean, I understand. So if you will let me telephone for a taxi, I think that will do better than the bus, which I find out does not run so often at night."

I looked at Ben, and he did the honors. "You're more than welcome to stay here. We've got plenty of room. I'll be happy to go and collect your suitcase."

"It's in your garden. I dropped it alongside the drive when I screamed. But are you sure you will not mind having me?" Pleasure and doubt were written all over Ursel's face. "I do not return to Germany for three days. It will be too much for you. You have your young children. Your father tells me about them. Sometimes he gets their ages mixed up. That sort of thing, the way even the best men do. But then, when I tease him, he fetches one of your letters, Ellie, and reads to me about them. The baby and the twins. Hilde and I are twins, so you will understand why I talk of her so often. Every week I go to visit her at the Christ Kirche parsonage."

I was wondering why I had the feeling that there was something I needed to remember when the door opened and Freddy came bursting into the room with his ponytail askew and his beard looking as though tufts of it were missing. Taking no note of Ursel, he fixed his anguished eyes on me alone.

"Ellie, your father's gone."

"What do you mean, he's gone?"

"I went with him up to his room, just like I promised, and I tried to talk him into a better frame of mind. But of course he could tell I agreed with you about Harriet. I'm not much good at faking the funk. He told me to buzz off."

"Get on with it," Ben urged.

"I went down to the kitchen and got bogged down trying to explain to Mumsie that you cook dinner; you don't incinerate it. And while we were going at it, I thought I heard a car start up, but I didn't think anything about it."

I remembered thinking I heard the same thing when the grandfather clock was striking seven. "Freddy!" I pleaded.

"After a while, I went back upstairs to reassure myself that Uncle Morley was all right. But he wasn't in his room. And I got this sinking feeling. So I hopped it out to the garage, and that Rent-A-Wreck car of his was gone."

In a distant sort of way I was aware that Ursel was fast absorbing my cousin's fear. Without putting rhyme or reason to it, she knew she was about to hear something dreadful.

"Ellie..." Freddy's voice was close to being tearful. "I'm afraid he may have decided to go back to the grounds of the Old Abbey. In case the vicar got it into his noggin to return there to sit reveling in the way moonlight doth with silver softness beguile the ruins of St. Ethelwort's monastery. And Mrs. Malloy told me there's been a fatal car accident at that bend in the road by the Cliffside B and B."

"I know," I said, but he was deaf to every voice but his own.

"I've been on the phone upstairs for the last fifteen minutes dialing around to see what I

258

could find out, but I can't get any info." His earring was spinning in circles. "Except that the all-knowing Mrs. Potter says she has it from her sister Mrs. Blum, who had it from a young man who climbed down the cliff to point where he could get a reasonably good look at the wreck on the beach, that it was a brown car. And the Rent-A-Wreck was brown. So I think, Coz"—Freddy gathered me into a rangy embrace—"you may need to be very, very brave."

CHAPTER 20

"THE RENT-A-WRECK WASN'T BROWN," I WAS insisting for the third time. "It was gray."

"Sweetheart, it was blue," Ben reasserted.

"Well, maybe a blue gray," I conceded.

"Neither of you is prepared to face the brutal truth." Freddy eyed us more in pity than censure. "I understand that; it's killing me, too, to think of Uncle Morley plummeting to his death. You have to wonder if his life flashed before him and if he called out for his mother. But that car was brown. A reddish brown."

"That was the rust." I refrained from raising my voice or adding, You nitwit!

"I'd say the best description of that car would be piebald." Ben took hold of my hand. "But whatever the color, aren't we putting too much credence in a second- or third-hand report? We're panicking, I'm sure for no good reason at all. I wish I remembered the car's license-plate number, Ellie. Damn it, I drove it into the garage. But there's no good in kicking myself now."

"Very true, Mr. H." Mrs. Malloy, entering the room, nodded wisely. "Having you hobbling around with a pair of cracked shins isn't about to help no one, Mr. H. There's them that might say you was just trying to make yourself the center of attention. Which I wouldn't take kindly to, seeing as I've always thought you a cut above most of the buggers that call themselves men. What's needed here is some common sense. Which is something that don't get better for being kept corked and saved for special occasions, you know. So there's no point in being afraid to use what little God gave you." She eyed each and every one of us sternly. "Even supposing Mr. Simons did go near where that accident happened, there's usually more than one car on the road at any given time. And like as not, he went clear the other way. Down to the pub in the village would be my guess."

"That I can think is so." Ursel looked like a woman clutching at a straw to paddle with as her canoe went over the rapids. "This pub, it would remind Herr Simons, perhaps, of the biergarten in Schönbrunn where he met Harriet Brown. Yes, this is a good thought. I find it not hard to see him there."

"Neither do I." Ben attempted a smile. "Morley with a pint in one hand and the photo of his beloved Harriet—the one Aunt Lulu took from the Hoppers—in the other. Asking the regulars if they would kindly throw darts at him to put him out of his misery."

"I never thought to phone the Dark Horse Pub," Freddy confessed.

"Or it could be that Daddy..." I got no further because Aunt Lulu appeared in the doorway. She looked like a child who had spent an unsupervised half hour playing in the flour bin. But that could have been because she had taken time to distractedly powder her nose after slogging in the kitchen.

"Dinner's ready," she announced in a disconsolate little voice. "If that chicken wasn't dead before it went in the casserole, it is now. I tried to make a cream sauce to pour over some peas. But it went lumpy. And when I tried to give it to the cat, he attacked me. So I had to hole up in the pantry. I'd be there now if Morley hadn't come in."

"Uncle Morley's back?" Freddy gave voice to the jubilation that flooded the room.

"Don't jump about like that, dear," scolded his mother. "You're getting too big a boy to leap into my arms, especially when I'm feeling horribly frazzled."

"We have been so much afraid that Mr. Simons is killed in the car accident." Ursel was trembling, but the color had returned to her cheeks, and her eyes were now the brighest of blues.

"Aunt Lulu, this is Frau Grundman," I said. "Daddy stayed at her guest house when he was in Germany, and she's going to be paying us a visit for a few days. Isn't that lovely?" This gained me a look from Mrs.

Malloy, the one that always made it plain that her nose was out of joint at not having been consulted on matters she believed required her stamp of approval. As we all filed out into the hall, on our way to the burned offerings awaiting us in the kitchen, she drew me aside, pursed her damson lips into a smaller bow, and planted her fists on her hips.

"I've nothing against that woman. Not everyone gets to be English when all is said and done. And it can't be easy being stuck speaking a foreign language your whole life. She looks a decent sort, although between you, me, and those banisters, she could do with coloring her hair and frilling herself up a bit if she hopes to catch your Dad on the rebound. Which is why she's come, as a blind man could see a mile off. And to show where my heart is, Mrs. H., I don't intend to put a spoke in her wheel, though it would be easy as wink, given that I've got more sex appeal in me little finger than most women have where men do the looking."

"Then what's the problem?" I watched the others go into the kitchen.

"I won't be turned out of my room for her." Mrs. Malloy had taken to occasionally staying the night since we had Rose.

"I wouldn't suggest such a thing."

"Well, but I wouldn't put it past you to have thought about it, Mrs. H. It's a nice room, with a lovely view of the sea. Now that I've got it all set out with my bits and bobs, who wouldn't want to sleep in it? And it's plain as can be you're out to make a good impression on Frau Grundman in case she does end up in the family."

I refrained from saying that Ursel might not be wildly fond of china poodles and pictures of Elvis Presley painted on black velvet. Nonetheless, I was upset. Just what did she take me for? A person of no loyalty or sensitivity?

"There's no question of your moving, Mrs. Malloy."

She sized up my expression. "In that case, you could put Frau Grundman in the tower."

"She's not Anne Boleyn," I countered. A silly reaction. The tower bedroom was charming. It was the one my in-laws always used when staying with us. It was reached by a short flight of steps leading from the gallery, and we had recently converted an alcove into a tiny bathroom. The reason I hadn't offered to install my father en suite was because of his size. He wouldn't have looked as though he were occupying a round room. He would have looked more as though he were wearing a baggy suit.

"Sometimes I'm surprised we don't have words more often." Mrs. Malloy's voice made it clear she was extending the olive branch. "There's always something going on to make us both touchy. I've worn myself out reading over the play till I could recite every line forwards and backwards. You've been having to deal with your father and everything that goes along with his troubles. And now there's this terrible car accident." She shuddered most effectively. "I can't shake the feeling that there's a dark shadow about to cast its nastiness over Merlin's Court."

Before I could say anything comforting, Ben crossed the flagstones toward us. He explained he was going outside to collect Ursel's suitcase from the bushes and that he wouldn't be a minute because dinner, a makeshift alternative for the chicken casserole, was almost ready. Feeling like a poor excuse for a wife, I preceded Mrs. Malloy into the kitchen. Here we found Freddy leaning up against the Welsh dresser like a broom that had been left there to get knocked over, Aunt Lulu seated at the table, and Ursel over by the Aga shaking pepper into a saucepan.

My father stood in front of the fireplace dwarfing every object in the room. His jowls dropped, his nose was reddened, and his pale blue eyes protruded. He did not look at me. It was as though I had come home from school dragging my satchel up the stairs to our fourth-floor flat and he was there. My father, who wasn't like anyone else's father. I had loved him then, as children do, without thought or reason. It had taken me a long time to realize that he wasn't perfect. Only now, as something knotted and hard inside me dissolved into tenderness, did I see this as a gift. Saints should be named Ethelwort and live in eleventh-century monasteries. Children need to know that their parents can be foolish and fallible in order to understand that sometimes it is how well we fail that counts more than all the successes. So that one day they can take the risk of stepping out onto the tightrope, with only the memory of a hand to hold on to, and take the wondrous risk of falling into the real world below.

I didn't rush up to Daddy and pour my feelings over him like a jug of warm milk. I could tell by the way he kept right on not looking at me that he had neither forgiven nor forgotten what he considered my unconscionable attack on Harriet's memory. It was Freddy, bless him, who spoke up to break the ice.

"I was saying to Uncle Morley, Coz, that it was a shame that he was out when Frau Grundman arrived."

"Especially when she was so shaken up after her fright and could have done with a strong man's shoulder to sob on. Or one with a cough sweet in his pocket to help soothe her poor throat after that scream she gave." It was Mrs. Malloy, revealing that she had indeed been listening at the drawing-room door.

"What's this about?" Daddy roused himself to register glassy-eyed surprise.

"It was nothing." Ursel began ladling steaming soup into earthenware bowls. "It is better that you do not hear of my foolishness or you will stop thinking of me as the sensible woman. And not anymore trust that I bring you good pickled cabbage."

"She saw a man lurking in the bushes," I began, but Daddy wasn't listening.

"You came all this way to bring me pickled cabbage, Frau Grundman?"

"Not so much that." She allowed the ladle

266

to dangle, dripping soup onto the working surface. "I worry for you, Herr Simons. You are so sad when you leave my house. I want to make sure that things go better once you reach England."

"But to go to so much trouble." He frowned quite fiercely at her. "It was unnecessary and really very foolish of you, Frau Grundman."

"She could hardly have expected men to come popping out of bushes at her," Freddy argued reasonably.

"Oh, I don't know," Aunt Lulu cheerily piped up. "Life is full of its little surprises."

"None's ever done it with me." Mrs. Malloy's disappointment was evident. "Except, that is, for the milkman, the one time I'd got behind paying him on account of losing big at bingo and having to pretend I was out when he came to collect."

"Any idea who this creep was?" Freddy pried himself away from the Welsh dresser and sniffed longingly at the soup.

"Course I do; he's been delivering my milk this twenty years."

"I think he means the man in the bushes, Mrs. Malloy," I said. "And if I'm any good at guessing, that was Mr. Price."

"Who?"

Luckily, before I was put to the trouble of explaining, Daddy readdressed himself to Ursel. "It was foolish of you to come, because you are not a seasoned traveler. By your own accounting, you have led a quiet, sheltered life in Schönbrunn, rarely venturing farther than Loetzinn. And your visits there were hardly of a gallivanting sort, your time being spent with your sister at the parsonage at the Christ Kirche. To think of you braving the terrors of the London underground, to be trampled underfoot by the madding crowd, or crushed in the closing doors of a train heading for Epsom brings chills to my heart, Frau Grundman, even though I see you standing whole and robust before me."

"I've remembered something." I took a couple of steps toward Ursel. "It nagged at the back of my mind when you mentioned the church where your sister Hilde is house-keeper to the priest. But I couldn't pull it into focus. There's been so much going on today. And this was such a small thing. When I was over at the vicarage earlier to talk to Mr. Ambleforth, his niece told me he was out but that I could wait for him in his study. He didn't return. But just before I left, I picked up an envelope that had dropped to the floor. It was addressed to Fader Bergdorff, the Christ Kirche, Loetzinn."

"Don't speak to me of that villain in a dog collar," Daddy roared.

"But you have never met Fader Bergdorff." Ursel had turned deathly pale.

"I'm talking about that rogue Ambleforth." He lowered his voice a notch the width of a thread. "Spouting on about this St. Ethelwort one minute and stealing Giselle's car the next! Can you guess, Frau Grundman, what precious entity, what peerless treasure, this motoring maniac abducted as he roared off into the daylight?"

Ursel stared at me, and nodded.

"Harriet's urn was in the car in a canvas bag just like the one in which you brought the pickled cabbage."

Ursel answered soberly. "I gave Herr Simons his bag."

"It was sturdy and wrapped snugly around the urn when I put it in my susitcase. Needless to say, Frau Grundman, I was not aware that you had one like it for the conveyance of such items as pickled cabbage." Daddy winced. "But I know you too well to conceive that any slight to my Harriet was intended. To return, however, to that felonious clergyman, after retiring to my bedroom earlier this evening"— Daddy directed a darkening look my way— "I was seized with such rage against the fellow that I went down to my car and drove to the vicarage, wasting several minutes due to turning left rather than right at the gates. Once there, I pounded on the door to no avail. But determined not to be denied the opportunity to plant my fist in his face, I camped on the front steps until I decided he was never coming back and then I headed back here."

It was what I had been about to suggest when Aunt Lulu came into the drawing room to say that dinner was ready.

"We were worried about you, Uncle Morley, old cock." Freddy gave him an affectionate grin.

"Very worried," Aunt Lulu agreed.

"Extremely worried." I realized that we were sounding depressingly like the Hoppers and hastened to explain. "You see, Daddy, while you were gone, we got word that there had been a terrible car accident on the cliff road near the Old Abbey. Very probably from the sound of it, at the same spot where you and I almost went off the road this morning."

"And you thought it was me?"

I could only nod.

"But here I am safe and sound, Giselle." He finally looked at me, and his voice was the one he had used when I would wake from a nightmare and he would be there before I thought I had called out, driving the monsters down into the dungeon, where they belonged, and telling me he had the magic key in his dressing-gown pocket. "And you don't know yet whose car it was?" he was asking as Ben came into the kitchen and Freddy and Mrs. Malloy passed out the bowls of tomato-and-basil soup.

"No," I said. But another memory had come, swift and sure this time, of standing with Daddy and the old gardener, Ned, outside Sir Casper's secretary's office and hearing Mr. Jarrow talking to someone on the telephone and, in the course of the conversation, confirming an appointment between that person and Sir Casper for this evening. I was about to say something, then changed my mind. We were all exhausted. What we needed was food and bed. Indeed, everyone else seemed to be of like mind. We gathered around the table and stuck to safe topics of conversation. Freddy and Mrs. Malloy even refrained from talking about the play, which would have brought up Mrs. Ambleforth and inevitably her husband. Aunt Lulu didn't try to slip the sugar bowl into her pocket. I noticed Daddy smiling a couple of times at Ursel, and I sensed that he did find her presence comforting. The soup was delicious, as was the salad, the selection of cheeses, and the crusty bread. It's amazing what good food can do to restore your frame of mind.

But two things happened to disturb me before the evening was over. When I was in the bathroom, giving my face a quick wash and brushing my teeth, I noticed that the silver powder box Ben had given me for my birthday was missing from its place by my collection of antique scent bottles. But it was when I went into the bedroom and Ben looked at me with a worried crease between his eyes that I felt a shiver run down my spine.

"Ellie," he said, "I've really taken to Ursel, and I can tell you like her, but don't we have to step back and ask ourselves if there may be more to her showing up here than meets the eye?"

CHAPTER 21

I OVERSLEPT THE NEXT MORNING AFTER HAVING A horrible dream in which Ursel suddenly turned into Harriet and chased me toward the edge of the cliffs wielding a jar of pickled cabbage while Mr. Price stood cheering her on. Naturally, this was all Ben's fault for putting nasty ideas about a very nice woman into my head. But I didn't get to snarl at him, for when I got up, he wasn't in the bedroom, and by the time I'd had a shower and washed my hair, my annoyance had gone down the drain with the soap suds. That's the trouble with husbands. If you don't catch them when you're at the boil, it's over; because you start remembering how wonderfully they scramble an egg and how they never seem to notice that you haven't won any beauty competitions lately.

When I came down the stairs, he was in the hall looking handsomer than ever. It had to do with the way his black brows were drawn into a straight line, the tightening of his classic features, and the way his eyes darkened so that when he looked at me it was difficult to tell if they were emerald green or midnight blue.

"I'm sorry." I looked guiltily at the grandfather clock, which showed twenty minutes past ten. "The morning seems to have gotten away from me."

"That's not the only thing that got away, Ellie."

"Meaning?"

"Why don't you come and sit down?" Ben took me gently by the elbow and propelled me into the drawing room. It usually looked restful, with the soft morning light touching the damask sofas and the peacock-and-rose Persian carpet. But now I didn't find its atmosphere the least bit soothing. Abigail's portrait above the fireplace looked braced for bad news, and the curtains stirred restlessly at the half-open windows.

"Please tell me what's happened." I sat down to a bleat of protest, and Tobias clawed his way out from under me. At least he wasn't missing.

"Drink this first." My better half handed me a glass of orange juice from a tray on the coffee table, also supplied with a toast rack and marmalade.

"The vicar showed up over an hour ago." Ben swigged down his own juice and stood looking as though he would have liked to send the glass smashing into the fireplace. Perhaps if it hadn't been from a set given to us by Mother, he would have done so. Instead, he placed it, as if hardly daring to trust himself, back on the table.

"But I don't see what's so bad." My hand fumbled toward a piece of buttered toast. "Unless"—a chill coursed down my spine— "Mr. Ambleforth didn't bring our car back because he managed to misplace it while he was stuck on the top of Mount Sinai with his head in the clouds. Are we destined never to see the urn again or find out what was in it?"

"Oh, he brought the car back."

"You're going to have to start at the beginning." As aids to staying calm, I munched on my toast with one hand and stroked Tobias with the other.

"I was out looking for that delinquent cat, Ellie." Tobias did not have the grace to look one whit abashed. "I had heard him meowing like a banshee while I was putting on the coffee. And I had just spotted him high in that tree by the gates when the vicar drove past. So I left Tobias to tumble out of the tree on his own, as he had been threatening to do, and raced after the car." Ben pulled a face at the obnoxious animal. "Fortunately, Ambleforth stopped to offer me a lift and inquire directions to Merlin's Court. After we got it sorted out who I was and he had thanked me for the loan of the car, I took the wheel and drove us back here. I was in such good spirits because the canvas bag was still on the floor of the passenger seat and I could feel when I picked it up that the urn wasn't broken, I decided to be not only grateful but gracious."

"I'm sure you were wonderful," I said soothingly, having learned that women aren't the only ones who cannot always be rushed through a conversation. Ben could sometimes take ages telling me about a recipe that could have been cooked and distributed to the needy in half the time.

He looked ready to tear every hair out of his head. "Ellie, I not only introduced the man to Tobias, who had come down from the tree as if it were a stump; I also invited Mr. Ambleforth in for a cup of coffee, figuring he had to be embarrassed at all the trouble he had caused. In his place I would have been ecstatic to know there weren't any hard feelings. But I needn't have worried. He was completely oblivious to the fact that he could thank his lucky stars he hadn't been arrested for car theft and had his face splashed all over the papers as another fallen clergyman. It was clear that only good manners induced him to make small talk about the Council of Trent as we walked to the house."

"Was anyone else up?" I asked.

"Not a one."

"What did you do with the urn?"

"I put it on the Welsh dresser."

"And did Mr. Ambleforth say anything about it?"

"He asked if there was a tin of cat food in the bag, adding vaguely that he rather liked pussycats but his wife didn't because a neighbor's tabby had once chewed the leaves off one of her plants. And she ended up getting only a fourth-place ribbon in the parish flower show."

"At least you got some information out of him." I sat chewing on another piece of toast. Tobias, deciding he wasn't going to get so much as a lick of butter, got off my lap.

"It was the last coherent thing Mr. Ambleforth said in a half an hour, Ellie. As soon as I brought him in here and handed him his coffee cup, his nose went between the pages of the book he had pulled from his pocket. He kept right on reading while I sat making attempts at conversation. All I could get out of him was 'Very nice dear, you must have your hair set more often.'"

"He certainly is peculiar."

"I wondered how long he would sit on the sofa turning the pages of that damn book." Ben leaned against the bookcase as if exhausted by the memory.

"He took no notice of you at all?"

"Sweetheart, I might as well have been invisible. A ghost who wasn't doing a good enough job of moaning and groaning, with some clanking of chains to get the point across, that one of us needed to leave. I was praying that you would walk in when suddenly Ambleforth got to his feet and, still without lifting his eyes from his book, said: 'I have sinned, my dear. Vanity of vanities. I have sought to see him return in glory and in so doing have violated what is most holy.'"

"Oh, poor man!" I experienced a rush of pity.

"Did he ask if you knew where he had left his hair shirt?"

"He said he would take a stroll around the garden. And before I could expound on how much I had enjoyed his inspirational visit, he wandered out into the hall and out the front door."

"Then what happened? Did he drive off in our car again?"

Before Ben could answer, the doorbell rang, and he darted from the room to answer it. He was back before I could swallow the toast in my mouth, bringing Kathleen Ambleforth with him. She was certainly worth a double take. The Edwardian-style skirt and blouse needed letting out to better accommodate her ample figure. And the enormous bunches of fruit on her hat looked ready to topple off if she didn't stop shaking her head.

She advanced upon me with arms outstretched. "Ellie, I didn't get home until very late last night. Dunstan was not at home when I returned. I sat up most of the night waiting for him to come back. But he never did. And finally I fell into an exhausted sleep from which I awoke only a short time ago. I rushed over here the minute I was dressed. I was in such a hurry I didn't realize I'd put on an outfit for the play I had brought home for repairs. And now I really don't know what to say to you both."

"Mr. Ambleforth has already been here," I said.

"He brought back the car?"

"It's back in the old stable that we use for a garage," Ben told her.

"What a relief!" Kathleen dropped into a chair. "Poor Dunstan, he does get himself into these pickles. I suppose he was sitting in the monastery ruins at the Old Abbey, reading his favorite book, before he went off in your car. It's the one he wrote nearly forty years ago when he first began devoting his intellectual life to the study of St. Ethelwort. And it never fails to hold him enthralled. When my dear husband is most powerfully in the grip of his own insights into the impact of the Ethelwortian rule on society today, he loses all touch with this earthly life."

"It would seem he can still drive a car," Ben pointed out.

"At such times, he acts completely on automatic." Kathleen clasped her hands, and an apple dropped off her hat. "What worried me in this situation, knowing as I did that you had been planning a trip to France, was that you might have left suitcases in the back of your car. And seeing them, Dunstan could have taken it into his silly old head that he was off on a pilgrimage to the ruins of one of St. Ethelwort's shrines. There's one in Shropshire and another in Kent. In the Middle Ages men used to flock to them in droves."

"I remember you saying that he was a man's saint," I said.

Kathleen nodded, and a pear went flying this time. "Ethelwort was the patron saint of men who, to put it bluntly, couldn't come up to scratch in the bedroom."

"And today he's been replaced by a pill." Ben barely repressed a smile. "I wonder if we can really call that progress."

"I've often pondered," Kathleen continued, "whether those poor dears in bygone times admitted to their wives that they were off in search of the ultimate miracle or if they salvaged their male pride by insisting they had to go off and pay fealty to their liege lords or attend a jousting tournament."

"I'm beginning to think it is a miracle we got our car back," I said.

Kathleen shook her head, but this time without dire results to the hat. "My dear, I can't tell you how relieved I am. I'm afraid I was a little preoccupied when I spoke to you at rehearsal yesterday. The last time something of this sort happened it was the verger's car at our old parish. Dear, silly old Dunstie! He was gone on that occasion for over a week. He had spent the time at a university library—I can't remember whether it was Nottingham or Bristol—scouring through a collection of illuminated manuscripts that sadly produced not one reference to St. Ethelwort."

Ben and I looked at each other. What was there to say? Kathleen got to her feet and stepped on Tobias, who resented being interrupted just as he had cornered a bunch of cherries. "I'm sure you must think my husband has stepped over the line between eccentricity and lunacy." She picked up the fallen apple and stood polishing it on her sleeve. "But then again, having a father like yours, Ellie, probably gives you a little more understanding than most. I'm sure he's just as lovely a man as Dunstan in his way, but definitely odd by most people's standards."

It was Ben who answered her. "He arrived here the other night after suffering a devastating bereavement."

"Oh, I am sorry." She went to take a bite out of the apple, realized what she was doing, and put it in her skirt pocket. "Believe me, I will keep him and your family in my prayers. Life is so hard at times, isn't it? Dunstan had dreamed of coming to this parish for so long. To walk the lanes where St. Ethelwort once trod and to be within daily reach of the monastery ruins was his idea of heaven and earth. But I am afraid that the move has not been entirely beneficial. Sir Casper has not answered any of his letters. And Dunstan was so hoping for the opportunity to see the chapel at the Old Abbey again. He was shown it years ago by Sr. Casper's father but wanted to refresh his memory for some footnotes he wishes to include in volume twelve."

"As lifetime studies go, it is a remarkable contribution." Ben again looked ready to tear his hair out.

"A reviewer for the Northumbrian Parish Preacher called it monumental." Kathleen stepped over Tobias, who was now after the grapes, one of which was trying to go into hiding under a chair.

"That says a lot." I wasn't able to work a lot of enthusiasm into my voice. It was hard to feel an overwhelming interest in someone else's husband when the need to know what mine wanted to tell me gnawed away at my insides. What could have gone missing now that the urn had been returned? I had a sudden nasty suspicion and avoided looking at Ben in case I read confirmation in his eyes.

"Dunstan has always needed coddling, which makes it a blessing in disguise that we never had any children." Kathleen smiled with rueful fondness. "Brilliant men do need to be spoiled more than most. They're so busy thinking lofty thoughts that someone has to be there to do their ordinary thinking for them. And that has been a big part of the problem lately. I've been neglecting the poor lamb shamefully. Murder Most Fowl is my most ambitious production yet."

"I'm sure it will be a huge success," Ben responded tersely.

Kathleen looked as though she might finally be making a move toward the door. "Thank you, Ellie, for the loan of the silver dish. May Mrs. Potter, who's in charge of props, stop by if we need to borrow anything else?"

"Certainly." I stood up.

"You wouldn't happen to have one of those gimmicky cigarette lighters in the shape of a gun?"

"We don't smoke."

"I just thought you might. They were popular years ago. Almost antiques, you could say. We're being lent a proper stage gun, but not in time for the dress rehearsal."

"I don't hesitate to ask"—she beamed at me—"because being an interior designer, you're sure to have lots of unusual things and possibly even some furnishing samples." She waved a hand at the bureau, possibly indicating it appeared to fall into such a category. "We really do appreciate your support of the play. As Freddy has probably told you, the dress rehearsal is tomorrow evening."

"That's lovely," I said, because clearly Ben had made up his mind that opening his mouth again would encourage her to stay for a week. We were getting to the point where we really didn't have any more spare bedrooms.

"I'm hoping that earlier in the evening Dunstan will hold a prayer service for the victim of last night's car accident." Kathleen stood with her hand on the doorknob. "Ruth told me about it just as I was rushing out of the house to come here. She said she'd heard from Mrs. Potter half an hour before that the victim was a woman, as yet to be identified. But whoever she was, we must not lose sight of the fact that we are all one in Christ."

"Very true." Ben broke his vow of silence.

"Did you know that Mrs. Potter's nephew is a policeman?" Kathleen finally allowed us to trot her out into the hall. "Single and eager to settle down, from the sound of it. So call me a meddlesome old aunt," she said with a deep-throated chuckle, "but I can't help thinking that it might be an idea to try to find out if he and Ruth would suit. At the moment, she has this mad crush on your cousin, Ellie, but I'm really not sure he's for her. Too much of the free spirit, if you don't mind my saying so."

"Not at all." I didn't add that Freddy would be delighted to hear it.

"And fond as I am of her, I believe Ruth is a girl who needs a strong man." Kathleen sent a couple of peaches toppling. "Behind that meek exterior of hers there is a way-ward streak. I've got an idea that she some-times leaves the dog tied to a tree and bikes on down to the pub. Her uncle and I aren't against her having a bit of fun. But if she's out late, she wants to lie in bed all the next morning. And that just won't do when she get's a real job. Which we know has to be what she wants, because all girls are wild to go to London and live in hostels on a shoestring. It's part of being young, isn't it? But Ruth doesn't believe us when Dunstan and I say we don't want to stand in the way of her making her own life after he completes the current man-uscript. Then again, if she were to marry this policeman..." Kathleen went out the front door still talking. And I finally got to ask Ben the all-consuming question.

"Is the urn gone again?"

"I'm afraid so."

"How?"

"Remember, Ellie, I told you I left it in the kitchen?"

"On the Welsh dresser."

"That's right." He took a couple of turns around the hall, glaring, as he did so, at the twin suits of armor that stood looking hope-lessly craven. "When I came out of the drawing room after my interminable stint with the vicar, the kitchen door was open, and I saw your father and Aunt Lulu and Ursel sitting at the table. They were chattering away, so I went into the study to read through the work I'd done yesterday on the cookery book. And when I came out about fifteen minutes later, Morley was gone. So, for that matter, was Aunt Lulu. Ursel said she had gone back to the cottage to cook Freddy's breakfast."

"A likely story." I was fuming. "And where did Ursel say Daddy had gone?"

"To Cliffside House to hand over the urn to the Hoppers."

"And she didn't try to stop him."

"She said she offered to go with him, but he refused."

"Oh, Ben!" I stopped being angry in order to feel terribly frightened. "And he's not back. What if those Russian dolls have come to life and are doing away with him as we speak? Dead men don't get to talk their lips off, do they?"

"Who said that, Shakespeare?"

"This is no time for feeble attempts at humor."

"Ellie"—he was using his reasonable voice, the kind guaranteed to drive any wife right up the wall—"if I had thought for a moment that your father was in danger, I wouldn't have sat listening to Kathleen Ambleforth dropping her fruit all over the floor, now, would I? It's the fact that we never got the chance to examine the urn that infuriates me."

"We'll just have to get it back," I said, "along with rescuing my father. You wouldn't happen to remember where we put Mr. Price's gun, would you, darling?"

CHAPTER 22

BEN AND I REACHED THE OLD INN THAT WAS NOW
Cliffside House within seconds of each other.
We had decided to drive separately because
we still had to return the Honda Prelude to
Lady Grizwolde. Stepping out into a wintry
chill under sullen skies, I shivered even
though I was wearing my warm hunter-green
jacket and wool slacks. The brave, bright
splendor of autumn seemed to have vanished
in the night. There was frost on the hedges.
Ben jogged over to me from his parking place
alongside the Rent-A-Wreck, and hand in
hand we crunched across the gravel and
mounted the steps to the door.

"Things are looking up, Ellie. He's still here."

"Yes, but is he still in one piece?"

"Of course he is." Ben lifted the knocker and
let it fall with an iron thud. "Even if the
Hoppers got into their heads to harm him, they
wouldn't do it here."

"Not in the reception room, perhaps, but Daddy, as we both know, is an easy prey. They would only have to ask him to come up to one of their rooms to see some of Harriet's etchings and he would go like a lamb to the slaughter. Then they'd be out of here like a shot with the urn."

"Come on, Ellie, it doesn't help to assume the worst."

"Why not?"

"Because Morley's only trouble right now may be that he's sitting drinking a cup of weak instant coffee and eating a stale biscuit. Served to him by Mrs. Blum, who, if she is anything like her sister Mrs. Potter, won't have left him alone with the Hoppers for fear of missing something worth gossiping about."

"They're nothing alike," I said while he again attacked the knocker. "Mrs. Blum is a very dour woman. It may come from living in a house that was a smuggler's den of iniquity."

I realized that I was carrying on in a way that would have tried the patience of St. Ethelwort. But I couldn't stop myself. The suspense of waiting for someone to open the door was killing me. Even Ben conceded that it seemed to be taking ages. I was about to suggest that he go down the steps, come back up them at a run, and kick the thing in when we heard the groan of hinges that must have needed oiling for at least twenty years. We were suddenly looking at Mrs. Blum. She was a tall, gaunt woman with a face that would have frightened away children willing to brave

286

green slime monsters rising out of swamps for a bag of sweets on Halloween night.

"Mr. and Mrs. Haskell? Come in," she urged in a voice that reminded me of a Hoover with something caught in the works. "I was wondering when you'd get here. Wipe your feet on the mat. No need to bring in half the outdoors. That's right." Ben and I knocked heads in obeying. She stepped around us to close the door and then proceeded on down the hall. The sloping pine floor creaked with every step, and under the faint smell of mildew I thought I caught a woody whiff of seawater-soaked brandy kegs rolled ashore in response to a lantern signal. But I didn't obsess on the Old World charm.

"What did you mean, you were wondering when we would get here?" I inquired of Mrs. Blum's back as she glided past the table with the visitors' book lying open next to a vase of flowers that might have wilted more from fright than a lack of water.

"Didn't you get my phone message?" She turned a corner into a narrow passage with only a couple of low-wattage wall lights to make it possible to walk without hoping a ghostly guide dog would materialize out of the gloom.

"What message?" Ben's voice had a hollow sound to it.

"The one I left for you with Mrs. Malloy."

"We left the house without seeing her." My heart was now pounding as if a dozen of the king's men were demanding admittance at the old inn door. "What was it you wanted to tell us, Mrs. Blum?"

She didn't ask what had brought us to Cliffside House if not for her message, but she did slow her stride, although without turning her head. "Mr. Simons showed up here about an hour ago. When I opened the door, he practically fell into the hall. There was no getting anything coherent out of him. I couldn't smell alcohol on his breath, but I'm sure he had to be drunk from the way he was staggering about and bumping into the walls." She stopped to place her hand on a doorknob. "Knowing my Christian duty, I brought him down here, where I wouldn't have to explain him to the other guests. This isn't that sort of establishment, you know. I left him to sleep it off on the sofa while I went to phone you. When I returned to check on him, he tried to sit up and babbled something about wanting to see the Hoppers, who are staying here. But I didn't go and get them. They're perfectly respectable people. I couldn't subject them to any unpleasantness, whatever their connection, if any, with him. My guests come here for peace and quiet."

"I'm sure my father-in-law did not show up here drunk." Ben returned her look for look.

"He has the nose for it." Mrs. Blum's lugubrious face revealed a resigned acceptance of the medical evidence as she saw it. "An uncle of mine had a red nose like that, and it didn't come from the tomato sauce he poured on his bacon and eggs."

"It's a cold day," I responded stiffly. "I expect my nose is red, too."

"With Uncle George's, it was the brandy. And in the end it was the death of him."

I was about to make another protest, but then I remembered that we did seem to have been pouring that particular substance down Daddy's throat at regular intervals since his arrival at Merlin's Court. Catching Ben's eyes, I realized he was thinking the same thing. We followed Mrs. Blum meekly into a small room. Its paneling was darker than that of the hall. There were dusty red-velvet curtains at the windows, and the scattering of furniture looked as though it had been relegated there when chair and table legs wobbled and springs began poking through the upholstery. Daddy's legs extended over the foot of the beige sofa that was three sizes too small for him.

"I'll leave you to him." Mrs. Blum turned to go but remembered her Christian duty. "I suppose I could bring you some coffee. It'll have to be instant. I still have some beds to make and the bathrooms to do."

Ben and I thanked the closed door, and I scurried over to kneel beside Daddy and pat the hand that trailed the floor. Until that moment I hadn't allowed myself to focus too desperately on what could have happened to him. I had clung to the fact that Mrs. Blum hadn't thought his condition merited sending for a doctor. Such reasoning was, of course, nonsense. She had made an instant diagnosis, based on Uncle George, and had never considered any other possibility.

"Where am I?" Daddy opened an eye just as I had decided he was in a coma from which he would never awaken.

"Cliffside House," I whispered, afraid to shock him back into retreat.

"What am I doing here?"

"You came to see the Hoppers." Ben spoke from behind me.

"Never heard of them," he said, sending my mind leaping to thoughts of amnesia.

"Harriet's relatives." I fought back tears. "You came to bring them the urn."

Daddy struggled to sit up, winced, and eased back down. For a few moments he lay rigid; then his lashes flickered, and as if drawing upon every ounce of his strength, he opened both eyes and looked at me with bleary recognition. "It is coming back to me by painful degrees, Giselle. The vicar must have returned the urn, because when I went down to the kitchen this morning, it was on the Welsh dresser in the canvas bag. I remember Lulu and Frau Grundman coming in, and after that"—his voice faltered—"everything is fuzzy."

"Give it time; it will come back to you," Ben consoled.

"My confounded head!" Daddy moaned. "I feel as though I've been hit with an iron bar." He lifted a hand, let if fall, and lay as if he were slipping back into unconsciousness. Then suddenly he gave a convulsive jerk. "I do remember. Light pierces the wayward darkness. I was in the car, and then I wasn't. I was standing gathering my courage to fulfill my promise to Harriet when I heard something behind me, the crunch of a footstep on gravel.

I started to turn, caught a glimpse of a face I recognized, and then, alas, oblivion."

"Daddy," I leaned over him. "You've got a bruise the size of an egg on the side of your head."

"Who was it you saw, Morley?" Ben was sticking to the basics.

"I appreciate your interest, Bentwick. It was that man. The one from the airport and then again at the house yesterday."

"Mr. Price." I ground out the name. "I think we are now entitled to assume he made an unsuccessful attempt to get the urn from Ursel last night. And this morning he lay in wait and followed you here." I could not keep the sigh out of my voice. "I suppose that this time he got it, Daddy."

"No, Giselle. I can at least reassure you in that regard. You may rejoice in the knowledge that the miserable miscreant did not lay hands on the urn."

"Oh, that's wonderful!" I would have hugged him again if I hadn't been afraid of inflicting permanent injury. "I suppose he must have been scared off by someone going in or out of the house before he could grab it. Where is it?"

"Still at Merlin's Court."

"You forgot to bring it with you?"

"Indeed not." Daddy rallied to look at me askance. "I do not suffer from the vicar's deplorable absentmindedness. It has come back to me now that conversation with Lulu and Frau Grundman in the kitchen. I was telling them that Herr Voelkel had selected the urn, and loath as I was to criticize the man in the performance of so anguishing a commission, I did believe he could not have done worse by Harriet. Both ladies were intensely moved by my impassioned rhetoric and the tears that I failed to stem. It was Lulu, whom I had intemperately taken for a foolish woman wallowing in self-absorption, who most generously provided a solution. She offered me a beautiful antique-silver powder box which she happened to have in the pocket of her skirt. The thought had crossed her mind that you might wish to have it, Giselle, and she was going to give it to you when you came down for breakfast."

"How extremely kind of her." This was no time to think about what I would like to do to Freddy's mumsie.

"An understatement, if I may say so, Giselle. However, Lulu said she now saw that the powder box would make the perfect receptacle for Harriet's ashes, and she was sure you would agree without a question. Her generosity moved me deeply. As did that of Frau Grundman when she said that the task of transferring the mortal remains from the urn might be more than my fragile emotions would bear. And she would be honored to perform the task for me."

"But, Morley, don't you see that the bad guys could still have won? It may not have been the urn they wanted, but the contents." Ben's brows came down in a black bar as he studied my father's face. "No, of course you don't; you've been hit on the head."

Before I could say a word, Mrs. Blum entered the room with a tray of coffee cups and a plate of biscuits that even from a distance looked stale.

"I see you're looking better, Mr. Simons." She imparted all the cheer of Death come calling. "I just saw Mr. Hopper, and he asked if perhaps you had telephoned. When I told him you were here, he said he would fetch his sisters and join you in this room. That's if you're up to it, of course." She didn't add that she wouldn't want to interrupt his hangover, but there was condemnation in every rustle of her skirt as she handed him his coffee cup.

"I think my father-in-law should go to hospital to be checked over," Ben told her. "He's got a bad bump on his head."

"My uncle George used to fall down when he'd had one too many. The wages of sin, Mr. Haskell, are not an extra five pounds in the pay packet." Leaving Ben and me to pick up our own cups of coffee, which was every bit as weak as he had anticipated, Mrs. Blum departed. Daddy was just saying he was glad we hadn't mentioned he had been attacked, because there was no point in raising questions he wouldn't have wished to answer, when in came the Hoppers. Today they wore matching red sweaters. Cyril wore black trousers, and Edith and Doris had on black skirts. Three roly-poly figures that didn't look as though they had a brain to divide between them. But what did I know about anything? I had taken an immediate liking to Ursel Grundman, and where had that got me or, I should say, Daddy?

The Hoppers sat down on a wooden bench, placed their plump hands on their knees, and peered at us with black eyes that looked as though they had been painted and varnished to match their slicked-down hair.

"Did you bring the urn?" Cyril asked in his wooden voice.

"Yes, the urn," said Doris.

"Harriet's urn," said Edith.

"Mr. Simons did bring it." Ben spoke before Daddy opened his mouth. "But unfortunately for him and all of you, he was attacked and robbed before he could reach the door. We want to know why. In other words, what are you prepared to tell us about the urn, because what we do know for damn sure is that Harriet isn't in it."

All three Russian dolls blinked. They looked at each other. They inhaled and exhaled in unison, and again Cyril spoke first.

"We don't know anything."

"All Harriet told us was that we were to collect the urn," said Doris.

"And not talk too much in case we let something slip," said Edith.

"But you just said you don't know anything," I pointed out.

"Not about what is really in the urn or who it's for." The merest flicker of intelligence strayed across Cyril's features. "Harriet didn't want us to say anything personal that might be different from what she'd told Mr. Simons or that might help him track her down if he ever realized he'd been scammed."

"She said she knew how to mix the truth with

294

the made-up stuff to be convincing." Edith lowered her head. "But she said it took lots of practice. And she was right. We shouldn't have let slip that she'd worked at Oaklands because that's where, after listening to the patients talk about how well crime paid, she decided to go into business for herself."

"It was after her husband left her." Doris raised her chin. "She needed money to look after us. We've always needed a lot of taking care of. We didn't always look like this. It's been one operation after the other for each of us. That's why Cyril was beaten up as a kid. Edith and me didn't have it quite so rough. We only got laughed at and called names."

"So Harriet really is your cousin?" I sat on the floor and held Daddy's trailing hand.

"Of course," said Cyril.

"This was going to be her last job," said Edith. "It was going to give us the rest of the money we needed to buy a house in Dawlish. That's in Devon. We went there on a caravan holiday once when we were kiddies and always dreamed about going to live there."

"What about the Voelkels? Where do they fit into the picture?" Ben asked. Daddy sat looking only semiconscious.

"Who?" Doris's face went blank. The other two black heads bent toward hers, and she sat nodding as if it would take the tug of a switch to make her stop. "Now I know who you mean. That's not their real name. It changes with every job. They sometimes worked together. The man and the woman and his old mother and Harriet. But it got that Harriet didn't like them so much. He kept pushing her to get into the big time when all she wanted was what she called honest pay for a dishonest job. And this time, she told us, he didn't like it because she started to have feelings for Mr. Simons."

"Harriet fell in love with you." Cyril looked with eyes that had lost their varnished look at Daddy.

"She didn't mean to," said Edith.

"It broke her heart," said Doris.

"Why are you saying all this?" Daddy finally spoke as if from somewhere far away.

"Because it doesn't matter anymore." Cyril's voice cracked like a piece of dry wood. "We thought there had to be something wrong last night when she didn't show up to collect the urn like she had written and told us she would. Then, when we heard about the accident, we knew that had to be why. It didn't take hearing from Mrs. Blum that it was a brown Vauxhaul that went over the cliff or for her to tell us the license-plate number. We already knew deep inside us that our Harriet was dead."

CHAPTER 23

"DEAD! DO I NOT ALREADY KNOW THAT?" MY FATHER rose up like a wounded lion roused from fitful slumber by someone treading on his tail. "Have I not already faced the unassailable truth that sweet Harriet's mortal being is gone, never to return?"

"Daddy, I don't think you can have been listening to what the Hoppers have been saying." I hurried forward to place a soothing hand on his arm but stepped smartly backward when he snarled at me, showing more teeth than I had thought he possessed.

"It has to be hard for you to accept." Ben wisely kept at a safe distance. "You've been cruelly tricked, Morley. Not too many people are ever likely to find themselves in your position—having to deal with the death of a loved one twice over. But that's how it is. There was no car crash in Germany. Ingo Voelkel lied to you. His meeting with you was staged.

The entire, unhappy Harriet episode was a ruse to get you to bring that urn into England. Only now she is dead and—"

"A terrible fear smites me, Bentwick." Daddy's roar shook the timbers of the old inn. "It is that you and my daughter are in league with these paltry specimens of humanity." He swiveled around one of the Hoppers, who squeaked piteously before ducking behind a table. "Perhaps, God knows, you believe yourselves to be acting in my best interests," he roared, clasping a hand to his heaving chest. "Defame my Harriet and I may the more quickly rebound from her loss. Yes, I can see that may be your thinking. But I tell you, nothing anyone says will weaken my faith in her goodness or tarnish my memories of our days together."

"We did say she loved you," whispered Edith.

"That's right," Cyril agreed.

"Indeed we did," said Doris.

Something in their unblinking black eyes must have gotten through to him because Daddy covered his face with his hands and began to sob. In great gulping gasps, as if he no longer believed in hope or comfort from this world or the next. I was thinking that my own heart would break when Mrs. Blum thrust open the door and informed us that we were disturbing the other residents.

"I think you'd best leave, Mr. and Mrs. Haskell, and take the old man with you. Cliffside House is a respectable establishment. A woman came looking for a room yesterday morning. A shabby, unkempt sort of person. Not at all our usual sort of clientele. And I was put to the trouble of getting rid of her."

"No need to worry about us," Ben said coldly, taking Daddy's arm. After murmuring some sort of good-bye to the Hoppers, I followed my two men through the maze that led us back to the depressing hall and outside, where the air didn't smell as if it were two hundred years old and the wind hopefully would put a little color into Daddy's cheeks.

Moving woodenly across the parking area my father insisted, with a pitiful disregard for common sense, that he didn't need medical treatment for the bump on his head. So we agreed that Ben would drive him home and telephone our wonderful family doctor to request a house call. Meanwhile, I would go on to the Old Abbey, return the Honda Prelude, and come home by taxi.

It made my heart ache to see the misery in Daddy's eyes as Ben helped him into the passenger seat, where he sat looking vacantly out the window. This was a different kind of grief than we had seen before, quieter, less close to the surface from which tears flow. His devastation was such that I feared it would be a while before he could rouse himself to again parade his grief in public. Was this how he had been after the immediate shock of my mother's death had worn off? Had he thus wandered in the desert of his soul until he met Harriet? I found myself wishing sadly, as I drove to the Old Abbey, that things might have been different, that they could have met as two people with no hidden agendas, eager to embrace the autumn of their lives, safe in the assurance of a steadfast love.

I had to make myself think of something else. So I settled on Mr. Price's gun. I hadn't been serious when I suggested to Ben that we take it with us to Cliffside House. Neither of us would have known how to fire the thing without the instruction manual. I also suspected that we would have been the ones getting into big trouble for being caught in possession of a stolen weapon. The judge would be vexed that we hadn't turned it into the police station after Aunt Lulu showed us what she lamentably viewed as sort of a door prize. Had the children been home, Ben or I would have immediately locked it away in a safe place while we were wondering how to turn it over to the authorities without landing Aunt Lulu in hot water. Now I couldn't remember where in the drawing room the gun had ended up. If it had been left on the coffee table, it hadn't been there this morning. I would have noticed a gun nestled between the marmalade pot and the toast rack. Our carelessness was really inexcusable; I got panicky thinking about Daddy's present state of mind. I really didn't think he would try to kill himself. But tragedies occur when people don't take the time and trouble to assume the worst.

I kept picturing the car accident as I drove alongside the wall enclosing the Old Abbey. And when I turned in at the gates and glanced toward the ruins of St. Ethelwort's monastery, stark and secret in the gloom of the day, I thought about the wages of sin, so dear to Mrs. Blum's heart. What a bitter irony that Harriet's manner of death had so closely mimicked her feigned demise in Germany. Was it possible that driving this winding road above the coast had impaired her concentration because the similarity of settings had reminded her of the story she and Herr Voelkel had concocted for my father's benefit? Or had she simply been driving too fast in her haste to get the urn, which the Hoppers would have collected as arranged but for Mr. Ambleforth's unwitting intervention? And if she were hurrying, was that because she had a second appointment to keep, one in which she was to complete her business deal with a purchaser who did not allow moral or legal nitpicking to stand in the way of achieving a heart's desire? Who was this villain lurking offstage? Had Mr. Price and his cohort hired her and the Voelkels to commit the robbery and then decided to cut out the middleman, or in this case, woman? Or was there some other shadowy figure standing in the wings? Someone every bit as wicked as Malicia Stillwaters in Murder Most Fowl?

I continued on down the drive and was struck again by the beauty of the Georgian house, so pure in its lines, so mellowed by time that it seemed as much an act of God as the sky above. Parking the car close to the old stables that now served as the garage, I slipped the keys in my jacket pocket, climbed out, and found old Ned the gardener standing a few feet away with a bunch of bronze and yellow chrysanthemums in his hands.

"Morning, missus!" He gave one of his

funny little hops, and his face broke into more wrinkles as his mouth formed a smile. "You've brought her ladyship's carriage back all of a piece, save that the horse is missing." He cackled a laugh and beckoned to me with a gnarled finger. "Come along inside. I'm on my way to take these flowers to the chapel. It used to be that the lady of the house took care of filling a vase for the altar one or two days a week. But the present her ladyship would rather have me do it. And Miss Finchpeck can't go there on account of the damp getting into her chest. She'll have told you how the fog got into her lungs the night she were born and how it's left her a poor dab of a creature."

Miss Finchpeck hadn't put it exactly like that. But I nodded and told Ned I had only come to return the car. If Lady Grizwolde was busy, I would leave the keys with him along with an apology for not having returned it yesterday.

"She ain't busy. She's come up poorly."

"Oh, dear!" I said, shivering as a gust of wind attempted to scalp me. "I hope it's nothing serious."

"It be her ankle." Ned had the advantage of hopping about to keep warm. "She went and sprained it last night. I wasn't there when it happened, not sleeping in at the house, but Cook says to me this morning, when she gives me my cup of cocoa, that Lady Grizwolde done it when she was trying to get Sir Casper upstairs after him having one of his spells. And Mr. Jarrow for some reason not being around to help her with him. Though he come along quick enough after her lady-ship started hollering. Cook said she heard her yell out and went to see what was up. And it was Mr. Jarrow that got Sir Casper up to bed and Cook that helped her ladyship back down to the settee in the library."

"I am sorry, and I hope Lady Grizwolde's ankle mends quickly." I held out the car keys. "I'd better let you have these, Ned, and not disturb her."

"Could be she'd be glad of seeing a fresh face, being stuck lying with her foot on a cushion. Miss Finchpeck's not what you could call jolly company at the best of times. Not that there's n'owt wrong with that. She's a lady born and bred, and it do sometimes takes them that way. All that there history of their ancestors having their heads chopped off and set up on spikes for the riffraff to laugh at. And I did hear tell from Cook as Miss Finch-peck offered to sit with Lady Grizwolde and prompt her with her lines for the church play. Not that there's no real need for that, her ladyship being a proper actress before she married Sir Casper. And anyhow, it don't make much difference now, do it? Not when she can't get off the sofa, let alone walk up on stage. Leastways, not for the dress rehearsal tomorrow evening." Ned gave another of his amiable cackles, while I wondered how Mrs. Malloy would react to this news.

"The play won't be the same." I tried to hold down my hair.

"You can tell I'm well up on it." Ned did

another of his hops. "My granddaughter Sarah, as works up at the house, is thick as thieves with the vicar's niece. And you wouldn't think it likely, given they're different as they come. Ruth's one of them lassies that's got to be shown how to have fun, while my Sarah's always up for a mite of mischief. The tricks she pulled when she were a kiddy, and still does from the sound of it! It's a wonder I've a hair left on my head. But I shouldn't be keeping you out in the wind, missus, talking your ear off. Come along up to the house. Even if you can't see her ladyship, Cook can fix you a hot drink."

I was about to refuse but remembered I needed to phone for a taxi. A cup of tea or coffee would be welcome while I waited. We walked around to the entrance we had used the day before, the one that took us along the corridor past Mr. Jarrow's office to a half-flight of steps that I now discovered led into the kitchen. Here a red-faced woman in a white overall was slapping out pastry for rolling— Mrs. Johnson, the superb cook whose quiche I hadn't sampled yesterday because Lady Grizwolde had been so eager to curtail my visit after Sir Casper put in his capering appearance. When told what I needed, she offered to ring up the taxi company for me but warned there could be a half-hour wait.

"They're always busy, but they do show up, which is more than you can say for some of the other ones. Why don't you go along with Ned, Mrs. Haskell, and take a look at the chapel. We're the only house in these parts that has one. The Grange doesn't, and neither does Pomeroy Hall. And then, when you're done, you can come back here for a cuppa."

I thanked her, said I would be delighted to return and have a cup of tea with her if she could spare the time to join me, and followed Ned through a green baize door and along a passage that opened onto the main hall. We were approaching the lovely room where Daddy and I had been installed for our visit with her ladyship, and I remembered how its ambience had changed so unpleasantly after Sir Casper came hobbling in and gleefully talked about redecorating the master bedroom. My pace slowed, and I heard Timothia Finchpeck's voice coming from behind the door, which wasn't quite closed. I was startled not only by what I heard but by the hard clarity of her voice; yesterday I'd had to strain to hear her downtrodden governess whispers.

"You're a murderer. Don't try to deny it. I followed you and saw what happened. I thought you were going to meet him, but I was wrong about that. Don't worry, I'm not going to tell; it's enough that you know that I know."

Ned chuckled in my ear. "That do be Miss Finchpeck."

I could only stand like a zombie.

"Her must be reciting lines from the play. Could be she's making pretend she'll have to take over for her ladyship."

"Someone else is understudying the part of Malicia Stillwaters," I whispered. If Ned had not been there, I might have inched the door open a crack and looked in to see who, if anyone, was in that room with Timothia Finchpeck. My heart was still knocking as if desperately trying to get my undivided attention when he veered to our left under the hanging staircase and we were in another passageway that branched off in two directions. He took the right fork and a moment later was opening an arched oak door.

The chapel was tiny, with three blackened oak pews on either side of a narrow aisle leading to the altar. It was exquisite; its stone carvings, stained-glass windows, and ornate pulpit reminded me of a cathedral the size of a doll's house. It had a typical old-church, musty smell, but for me that only added to its charm.

Ned stood beside me, the chrysanthemums bunched in his hands. "Did I tell you afore, missus"—his voice echoed with every syllable—"as how the stone for these here walls was dug up from what's left of old Worty's monastery?"

I nodded, although I couldn't remember whether or not he had.

"You take a look around while I takes out the old flowers and put these fresh ones in the vase on the altar. That's been done since Sir Casper's mother's time, although..." He shook his head and went nipping up the aisle, leaving me to look up at the biblical figures reclining at their ease on banks of clouds as if at some heavenly banquet. I then wandered up and down the sides of the chapel, stopping to admire a carved angel here and a gargoyle there until Ned called out to me.

"Would you like to come see where he used to be, missus?"

"Where who was?"

"Old Worty."

Completely bewildered, I mounted the stone step and joined him in front of the altar. "You mean this is where he would have stood? But surely this area didn't come complete from his monastery."

"I'm talking about a real piece of him. There's a word for it, and if I scratch me head for a minute, it'll come to me." He suited action to words. "I've got it now, missus. A relic, that's what it's called. A holy relic. It was kept in a space in there," he said, tapping at a rectangle of stone. "For centuries, it do be said. And old Worty made a promise to that lady of the house, right back in Elizabethan times, that so long as he was left be, there'd always be an heir for the Old Abbey. But Sir Casper's mother didn't pay the old legend no heed. She was reared up Catholic—they're big on relics—and it so happened she come from the very town that was old Worty's birthplace. A funny sort of name, but so they mostly are in foreign parts." He stood scratching his head.

"Was it Loetzinn?" I felt as though the stone floor was about to drop out from under me.

"Aye, that do sound right. And Sir Casper's mother, Lady Grizwolde that was, her do be bound and determined that the relic go to the church that's said to be built over the place where old Worty's family's home once stood. And she talked her husband round to letting her have her way. But not till after she'd give him an heir. Maybe Sir Walter thought the old story was just that—a story. But when it come time for Sir Casper to do his duty by the Grizwoldes, he didn't have no luck in filling up the nursery. When his first wife passed on, I guess he could have told hisself, it was just one of them things. Lots of couples ain't blessed with children, but men of his age can still pull something out of the old bag of tricks. So he looks around for a young wife. But it don't happen for them. No nappies flapping on the line. Sir Casper, he's looking at the end of the Grizwoldes. When he passes on, the house goes to Miss Finchpeck. After her it'll be strangers at the Old Abbey." Ned picked up the bunch of dead flowers he had laid beside the vase now containing the chrysanthemums. "There's another part to old Worty's legend." He cleared his throat. "It's said as how there was miracles for men past doing the job, if you do be getting my meaning, missus. And I think Sir Casper, he's been hoping for one of them miracles."

I stood looking at the chrysanthemums. No wonder Mrs. Johnson, the cook, had said the Old Abbey was at sixes and sevens. All sorts of emotions had to be steaming up the atmosphere. Sir Casper would be distraught that having hired Harriet in hope that by appeasing St. Ethelwort his virility would be restored, things had gone fatally awry. Assuming she didn't keep her appointment that last night to complete the transaction, he must have feared the worst when informed that a car had gone off the cliff almost outside his gates. How could he hope the urn had survived the crash? And what of her ladyship? I remembered how eager she had been, surprisingly so for a woman of her almost pathological calm, that I bring my father with me for her meeting. And how she had steered him toward talking about his time in Germany. I also recalled how she had left the room supposedly to look for the magazine that Miss Finchpeck had failed to find after he mentioned that the urn was in the car. I saw in my mind's eye her returning to the room, her complexion dewy and that additional shine to her satin smooth hair. Had she gone out into the rain to get the urn Daddy had told her he had left in the car? Had she been intent on ensuring it never reached her husband, who was alrcady showing renewed sprightliness at the prospect of being able to fully function once again? What had been her feelings upon discovering that Mr. Ambleforth had gone off in our car? Had she married Sir Casper instead of an equally rich younger man in the hope that at his age he would not long be capable of the overtures that her cold nature found repugnant? Did she in her own way love Mr. Jarrow? Was he hostile toward her because she had rejected him for a life of married celibacy? Had he perhaps been the one to introduce her to Sir Casper? And had he taken a twisted, malicious pleasure in watching his employer's lewd pursuit of her yesterday? The questions kept racing through my head. Could it be that Sir Casper had sent Mr. Jarrow to Schönbrunn to keep an eye on Harriet to make sure she was acting in accordance with instructions and would deliver the genuine article? And what of Timothia Finchpeck? Was she rejoicing today that there would be no miracle heir to deny her the opportunity to one day rule as mistress of the Old Abbey? The chill from the stone floor crept into my feet and all the way up my legs. I knew, as surely as if I had the evidence in my hands, that Ned and I hadn't overheard her speaking Malicia Stillwater's lines. Miss Finchpeck believed there had been no car accident outside the Old Abbey gates last night. Someone had deliberately sent it off the cliff. Someone who now had a sprained ankle to show for her trouble. From the sound of it Miss Finchpeck had been a witness and was now empowered by her knowledge to turn the tables and make Lady Grizwolde toe the line.

"I do be inclined to ramble on about the family, but the Old Abbey's been my life, missus, since I could barely toddle." Ned turned with the dead flowers in his hand to descend the altar steps, and before we were halfway down the narrow aisle, Mrs. Johnson poked in her head to say my taxi was at the front door.

It was as though I had been informed that a spaceship was waiting to transport me to Mars. I continued to feel disoriented on the drive home. As I crossed the moat bridge to the courtyard, Mrs. Malloy was coming down the steps in her fake leopard coat carrying the bag that held her cleaning supplies and today almost certainly the script for Murder Most Fowl.

"I'm off home," she said with a compression of her butterfly lips. "I just heard from Mrs. Potter that Lady Grizwolde's broke her ankle or at least sprained it bad. And I need to commune with me own things—in particular one of me china poodles that understands me like no one else does—if I've a hope of getting through the rest of today and tomorrow morning. Then, if I can make it through the dress rehearsal tomorrow, I can tell meself I've only got to walk into the lion's den three more times. Doctor was here to see Mr. Simons, and when I had a word, he said there was pills I could take to calm me nerves but they'd make me sleepy. So what the bloody hell good was that? Oh, and by the way"—she didn't appear to notice my silence, probably because she rarely let me get in three words straight—"he said he didn't think there was much wrong with your dad, but he had Mr. H. take him down to outpatients at St. Mary's just to be on the safe side. Your hubby said not to worry if they're gone hours because there's always a wait. Freddy and his mum are down at the cottage, so you'll have the place to yourself except for Frau Grumble."

"Grundman," I automatically corrected, but she was already off down the drive, and I went into the hall to find Ursel standing there as if she had been waiting for me.

"I need very much for to talk to you." She looked genuinely unhappy.

"Is it about your supporting my father in his decision to take Harriet's 'remains' to the Hoppers?" I stood peeling off my jacket and then tossed it along with my handbag on the trestle table.

"That, yes, but first there is more."

"Why don't we go and sit down?" I said, and without waiting for a response, led the way into the drawing room. Once there, I waited for her to take her seat on the sofa facing the windows before settling myself somewhat rigidly on the one across from her. The clock on the mantelpiece seemed to tick more loudly than usual, as if impatient for one of us to begin talking.

"All of what I tell you last night is true." Ursel met my eyes squarely. "That I wish to see that Herr Simons is all right and everything about my visit to the house on Glatzerstrasse. But there is something I do not tell you. I have make a promise to my sister Hilde that I will not speak of it. She is not so sure in her head that Herr Simons is the good man I tell her he is. She thinks he may be Harriet's partner of crime. I say it is not so, but she tells me: 'Ursel, you are not thinking clear. You are in love with this man. It was the same when your Heiko was alive; you do not see that he drinks too much the schnapps.'"

"You've lost me?" I said.

"Then I explain better. Hilde is very upset. I tell you last night she works as housekeeper for Fader Bergdorff at the Christ Kirche in Loetzinn."

"Yes." I was beginning to get a glimmering of understanding.

"He is a kind man, a good priest. And one day he comes to my sister very worried. He says, 'Hilde, the relic of the saint has been stolen from the church. You know I do not believe much that a piece of bone and the dried flesh is what makes for holiness. To me it is the invisible that is most real. But our church is packed always on Sundays and often in the week. The women they would come, anyway, but the men, many of them, come to be sure of the miracle of St. Ethelwort in their hour of need. Hilde,' Fader Bergdorff say, 'it matters not to me why they come, only that they come. If I tell that the relic is gone, some will stay home. So I will say that the reliquary has gone to be cleaned....' "

"The what?" I almost slid off the sofa.

"Perhaps I do not have the word right?" Ursel spread her hands.

"Yes, you do, it's just that I hadn't thought... But of course. That's why the urn was so ugly. It had been camouflaged in clay, but they are often of odd shapes, which explains the lumps and bumps and why Mrs. Malloy said it looked like something a child might have made in play group. My goodness! It has to be incredibly valuable."

"That is so." Ursel's face had more color and life to it now. "It once had in it the relic of another saint. Such things get lost over time. This is what Hilde tell me. But the reliquary has been in the Christ Kirche for many years, before St. Ethelwort was given back to his birth-place. Fader Bergdorff does not want to notify the police because the word of the theft will be in the newspaper. And he does not want the men to stop coming to mass. He cares always first for the souls of his people. It is why I get upset last night when you talk about telephoning the police. I must keep faith with him. When I tell Hilde about the empty house on Glatzerstrasse, we think we begin to see. And when we talk to Fader Bergdorff, he tell me to come and see what I can find out but not to put my life in danger or the Christ Kirche in the papers."

"But I don't understand about this morning."

"It is simple." She was actually smiling at me. "Herr Simons was determined to fulfill his promise to Harriet, but he worries that the urn is ugly. Your Aunt Lulu, she happens to have a silver powder box in her pocket; I say I will put the ashes in it. And so it is I do. I take them from the fireplace."

"Oh, Ursel!" I said. "Where is the reli-quary?"

"I put it on a shelf in your Ben's study, where it is hidden behind books. Old ones that I think no one would often pick up."

"Let's go and get it!"

And so we hurried like a pair of excited schoolgirls across the hall. But there was no joy ten minutes later after we had pulled every book off the shelves. The reliquary was gone. So, we soon discovered, was Mr. Price's gun, which Ben had also thought to conceal behind a volume entitled How to Safeguard Your Home, chapter one of which dealt with the importance of securing doors and windows even when at home. Something we had failed to do. Sadly, I remembered noticing the curtain stirring in the breeze at the drawing-room windows when Ben was talking to me about his visit from Mr. Ambleforth. But it was too late to kick myself; besides which, I preferred to save my energy for the next time—if there should be one—that I saw the obnoxious Mr. Price.

CHAPTER 24

"NOW GUESS WHAT'S MISSING?" I THREW MYSELF BACK
on the bed and eyed Ben with utter hopelessness when he entered our room at around
ten that evening. Hair damp from his shower,
he looked dashingly debonair in his black-silk
dressing gown.

"I dread to think." He bent to stroke one
of my dangling feet. "But at least it isn't
your father. I just checked on him, and he
appeared to be asleep."

"That's good." I stared dully up at the
ceiling. "He has to be all in after what this day
has put him through. I'd feel easier about him
if he'd got some of his feelings off his chest
instead of refusing to talk about Harriet's
second passing. I suppose it's not surprising
that he didn't respond when I told him about
St. Ethelwort's mummified finger or so much
as blink on hearing that Mr. Price had called
to collect the reliquary while we were at

Cliffside House. What can any of this matter to him? This morning he lost all that was left to him. His faith in the woman he loved. But even so, I'm beginning to wonder how long he's going to stay this way—shut up inside himself, not rousing himself to do more than sniff at his dinner? What if he never comes out of it? What if he ends up spending the rest of his life in a hospital staring glassy-eyed at four walls year in and year out."

"Ellie, now you're the one going off the deep end."

"Thanks a lot," I told the ceiling.

"All I'm saying, sweetheart, is that you're overtired and stressed out."

"You're right." Sitting up, I began unpinning my hair from the squashed bird's nest it had become after being retucked into place during the day and finally lain on in weary despair. "It just seemed the last straw when I came in here after having my bath and found that someone has made off with my brand-new pink nightie and negligee. The ones I bought for going to France and left off packing until the last possible moment. Because looking at them lying on the bed, in all their lovely gossamer perfection, was enough to make me feel Parisian."

"So that's what's gone missing." Ben did not sound particularly devastated as he shrugged out of his dressing gown and tossed it on a chair. He was wearing a rather nice pair of claret pajamas with turnups on the legs and double-buttoned cuffs. And it was wrong of me to feel a flicker of resentment. It wasn't his fault that there I was in faded flannel after deciding that pink nylon and lace might provide the emotional lift I needed at the end of this extremely trying day. But did he have to look quite so much the suave man about the bedroom, contemplating a final cigar before his valet materialized to tuck him into bed?

"I expect Aunt Lulu helped herself." I went over to the mirror and began brushing my hair until the electricity sizzled.

"But they—the nightdress and negligee—wouldn't be her size."

"True, if hardly tactful."

"Ellie!"

"Sorry. I know I'm being difficult." Discarding my brush, I began slapping night cream on my face as if it were cake topping. "It doesn't matter if it fits. We both know Aunt Lulu didn't take it because she traveled light and forgot to pack anything to sleep in. To her its all about the thrill of being a naughty little girl pulling something over on the grown-ups."

"You're still angry about the silver powder box." Ben came up behind me and nuzzled the top of my head with his chin.

"Of course I am. It was lovely, and more important, you gave it to me for our anniversary. It really would have served Aunt Lulu right if she'd poked around inside and found St. Ethelwort's nasty old finger. She'd have thought it was a piece of Harriet that hadn't been reduced to ash; but even so, it might have brought her up short. Now nasty Mr. Price has both the ashes and the reliquary, and poor Frau Grundman has failed to recover them for that nice-sounding Father Bergdorff." I rubbed in the last dollop of night cream and replaced the lid on the jar.

"You know, we really can't be sure it was Price who broke into the house." Ben paced away from me and, after circling the room a couple of times, turned back the bedcovers. "We zeroed in on him because he wheedled his way in here yesterday."

"And he was the man with a gun," I pointed out.

"I know." Ben lay down and tucked his hands behind his head. "But let's not forget we're dealing with a whole bunch of questionable people. Lady Grizwolde, for instance. Don't you think she would have stopped at little to prevent Sir Casper from testing his faith in miracles by climbing into bed with her at night?"

"Yes, but she's got an injured leg."

"Or so she claims."

"I've been picturing her doing it pushing that car over the cliff."

"Then maybe she sent Mr. Jarrow over here this morning."

"There is that." I finished tying my hair back with a rubber band and snuggled in alongside Ben. "All that chilly animosity of his toward her strikes me as a ruse to hide the fact he's madly in love with her and suffers the pangs of the damned every time she's within a mile and a half of him. And when she asks him to do something for her, even something illegal, he sobs with delight into his hanky. But maybe I'm just an old-fashioned romantic. Maybe what motivates Mr. Jarrow is all about economics—keeping his employer happy in hope of a sizable inheritance when the time comes. He could have showed up here at Sir Casper's request. And let's not forget Timothia Finchpeck, although the idea of her climbing through our drawing-room window does rather boggle the mind."

"If we went to the police, we could let them sort all of this out." Ben screwed up his eyes and smothered a yawn with the top of the sheet.

"We've been all through that. We can't talk to them for the same reason that I'll bet the Hoppers are still dithering about whether to go down to the station and report that the car that went over the cliff was owned by their cousin Harriet. They'll be afraid of being roped in as conspirators. Which they are, poor things, after their sad fashion. And I'm afraid for Daddy's chances if he owned up to bringing the reliquary out of Germany into England. Can we really count on the police viewing him as an innocent pawn? Especially now, when there's a death here in Chitterton Fells to be cleared up and he can't produce the stolen object. They might even think he went out last night and engineered the car crash after a row among thieves with Harriet. There's only our word for it that he was here at the time. For that matter, can we even be sure that he didn't slip out for a while when we thought he was in his room? And then there's Mrs. Ambleforth."

"What about her?"

"She might feel morally obliged, if questioned, to tell the police about Daddy's behavior that night she came looking for her husband. She obviously thought it very odd, because she told her niece Ruth about it."

"I would think she'd be used to odd behavior after being married all the years to the vicar. Your father's not half the crackpot he is."

"Yes, but we all have blind spots when it comes to our mates."

"Thanks a lot." Ben patted my hair while giving vent to another yawn.

"I'm saying that what passes for charming eccentricty in a husband could scare you up a twelve-foot wall in a stranger. I think Kathleen was afraid Daddy was going to ravish her on the spot that night, with me watching, and it could have set her against him. I get the feeling from the way she keeps trying to find a husband for Ruth that she's got some rather outdated ideas about marriage—that women need it to make themselves respectable and men need someone to cluck over them. And it isn't just Kathleen who could put in a bad word for Daddy," I sighed. "If push comes to shove when it comes to saving their own necks the Hoppers could truthfully say that I had admitted to them, when saying Daddy wasn't ready to give up the urn, that he could turn violent. Are you listening, Ben?"

"I've been thinking," he murmured drowsily.

"About what?"

"Maybe it wasn't Aunt Lulu."

"What wasn't?"

He struggled to open his eyes, but he words grew slurred.

"I mean, perhaps she didn't take your nightdress and that thing that goes over it. Couldn't they be in a drawer or on a hook somewhere?"

"No. I looked everywhere. Practically ransacked my dressing table and the wardrobe. It is nice of you to try and get her off the hook, and I'm fond of her, too, but she really is the limit. She wasn't more than politely contrite about the silver box. Freddy was the one who was upset. I really think he's ready to get hold of his solicitor and put himself up for adoption. But I told him to hold out and hope that something does happen to scare her into her senses."

A muffled snore informed me that I was talking to myself. And as women tend to do, I blamed myself for not being able to hold his attention. Even in a crisis I was boring. But then we can't all be born fascinating like Harriet. I turned with as much eloquence as I could muster over on my side and even gave the pillow a couple of thumps without getting so much as a drowsy, incoherent mumble in response. There was nothing for it but to try and get some rest myself, so that in the morning I would be up to coming up with some ideas on how to save Daddy. To that end I switched off the bedside lamp. But sleep wasn't easily come by. I started wondering if Harriet and Herr Voelkel had been lovers and whether his wife, Anna, had minded. Or were they, and the black-garbed housekeeper, all just longtime business associates hired by rich people to acquire treasures for their private collections? Presumably, Sir Casper hadn't got Harriet's name from an employment agency, but he was, or had been, a man of the world, and I imagined that there are always people who, when asked, know someone who knows someone who for the right price would steal the Taj Majal. And gift wrap it before handing it over.

It was impossible; I was never going to get to sleep. Slipping out of bed as stealthily as possible and feeling my way into my slippers, I crept across the shadowy room and lifted Ben's dressing gown off the chair before tiptoeing out the door. I stopped at the top of the stairs to tie the silk sash around my waist. It would have put the lid on a difficult day if I had tripped going down and broken my neck, creating more heartache, along with another accident, for the police to investigate. While standing there, my eyes went to my father's bedroom door. It stood just a little ajar. Ben, I decided, must not have closed it properly after peeking in to check on Daddy. It never occurred to me as I crossed the gallery that he wouldn't be in his bed. But one look told the story. The covers were thrown back. His clothes were gone from the chair; his shoes, from beside the bed.

Something drew me to the window. It may have been the memory of thinking after putting him in here that it might not have been such a bright idea to give him a room with such an excellent view of the sea. Had the sound of the waves spoken to him in his sleep? A soothing, seductive voice—something between a summons and a plaintive wail—urging him to drown his sorrows once and for all? With trembling hand, I pushed aside the curtains. The moon was sitting among the trees like a ghostly canoe, and there, standing in the drive like a lost soul, was my father.

I'm not sure how I got down the stairs or out the door, but suddenly I was holding on to his arm and walking with him in the near dark toward Freddy's cottage and back again. It was cold and damp, but I didn't shiver. Relief warmed me as nothing else could.

"I woke up and couldn't get back to sleep, Giselle."

"That's understandable," I soothed, wondering when the moment would be right to suggest that he come back inside and have a hot drink.

"So I came outside to talk to your mother."

"Did you?"

"It's something I've done quite often through the years. Gone for a walk and imagined her stepping alongside me, her hand tucked in my arm, just as yours is now. I don't speak of her very often. At first, it was too painful, and then I found I preferred not to share her with others. Selfish of me, no doubt, but I've always been a man who put himself first. Think of what I did to you, walking out on you when you were seventeen."

"You were inclined to drag me with you through the slough of despond, as some parents would have done."

"That is one way of looking at it." Daddy's voice had brightened.

"One should always look back on the past through rose-colored glasses." I turned him around as we reached Freddy's cottage for the second time.

"Where did you hear that, Giselle?"

"From you. Lots of times when I was growing up."

"I was a fool." His face was lugubrious in the moonlight. "And now I'm an old fool. How could I have loved Harriet so blindly and so ill?"

"You saw something good in her. Something that the Voelkels and a life of crime hadn't been able to extinguish. That's what Mother would have said."

"How do you know?" He turned to me with a piteous droop of his jowls.

"Because I talk to her, too." I reached up to kiss his cheek. And when we turned to go inside, we saw a light on in the kitchen. We were to discover that Frau Grundman was up, dealing with her inability to sleep by preparing a breakfast casserole dish from a recipe that Ben had given her (from the cookery book in progress) earlier in the day. And when I finally returned to bed, for a while I lay hoping that if there had been any ghosts in that garden, they, too, could go peacefully to their rest.

CHAPTER 25

BUT THERE WAS NO USE IN KICKING MYSELF—
which, in any case, it would have been difficult to do, seeing as the following evening I
was squashed in a pew at St. Anselm's Church.
The congregation was becoming decidedly
restive due to the harsh reality that we had
already spent an interminable amount of
time waiting for the vicar to show his face in
the pulpit.

Almost the entire parish had turned out to
participate in the evening prayer service for
the recent car-crash victim. Our household
had arrived a scant two minutes beyond the
scheduled time and had been unable to sit
together. My father, needing a minimum of
two places, stalked up and down the aisle
several times before spotting a place, at which
time he announced, in a voice that shook
the rafters, that it was a sorry state of affairs
when a man came to church once in twenty

years and couldn't find a seat. Far from shriveling with embarrassment, I was intensely proud of him, knowing, as I did, that he had the most compelling of reasons to believe that the woman killed in the accident was the one he had loved and already mourned for as dead. I shifted in my seat and lost an arm and a leg in the process. After finally wrestling myself free, I took care not to budge an eyebrow until all heads turned, forcing mine to do likewise in one of those chain reactions that get people injured or even killed.

Lady Grizwolde was being wheeled down the aisle by Ned's granddaughter, Sarah, of the rosy cheeks and cheeky expression, although if there was anything cheekier than her ladyship showing up for the service, I couldn't think of it. Not if it was she who had murdered Harriet. I had lain awake in the early morning chewing the whole thing over for the third or fourth time. Had the classically beautiful woman now being wheeled into a place close to the pulpit gone out to the Old Abbey gates the night before last to intercept Harriet before she went up to the house to deliver the urn to Sir Casper? Had she acquired the injury to her ankle either in struggling with her out on the cliff road or while straining to shove the car over the edge after having first hit Harriet over the head with a rock? And why the wheelchair rather than crutches? Was she acting her heart out for sympathy?

Temporarily setting aside her ladyship, I had gone over the list of other suspects. I had even toyed with the idea that Sarah, having heard things as she flitted about the house with a feather duster or tea tray, had told her friend Ruth of the impending arrival of the relic. And Ruth, fearing this would effectively write end of story to the life and times of St. Ethelwort, meaning she would be shoved out of the vicarage nest and be forced to find a job in an office with a water cooler outside the door, had biked up the cliff road. And while pretending to be out walking the dog had been the one to waylay Harriet. But even at three in the morning this had struck me as a bit thin.

A person with a stronger motive to prefer that the saint not be allowed back in his anointed place and in so doing provide a miracle in the person of new heir was Timothia Finchpeck. I realized, of course, that it was possible that she had staged a soliloquy on hearing footsteps coming down the hall yesterday when I was with Ned. She could have hoped that if she was heard accusing someone of murder, she might be crossed off as a suspect. But from my meeting with her, I had gained a strong sense that duty to the family was all, and much as she might dislike, even loathe, the present Lady Grizwolde, she would not risk upsetting her Elizabethan ancestress. Then there was Mr. Jarrow. He might have decided to steal the urn after discovering, from Harriet's demand for increased payment, that it was actually a reliquary that he could peddle for a fortune. Or he might have been motivated by a love for

Lady Grizwolde that had survived all odds.

Risking wiggling one toe to ward off an attack of pins and needles, I shifted my suspicions to Mr. Ambleforth, who was obsessed to the point of mania with St. Ethelwort. There was that letter to Father Bergdorff on his desk. Had they corresponded for years on the subject of the saint? Perhaps the two men had even become friends, making it more than probable that the German priest would confide in the English vicar when the theft occurred.

Last but certainly not least on my list of suspects was of course Mr. Price. Had word of the reliquary's theft leaked out despite Father Bergdorff's best efforts, to be bandied about the underworld? And had he murdered Harriet in one of his botched attempts to get his hands on it?

The organist struck up a hymn, and Mr. Ambleforth finally ascended the pulpit. "My very dear friends..." His white hair stood on end, and his gaze wavered before lighting, like a fly that had been swatted once too often, on her ladyship's bowed head. "My esteemed colleagues of the Society for Monastic Research. I stand before you today humbled by the enormous tribute paid to me in the presentation of this handsome award." He picked up a candle snuffer that we had all seen him previously use for a bookmark. "I am immensely moved by this generous recognition of my work in restoring interest in the Ethelwortian rule. I know there are many worthier recipients whom you might have selected to so honor. That said, I am proud of what has been a life's work of inestimable joy. I am, however, aware that I have at times neglected other duties—to my wife, Kathleen, and to my former parishioners at St. Paul the Evangelist. And today I make the decision to step down"—he suited actions to words in beginning to descend the pulpit—"from my position of leadership in the S.M.R. and focus all my energies on my roles as husband and clergyman."

Before anyone could audibly voice his or her confusion, having thought this was to be a prayer service for the accident victim, people began piling out of the pews. A half-dozen heads in front of me was Freddy, and I was almost sure that the blond curls bobbing along behind him belonged to Aunt Lulu. Then I saw Ben's profile, and a couple of moments later I spotted Ursel, with Daddy towering behind her. But either I missed Mrs. Malloy or she was not in attendance. Naturally I began to worry about her. Was she bedridden with stage fright? Should I have an ambulance sent to bring her to the church hall, where dress rehearsal for Murder Most Fowl was set to start within the hour?

Outside in the drizzling rain a substantial number of people headed toward their cars or the bus stop. Those who lived close by, in the houses along Hawthorn Lane and Crescent Moon Close, would probably walk if going straight home. But a fair-sized group put up their umbrellas or turned up their coat collars and shifted over to the hall, a modern building that looked as though it had attached itself to the rear of St. Anselm's without being invited to do so.

It had been several years since St. Anselm's had put on a play. So it was not surprising that those with nothing more enticing to do took the opportunity to get out of the rain, hang up their outer apparel on the iron hooks in the vestibule, and cluster in tongue-clicking groups behind the rows of folding metal chairs. The curtain was due to rise at 7:30 on the dress rehearsal and there was yet a half hour to go.

Catching sight of Kathleen Ambleforth bustling about below stage checking the footlights, I got the impression, more from the set of the hat on her head than anything else, that she was not delighted by the size of the turnout. I knew from Freddy and Mrs. Malloy that family and friends were encouraged to attend the dress rehearsal so that the cast could get the feel of playing to an audience. But such a large attendance was likely to mean a loss in ticket sales. Unless of course, Murder Most Fowl proved so riveting that its fans turned out for every performance. But from the droop of the feather on Kathleen's hat, I did not sense that she held out high hopes for such a happenstance.

Ben went off to fetch me a glass of lemonade from a table positioned along the rear wall of the hall. While he was gone, which was quite a while, since the queue for free refreshments stretched into the vestibule, I searched out familiar faces. There were my friends

Bunty Wisemen, the Marilyn Monroe of Chitterton Fells; Frizzy Taffer, proud mother of Dawn, who was playing the maid; and Clarice Whitcombe, a sweet woman newly engaged to Brig. Lester-Smith, Murder Most Fowl's Major Wagewar. She had a Norfolk terrier with her on a red lead. It was generally known that she took it to church with her, but as it was a good little dog and only barked when the organist struck a wrong key, the Parish Council had refrained from taking action. I was about to cross the highly polished tile floor to chat with some of these people before the curtain went up when a hand tapped me on the shoulder and I turned and found myself looking at the Hoppers, lined up in descending order of height.

"We had to come for Harriet's sake," said Cyril.

"For our dear Harriet," said Doris.

"Our very dear Harriet," said Edith.

"We thought the vicar was to say prayers for her." Cyril made this contribution.

"It would have been nice if he'd at least said her name." Doris looked as though tears in the form of tiny wooden beads might slide down her cheeks. I hastened to explain that from what I had heard, the accident victim had yet to be officially identified.

"Haven't you notified the police that it was her car?" I was asking them when Ben showed up with my glass of lemonade and, after nodding in their direction, drew me aside.

"Ellie, I was just talking to Brigadier Lester-Smith, who has been told by someone who got the information from the ubiquitous source, otherwise known as Mrs. Potter, that another body—that of a man—has been recovered from the accident. He wasn't in the car. The theory is that he managed to crawl out a window, but his injuries were severe, and he was found last night close to where the car was recovered."

"A man!" My expression had to have been every bit as blank as that of one of the Hoppers. "Whoever could he be?"

"It's only a wild guess"—Ben took the glass of lemonade away from me before I could drop it—"but I'm wondering about Ingo Voelkel, of whom it might be said a crook by any other name is still a crook."

"It's not so wild an idea. Herr Voelkel didn't just vanish off the face of the earth after his meeting with my father," I was saying when Kathleen Ambleforth came charging up to us, looking much more the stereotypical vicar's wife than she had yesterday. Now she was wearing tweeds and the sensible brown felt hat with the feather.

"Here you are, Ellie." Her smile was at low beam. "The very person I've been looking for." She completely ignored Ben and the Hoppers. "I've been wondering if you've seen or heard from Mrs. Malloy this morning?"

"No." Out of the corner of my eyes I caught sight of Aunt Lulu talking to a thickset woman in a camel coat who even from a distance looked vaguely familiar, but it wasn't hard for me to refocus on Kathleen's worried face. "What's wrong?" I asked her. "Hasn't Mrs. Malloy shown up?"

A demoralized shake of the head. "I've been trying to get through to her on the phone for the past fifteen minutes."

"Perhaps she went to our house to sit quietly for a while before walking down here. Why don't I give a ring there?"

"Would you? You're so good. Mrs. Potter couldn't stop talking about your willingness to help out with the props."

"Really?" I said.

"She couldn't get over how good it was of you to leave instructions with Mrs. Malloy yesterday to let her browse around and take what she wanted. On condition, of course, that everything was returned as she got it."

I couldn't get over it, either. But I mustn't dwell on the matter. Kathleen now looked ready to fall sobbing into my arms. And who could wonder, given her husband's performance in the pulpit and now this panic? I also was very uneasy about Mrs. Malloy's failure to show. Her pride would suffer horribly if she ruined the dress rehearsal. She might even talk of immigrating to Australia. Rather than stand shuffling my feet, I headed back out to the vestibule, where there was a phone on the wall. I was about to pick up the receiver when the outer door opened and my heart leaped. Surely this was Roxie at last. But it was Lady Grizwolde who appeared, with Mr. Jarrow pushing the wheelchair, and I had to take the time to say I was sorry about her sprained ankle.

"I'm afraid that's the least of my problems." Her manner was cool but gracious, as always. "It turns out I also injured my back. And may have to have an operation. The pain didn't set in until yesterday. You probably heard how it happened when you brought back the car. Ned and Sarah are both chatterboxes."

"Ned did tell me you were trying to get Sir Casper upstairs after he was taken ill." Again I felt compelled to ask, "Is he recovering?"

"I'm afraid not; the doctor doesn't hold out much hope that he will last more than a few weeks or months at most." She could have been talking about the unlikelihood of the rain clearing up by the afternoon. I said I was sorry to hear that and hoped she at least would soon be on the mend. Whereupon Mr. Jarrow dipped his overgrown mustache in my direction and wheeled her into the hall proper. Again my hand went to the receiver, but before I could dial, I felt someone touch my shoulder.

"How'd you like to have your fortune told by a true Gypsy?"

Slowly I turned to face her. The voice was the same, as was the face, other than for a trace of red lipstick and green eye shadow. Today she wore the camel coat, and her hair looked as though it has been recently washed.

"I'm not interested in any more of your predictions." I was surprised at the firmness of my voice.

"You should be, lady, because here's one that's important. There's worse in store for you than black cats crossing your path if you don't persuade your father to hand over that urn."

"It's called a reliquary."

"So it is." She reached into her pocket for a packet of cigarettes and a box of matches and lit up. "Isn't it lucky that we understand each other?"

"And who's my father to hand it over to?" I was shaking, but only on the inside.

"Why, me, of course, lady." She dropped the match on the floor and puffed smoke in my face.

"And just who are you?"

"I've got lots of names. I have one for every day of the week."

"Would one of them be Harriet?"

"It's a pretty name, isn't it?" Her smile was genuinely amused. "It seems to go with platinum-blond hair and blue silk frocks and sapphire earrings. But don't you go worrying your head about details. I'm sure you've had your hands full these last few days with your dear Daddy spilling tears everywhere he goes, ranting on and on about his grand passion. All you need do is to see sense and be ready when I get back in touch. It will be soon. And remember, it won't be you that gets hurt if you don't play by my rules. It will be that handsome husband of yours or one or all of those adorable kiddies. For now you can just sit nice and quiet watching the play. Not a squeak out of you or you'll be sorry. I can see it in my crystal ball."

Before I could pry my lips open, the outer door opened once more, and Mrs. Malloy came clicking in on those ridiculous heels of hers. When I turned my head, the woman in the camel coat was walking back into the church hall.

"What's got you by the throat?" Mrs. Malloy demanded in a voice steeped in something stronger than tea.

"Kathleen Ambleforth was afraid you weren't going to show up."

"Well, that's no excuse for you to look like you're getting ready to fall to pieces, Mrs. H. You know me, always the professional. Just point me to the stage and I'll be Malicia Stillwaters come to life." She was now standing at a most peculiar tilt. "Wish me luck!" She went to go back out the door, but mercifully Kathleen appeared and airlifted her through another one at the far end of the vestibule. Somehow I found my way back to the rows of folding chairs and sat down in the nearest one before my legs gave out. What, I wondered in numb terror, did the Gypsy woman have in mind for this evening's performance? How could she be Harriet if Harriet had died in the car crash?

While I was still batting this question around inside my head Kathleen stepped onstage to announce that because this was a rehearsal there would be no intermission between the second and third acts. And almost immediately afterward the curtain parted. The audience was treated to the sight of Mrs. Malloy seated at a writing desk, wearing my missing pink nightie and negligee.

"How am I supposed to be writing a poison-pen letter?" She swiveled around to glare at the audience. Her voice was slurred, and even in my dazed state I realized she wasn't just tipsy. She was drunk. "Look what I'm given to do the job. A Biro"—she was waving it wrathfully—"with not a drop of arsenic or cyanide in it! If it isn't enough to make you spit. As I tell Mrs. H. every day of the week, if you want a job done right, you've got to have the tools. Now what's that blinking noise?"

It was Freddy knocking on the set door. He came into view when it fell down before he could open it, but luckily it was only made of cardboard, and he stepped over it with commendable aplomb.

"Greetings, Mrs. Stillwaters!" His voice projected to the back row of the tombstones out in the churchyard. And Freddy continued to enunciate every syllable as if it might be his last. "Or may I have the rare privilege of addressing you as Malicia?"

"You can call me what you damn well like so long as it's not Mother."

"And I am Reginald Rakehell, a hero to my valet..."

"Go on with you!" Mrs. Malloy snorted. "You're Freddy Flatts. And if I was your mum, I'd smack your behind, big as you are, for telling lies with all them people sitting out there listening to you." She swiveled around again and stared down at the audience. "Don't you lot go encouraging him by snickering, especially after you just come from dancing into church to watch the vicar nod off in the pulpit!"

I was able to sit in my seat and on some distant level absorb the disaster in progress even though the questions kept hounding me. If Harriet hadn't perished in that accident on the cliff road, as the Hoppers claimed to believe was the case, who was the woman who had died? Did it still make sense to think Herr Voelkel might have been her fellow victim in the crash? How many rows of chairs separated me from Ben? How long would it take me to reach him after the curtain came down? Was Kathleen Ambleforth so stunned by Mrs. Malloy's reconstruction of her part that she was physically incapable of calling a halt to the proceedings?

The second act started, and I became fixated on the books lined up on the fake mantelpiece. There was such a compelling familiarity to them, especially one with a blue-and-white dust jacket. It was the cookery book Ben had written shortly after we were married. I sat mulling this over in a deadened sort of way until the obvious solution slid into place. Mrs. Potter had taken it from Ben's study along with the other volumes when she came to see what props I could contribute. And because I wasn't there, Mrs. Malloy, intent on boning up on her understudy role, had left Mrs. Potter to wander at will, taking whatever props she needed. What did it matter? What did anything matter given the warning I had been issued in the vestibule by the woman who had called herself a true Gypsy? Would she now be true to her terrible words?

Suddenly the curtains were opening on the third act. I was now completely numb. Or so I thought until I saw what was now on the mantelpiece alongside the row of books. It was supposed to be an Indian vase containing incriminating evidence against Malicia Stillwaters and bequeathed to Reginald Rakehell by Major Wagewar. As I found myself rising up in my seat, I remembered what Mrs. Malloy had told me about what was to happen next. Malicia Stillwaters would produce a gun and shoot at the vase. Shattering it into shards. In reality, it would probably be made to fall by being poked at by a stick from behind the paper-thin wall because the gun would be a stage one. Not the real thing. Except for this particular performance, that is. Mrs. Malloy, who at the worst possible moment had sunk herself into her role as Malicia Stillwaters, was pointing—I recognized with the awful clarity bestowed by ice-cold fear—Mr. Price's small, almost-toy-sized gun at the urn. I knew now what had happened. Mrs. Potter had not only helped herself to some books; she had also found the urn, which she understandably thought was so ugly, we had hidden it away and would not be upset if it were sacrificed in a good cause. As for the gun, hadn't Kathleen asked me if I might happen to have one of those gimmicky cigarette lighters?

I was on my feet, but I couldn't open my mouth to shout out. Never mind. There were two other people who weren't at such a loss for words. One was the woman in the camel coat. The other was Mr. Price. Mrs. Malloy was so startled by their frenzied yells and their assault upon the stage that her arm swung wide and the gun went flying straight into my father's hand. Thank God for his oversized reach and for the aplomb with which he turned it on a pair of villains. For once he didn't emote. He didn't cry out the name Harriet. There was a very good reason for that, because the Hoppers rose out of their seats as one.

"That's Herr Voelkel's wife," said Cyril in an aggrieved voice, pointing at the Gypsy woman.

"So it is." Edith nodded her wooden head.

"It most definitely is," said Doris. "I remember that Harriet brought her to the flat once and we didn't like her."

"She laughed at us," Cyril agreed, "but she's not laughing now, is she?"

CHAPTER 26

"YOU'RE GOING TO HAVE TO EXPLAIN THINGS TO ME
very slowly. I didn't get more than a wink or
two of sleep last night." Freddy was sitting at
our kitchen table the following afternoon,
tucking into his third piece of Frau Grundman's
delectable blackberry-and-apple strudel. He
deserved to pamper himself after spending the
better part of the last twenty-four hours listening to his mother's tearful assurances that
finding herself in danger of being shot in
the fray at the church had cured her of kleptomania. It was clear he had minded very
much having to wait so long to get the story.
"Who was the Gypsy woman?"

"Anna Voelkel," I told him.

"Herr Voelkel's wife?"

"His widow; he was killed along with his
mother when that car went over the cliff near
the Old Abbey. His body wasn't found at
once because miraculously he managed to crawl

out of the wreckage into a cave a few yards away. It was dark, and I don't suppose the rescuers thought anybody could have survived the impact."

"Hold on a minute." Freddy sat tugging at his beard, a sure sign he was perplexed. "You say Herr Voelkel's mother was in that car with him?"

"That's right." I took the cup of tea Ben handed me and joined my cousin at the table. "She was the housekeeper, the old woman dressed in black who opened the door for Daddy and took him into that room with the picture of the dead cat."

"But, Coz, aren't you missing someone?"

"What do you mean?"

"I thought Harriet was killed in that accident."

"That's what the Hoppers thought because it was her car, but Harriet was already dead, murdered by the Voelkels in Germany."

"When did you find all this out?" Freddy, finding himself in need of a restorative, drained his teacup and picked up mine.

"At the police station. They were pretty decent to Morley because he did save the day down at the church hall," Ben spoke from over by the Aga. He was stirring a saucepan that contained ingredients for a recipe Frau Grundman had given him, and he hadn't been able to wait to try it. He had told her that if it worked out as he hoped, he would put it in his new cookery book and give her credit.

"The detective told Daddy that he'd known

people charged with stupidity to get twenty years, but he smiled when he said it." I smiled too, remembering. "And Mrs. Potter's nephew kept coming in with cups of tea. That's Chitterton Fells for you. All rather friendly and casual. Although I don't suppose Anna Voelkel had much of a good time."

"There is something about having the handcuffs snapped on that kills the 'we're all mates together' feeling," Freddy agreed.

"I don't think anyone's wasting time feeling sorry for her." Ben spooned the contents of the saucepan into a baking dish and sprinkled on a generous handful of buttered bread crumbs.

"I expect those were her cigarette butts that Daddy said stunk up the room the day Ingo Voelkel told him Harriet was dead and that his wife was too upset to come down and talk to him." My mouth twisted in distaste. "Poor Harriet. It's impossible not to feel terribly sorry for her. When Sir Casper hired her to steal St. Ethelwort's relic from the Christ Kirche in Loetzinn, he didn't know that it was a reliquary. At the Old Abbey it had been stored in a simple wooden box. So Harriet wasn't prepared for the discovery that she couldn't simply slip the relic into her makeup bag. It was this complication that made it necessary for her to find someone who wasn't known to the authorities to smuggle St. Ethelwort—or rather, his finger—out of Germany into England. Daddy, with a daughter living in Chitterton Fells, must have seemed like the gift of a kindly fate. Things could be done pretty much in one spot."

"Convenient. But as things turned out, not such a bright idea." Freddy had extracted a few crumbs of strudel from under his plate and was again munching away.

"Poor Harriet. The Hoppers said she was tired of her way of life," I told him. "She really had been seriously ill, and that had caused her to rethink things. She refused to up the price she had agreed on with Sir Casper before she knew about the reliquary. But she didn't count on the outrage of the Voelkels, with whom she had worked, on other jobs involving art and jewelry thefts. They weren't content with a percentage of fifty thousand pounds. Not when they knew the reliquary would be worth infinitely more to a collector willing to forgo asking too many questions."

"They really were an evil trio." Ben joined us at the table. "From the sound of it, the foul old mother pulled the strings, but the other two seem to have been more than willing to dance. They decided to murder Harriet in the manner that was to have been staged for Morley's benefit. Anna and Ingo persuaded her that it would be a smart idea to drive the route to be described to Morley on informing him of her supposed accident. They stopped the car at a suitable spot, delivered her a blow to the head, and sent the car off the road into the river."

"I want to think it was quick and she didn't suffer," I said, and felt Freddy reach for my hand.

"Then what happened?" he asked.

"The Voelkels proceeded with the plan as scheduled." Ben again picked up the story. "I suppose it made good business sense for them to offer the reliquary to Sir Casper at an inflated price, rather than to an outside buyer, because his instigation of the theft placed him in an extremely vulnerable position. Besides which, a man in search of a miracle isn't likely to count pennies. They must also have thought it a good move to let the Hoppers proceed as arranged to collect the urn from Morley. After all, who would suspect those simpleminded characters of being up to no good."

"So how did the Voelkels—mother and son—come to be in Harriet's car the evening of the crash?" Freddy stood up, stretched, and sat back down.

"They collected it from the garage of her flat," I said. "They had a key. It probably seemed less risky than renting a car and giving someone the chance to identify them later if things went wrong. Anna phoned while Daddy and I were at the Old Abbey to speak to Mr. Jarrow and confirm the appointment for that evening. He was acting for Sir Casper in the matter and had been over to Germany, as we suspected, to keep an eye on Harriet to make sure that she was doing what she had been paid to do. But sensing that Sir Casper might balk at coughing up more than the fifty thousand, the Voelkels decided that Ingo's mother—who presumably was the most adept at turning the screws—would accompany him to the meeting. And if all went well, arrange to hand over the urn. Anna had been to Cliffside House that morning hoping to see the Hoppers and advise them how to behave when they came to Merlin's Court to collect it. But they had already left to come here. It was then that she dropped the button from her coat. The one Doris later picked up and put in her handbag, meaning to give it to Mrs. Blum in case someone was looking for it. That sent me down the wrong track, because it matched the one the Gypsy gave to me supposedly for a good-luck charm and I leaped to the conclusion that the Gypsy was Harriet."

"I wonder why she spoke to you in the square that afternoon." Ben got up and poured the three of us more tea.

"I think she did it on a malicious whim," I said. "She must have recognized me from the family photo Daddy gave Harriet and was able to reel off information about my life from what Harriet had told the Voelkels about her conversations with him. Probably she got the idea from Harriet's own meeting with a true Gypsy, but didn't give enough thought to the possibility that she had told Daddy about it. And that the coincidence would set off alarm bells. Cold-blooded murderers must have enormous egos. I lay in bed last night wondering why she became worried when I said we were going to France, Ben. And I think it must have been because she was afraid that if we were gone, Daddy would head out of the area, and there would be all the bother of tracking him down. And it must have already been crystal clear to all three of the Voelkels—having met them before at Harriet's flat—that Cyril, Doris, and Edith were not readily adaptable to a change of plan."

Freddy leaned forward in his chair. "But there still remains one burning question. Was the car crash the other night an accident that couldn't have happened to two nastier people, or was it another murder?"

"Desperate to save herself from what she considered a fate worse than death," I continued, "Lady Grizwolde went out onto the cliff road, hoping to confront the Voelkels before they had a chance to see Sir Casper or Mr. Jarrow. Her idea was to talk them into giving her the relic and taking its container away with them to sell to someone else. Whichever one of them was driving, either mother or son, must have swerved toward the cliff edge when she appeared as a dark shape in their path. Her ladyship twisted her ankle and wrenched her back in avoiding being run over. Mr. Jarrow, who had followed her when she left the house, took her back inside. At which point there followed a scene with Timothia Finchpeck, who had been out in the garden spying on her ladyship and seen enough to be convinced she had witnessed her enemy shove the car over the cliff. But the police have now assured Miss Finchpeck, on the basis of skid marks, that she was indulging in wishful thinking."

"And that about sums it up," Ben said, eyeing the kitchen clock.

"Except to say," I reminded him, "that Lady Grizwolde hired Mr. Price's boss to steal the urn for a second time—from Harriet and company, before it could be handed into Sir Casper's eager clutches. Her ladyship might not believe in the St. Ethelwort legend, but she understood the power of suggestion upon a susceptible mind. Sir Casper was already capering after her with renewed, if wobbly, vigor, and talking about installing fairy lights in the matrimonial bedchamber. And this only in anticipation of the relic's return! How could she not be terrified that with the thing actually back in the chapel he would become sufficiently energized to make repulsive attempts at restoring connubial relations?"

"It's a sad thing when husband and wife are at cross-purposes," Freddy said, looking dolefully around for something else to eat. "But there is a lesson to be learned in all this if we will but heed it. You get what you pay for in life. I expect Lady Grizwolde had to hire Mr. Price out of the housekeeping money. And a right mess he made of things."

"Well, you do have to bear in mind that he is, as Ben guessed, a butler who happened to work for a crook," I pointed out. "He only took over when his boss was injured trying to get hold of Daddy's suitcase on the escalator. So it isn't all that surprising Mr. Price bungled his attempt to snatch Frau Grundman's canvas bag. And when his second attempt at acquiring the reliquary resulted in finding the silver powder box filled with fireplace ash, he must have thought we had tried to trick him. So when he heard about the church service for the accident victim he showed up first in the church and then at the dress rehearsal, planning to nab Daddy and get him to see sense. He must have got the shock of his life when Mrs. Malloy pulled out that gun onstage."

"Desperation tends to do away with common sense," said Ben. "Hence Anna Voelkel showing up."

"Oh, I think—from her Gypsy stunt—that she was probably always the loose cannon among the Voelkels." I stood up and stretched. "That's probably why Ingo didn't have her come down and speak to Daddy when he broke the news to him about Harriet's death. And with him and his crone of a mother gone there was no one to keep a reign on Anna."

"Imagine what she had to be thinking when Mrs. M. fired and hit the reliquary." Freddy had wandered off to help himself to the last slice of strudel.

"Luckily, the only damage was to the plaster casting that had been put on to camouflage it. And hopefully Father Bergdorff will get it back safe and sound after the powers that be at this end are done with the red tape." Ben handed Freddy a plate to prevent a trail of crumbs, and we both followed him to the door, where he bade us an affectionate farewell.

"Don't count on seeing much of me in the immediate future," he called back as he went down the steps. "I'll be on the go every minute keeping Mumsie up to scratch and doing the play. I suppose you've heard that Mrs. Potter is taking over the role of Malicia

Stillwaters. As prop manager she's been at all the rehearsals and knows the part backwards and forwards."

We hadn't heard, but we doubted that Mrs. Malloy would be horribly disappointed.

"See you at opening night!" Freddy's voice faded into the dusk, and Ben and I quickly went inside. Moments later, we heard footsteps out in the hall. We found my father and Frau Grundman standing there with their suitcases at their heels.

"You're not going yet?" I exclaimed.

"We thought you were staying at least another couple of hours." Ben eyed them worriedly. "I was just about to put the casserole in the oven for dinner. It won't take more than forty-five minutes."

Frau Grundman nodded at us. "This I know, but Morley"—she blushed—"Mr. Simons, he thinks we should be on the road if we are to catch our plane in good time."

"Ursel can't continue to delay in getting back to the guest house in Schönbrunn." Daddy cleared his throat. "And I have to say, I want—need to return and confront my memories in order to try to put them behind me."

"We'll miss you." My smile included Ursel as Ben bent to pick up both suitcases.

"My dear Giselle." I was relieved to hear that Daddy was back to emoting. "I lament the need to part with you and Bentwick after so short a duration, but if kindly providence allows, we will be reunited before too long."

"And you make the promise to write?" Ursel was misty-eyed. "I want to know all about how life stays here at Merlin's Court and if there should be any interesting news from the Old Abbey now that the relic is back in the little chapel."

"It was good of Father Bergdorff to agree to that," Ben said. "Mrs. Malloy, being practical to the core, thinks Lady Grizwolde should take the miracle into her own hands by being artificially inseminated before Sir Casper passes on."

"Alas, charming as it is to do so, we can't stand here saying good-bye all day." Daddy kissed my cheek, dashed a few drops from his eyes, and told me not to come outside. So I stood waving at the door while Ben went with them to stow the luggage in the boot of the Rent-A-Wreck. Unable to stay watching as they drove away, I retreated into the drawing room and sat in what I had come to think of as Daddy's chair, staring at the floor until Ben came in.

"Don't say it, Ellie," he admonished with a lowering of his black brows.

"Say what?"

"That Ursel would make your father a splendid wife."

"But she would," I protested, getting to my feet. "She's in love with him. And she's patient. She'll be willing to wait until one morning he looks at her across a crowded breakfast table and realizes she is the love of his life. But I must say that being who he is, he's bound to give her a lot of trouble from time to time."

"What's wrong with that?" He lifted my face

to his kiss. "Life without trouble isn't worth living."

"Are you sure of that?" I asked him tenderly.

"Quite sure."

"Good," I said, "because I just looked out the window and a taxi has deposited two Asian gentlemen on the drive. I have this sinking feeling they are the Japanese ones Daddy spent an evening chatting with at the guest house and graciously invited to come and stay with us at Merlin's Court for as long as they like."

"They do have rather a lot of luggage with them." Ben drew back after taking a cautious peek out the window. "Quick, we'll have to hide in the pantry in case they come around looking in the windows."

"There's no need for that. We've got time to run upstairs."

"The pantry will be cozier." Ben spoke firmly as he took hold of my hand and tugged me along. "Plenty of food and bevs on hand if we're holed up for a long siege. And"—I could hear the smile in his voice— "just the right amount of room in which to experience what it means to be alone at last."